A TASTE
of
PLEASURE

A TASTE
of
PLEASURE

ANTOINETTE

ATRIA PAPERBACK

NEW YORK   LONDON   TORONTO   SYDNEY   NEW DELHI

ATRIA PACKAGE

An Imprint of Simon & Schuster, Inc.
1230 Avenue of the Americas
New York, NY 10020

First Atria Paperback edition September 2015

ATRIA PAPERBACK and colophon are trademarks of Simon & Schuster, Inc.

For information about special discounts for bulk purchases, please contact Simon & Schuster Special Sales at 1-866-506-1949 or business@simonandschuster.com.

The Simon & Schuster Speakers Bureau can bring authors to your live event. For more information or to book an event contact the Simon & Schuster Speakers Bureau at 1-866-248-3049 or visit our website at www.simonspeakers.com.

Interior design by Kyoko Watanabe

Manufactured in the United States of America

10 9 8 7 6 5 4 3 2 1

Library of Congress Cataloging-in-Publication Data

Antoinette, (novelist)
A taste of pleasure / by Antoinette.
pages cm
I. Title.
PS3601.N569T38 2015
813'.6—dc23   2015021250

ISBN 978-1-4767-8226-3
ISBN 978-1-4767-8227-0 (ebook)

To all those who have loved and lost,
and dared to love again.

TOUCH ME

by Antoinette

Her lips brush his cheek, air full of words and requests.
His body leans toward hers as they move in the dance of love.

Will he be the one? she asks herself with reserve.
So many have tried to win her heart, a heart lonely and unloved.

Her body reaching out for another taste . . . another touch . . .
she is living through another day of life.

Open the pages and feast on her fantasies . . .

Chapter 1

CROISSANT AND FRUIT

Love is worth waiting for are among the words of wisdom that were a part of London Shelby's inheritance from her grandmother. That thought occurred as she leafed through a scrapbook while sitting on an antique fainting couch in Château d'Amour, an heirloom-filled home that Catherine Shelby had bequeathed to the grandchild she'd raised.

London had a day off from work in a law firm and was intent on spring cleaning her attic. She made herself a breakfast of a jelly-filled croissant and fruit, which she took to the attic with her. She plucked the grapes from the bowl and sucked each one into her mouth. Then she took a bite from the croissant, licking the overflow of jelly that trickled down her hand, then pondering how she would sort through good and bad souvenirs of the past to clear her way forward.

London had come to live with her grandmother at the age of ten in the aftermath of a car accident that killed her parents. She inherited the château at the age of twenty-four when her grandmother passed away. Catherine was a special and generous woman who not only left her granddaughter a few million dollars and a great home, but also a priceless journal titled *Life Lessons* that she hoped would help London to lead a fulfilled and independent life. Among London's favorites of her grandmother's words was "pleasure without pressure."

London was raised to enjoy life, but also to value an education and the virtues of hard work. She earned a degree from New York University while she was a member of Kappa Kappa Delta sorority, and she made friends easily. She came across a photo of her two best friends, Jen Gibson and Laura McCarthy. She wiped her hands on a wet cloth and traced their silhouette with her fingers. She had lost touch with Laura after they graduated, but Jen remained close to her. She turned the page and found a valentine from her first love—Deacon Wayne. A lacy white heart with such warm words it brought tears to her eyes as she read, "You're deeply in my *heart* this day, where you will always stay." She took it out of the scrapbook and held it in her hands, pulling it to her chest, reflecting when she met him ten years ago.

She was seventeen years old when she met Deacon in the College Ice Cream parlor. He took her heart away at first glance. He was a freshman in college and she felt so grown-up as he asked her if he might sit down. She lowered her eyes as she said, "Yes."

"I am Deacon Wayne," he said as he held out his hand for hers. She touched him and felt a tingle all the way to the floor.

"I am London Shelby."

"So, London, what brings you here?"

"I am filling out my application to the university and picking out classes," she said as she continued to leaf through the catalogue, her hands shaking with excitement as she looked up into his dark brown eyes. He was so handsome, she could hardly contain herself.

"What brings you here?" she asked.

"I attend the university here and stop by for a hot fudge charge once in a while. I can help you if you wish. What field are you planning on going into?" he asked.

"I would like to be a paralegal," she nervously responded.

"Well then I can help you. I am a second-year law student. You must take Professor Robinson's class; he is terrific." She smiled at his suggestion and let the pages fall as she searched for his class. "There it is." He placed his manicured finger on the class and smiled. "Well, London, I need to run, hope we run into each other again, nice meeting you," he said as he spun around and left. A faint whisper of his cologne lingered. She inhaled deeply as she sighed, watching him walk down the brick sidewalk.

They would bump into each other often and she found herself going to the parlor just to see him. They had many conversations and she was very taken by him, plus the fact that he was studying law made him even more interesting. She also felt a dying urge to ravish his body. After several talks, he asked her out on a date, which she accepted, and they went to a movie. He held her hand. She was in heaven. When he took her home, he kissed her at the door and she floated into the house. The feeling she had for him had grown deeply and she told Grams how she felt. "Well, my dear, you're approaching the most wonderful time of your life. You're a beautiful girl and you're going to have many lovers, I am sure, so don't get all hung up on the first one. You're too young." But London knew better. Deacon was for her and her alone. When he asked her to go to his family's cabin to celebrate Valentine's Day she felt he was going to ask her to go steady. "I'll pick you up Friday night around seven. We should be at the cabin by nine."

"Okay."

"Pack lightly and bring a warm sweater and coat; nights in the mountains are a bit cold."

"Okay, see you tomorrow night, bye." She was awake most of the night, thinking about Deacon and what was about to happen. She rubbed her hands over her body, feeling the curves and the fullness of her breasts. Her nipples, which stood proud and waiting for his lips. Her hands moved down as she opened her legs and her fingers felt wetness.

The next morning she told Grams that she was going to spend the weekend with Deacon, and Grams looked concerned. "My dear, are you sure you want to be with him intimately?"

"Yes, I am. I want him to be my first." Her grandmother came over and held her head in her arms. "It is your choice, my dear. Just hold on to your heart. I will be here if you need me." London ate a small breakfast. Her stomach felt like it was in her throat. She thought about tonight and the fact that she would be with Deacon for two days. The day in school dragged by and finally it was time for her to go home and finish packing. When she got home, Grams had put a lovely cream satin nightgown on her bed with matching sheer negligee and satin slippers with a note. "I won't be home when you get here, but I wish you a wonderful weekend." London took the items and held them up to her, spinning around. She could smell her grams's cologne on them. She carefully packed them in her suitcase and felt butterflies in her tummy. She showered and dressed. She heard the buzz of the front gate and watched Deacon drive down the driveway that led behind the château. He came to the door as she opened it, gathered her in his arms, and kissed her. That was all she remembered until they pulled into the parking space behind the cabin in the Adirondack Mountains. He opened the car door and helped her up the stairs to the front door, where he carried her over the threshold, kissing her as he placed her feet on the floor. He showed her around the log cabin, holding her hand and bending down to kiss her more, and then they unpacked. He walked her into the bathroom where there was a hot tub. Deacon felt she would be less embarrassed covered by water than standing nude in a shower. He tenderly kissed her more as she whispered, "Oh, Deacon, I have dreamed of this day." He smiled as he helped her undress. She had on blue jeans and a white wool sweater. His hands massaged her body, and he held her close as he kissed her neck and face. When her bra fell on the floor his lips touched her swollen nipples, and her head flew back as she moaned. He covered her with a towel until she was under the water. Then he sat across from her and extended his feet toward her and magically touched her body while skimming her private parts with his toes. He then moved toward her and took a nipple and sucked on it as his hands moved farther down. She opened her legs to a new touch and moaned as the surge of water touched her virgin parts followed by his talented fingers. "Are you ready, baby?" he whispered as he rubbed her shoulders and kissed her neck. "Yes," she said. She stood up as he wrapped her in a fluffy white terry cloth robe and handed her a glass of champagne, helping her to the bedroom. When he kissed her again, his tongue slid into her mouth and a new sensual world opened up. He led her to the bed, where he kissed her lips and neck and sucked on her nipples. He massaged her body as his lips followed his fingers down to her passion zone. He took one finger and slid it between her legs and touched her button. She moaned and squirmed, then he opened her legs farther, his body fell on top of hers, and he kissed her again. "Are you okay?" he asked.

"Yes, oh yes," she answered, her mind dazed with passion

and champagne. He pushed into her. She felt a burning sensation and then fullness. He filled her every desire and even more. After he made love to her, he held her in his arms as she toyed with his chest hair. They made love over and over as they feasted on each other. They got up and enjoyed wonderful barbequed hamburgers, ribs, potatoes, and chips, then back to the hot tub and more sex. On Valentine's Day he had pizza delivered. It was in the shape of a valentine, and he handed her a special white one. "Oh, Deacon, this is so beautiful. I will keep it forever." She snuggled next to him as he drove her home. After the weekend together, she heard from him frequently. The connection they had stayed intimate and wonderful. The conversations were mostly about the passionate time at the cabin, then, turned on by the memories, they would meet and have a quickie in the backseat of the car. "I can't believe how beautiful you are," he said many times when they were together, and she would blush and reply, "Thanks, I enjoy you too."

After several months one special conversation played back in her mind over and over again. "London, I have something to tell you. There is someone else in my life. She is in college with me and we are in the same class. We have been studying together and getting very close. I hope you understand, our families are friends and have been encouraging us to get together. I think we might. Even though I don't feel the same about her as I do you, it is for the best, I guess." London felt her eyes fill with tears as she placed the phone on the hook and fell crying on the bed. Her grams was walking by the room and heard her. "May I come in? Looks like you need a friend."

"Oh, Grams, I did what you told me not to do. I gave my heart away." Her grams held her close and let her cry, then they went downstairs and ate a huge bowl of ice cream drizzled with chocolate sauce and whipped cream oozing over the sides of the bowl. "London, pleasure without pressure is my motto. I have lived that way since your grandfather passed and it is the only way for me to protect my heart. Sex is just that . . . sex. It is the lust one person has for another. When the lust leaves, so do the feelings. However, love never leaves. It lingers through the good times and the bad. It gives you strength to get through what you felt you could never get through. Lust leaves at the first sign of trouble. When you find the right person, you won't ever have to say good-bye."

London looked up at her grams and smiled. "I have found that person, but he has another."

"If it is real, he will be back in time."

London smiled and then her mind came back to the present day.

She felt that strange feeling in her tummy for some ice cream. She smiled and left the attic. Took some things with her and placed the valentine in her purse, having gone through enough memories for one day. She hadn't counted on the task of cleaning out clutter in her life to be so emotional. For the most part she was a happy-go-lucky woman who lived life on her own terms. She worked, because she wanted, not needed to. She loved—or rather lusted for—when and whom she wanted to since lust was sometimes the best medicine to use when life got painful.

She picked up her purse, checked the mirror, looked at the pile of memories she had placed on the table, and thought, *I can do that some other time. I need a breather.* She walked down into the four-car garage under the house and patted the antique Rolls-Royce, her grandmother's car, as she strolled past. Her mind was in search of trouble and her body was crying for a lover's touch as she eased into her black convertible Beemer. The supple leather felt cool and luxurious on her hotness.

She selected Lady Antebellum from the playlist and "I Need You Now" resonated through the Bose sound system, sending chills across her skin. She eased the tan convertible top down and let the wind tousle her hair like it was blowing memories out of her mind. The breeze felt exhilarating as she sped off. She was going to find a frame for the valentine and stop in the ice cream parlor for a hot fudge sundae with whipped cream.

The afternoon sun beat down over the steamy city, and the streets were alive and hustling with commotion. London traveled by a few haunts and finally found a parking place. Ice cream parlors were scarce today, but she found a place to frame her valentine and right down the street was hers and Deacon's nostalgic ice cream haunt. She smiled as that was the only place she wanted to be right now. She shouldn't have been shocked after the earlier sentimental trip to feel familiar eyes on her. But she was and when she turned around how appropriate it was to find Deacon staring at her as she screamed his name. "Deacon, is that you?" She got up, ran over to him, and gave him a hug before she realized what she was doing. "I was just thinking about you. It's been years. How are you?" she asked, her heart beating so fast she could hardly contain herself. His white shirt opened up at the top, his dark hair accentuating his olive skin. He had matured and looked like an Italian model with his lips in a half smile as he looked down at her and whispered, "You're more beautiful than I remembered," his breath hitting her neck. She tingled.

She tried breathing more deeply without calling Deacon's attention to her anxiety as she felt a sudden coolness settle within him. She smiled and listened, even as he told her that he'd married the girl he was committed to so long ago. He got up to leave as they both said, "Let's keep in touch." They laughed as they exchanged cards. He looked at hers. "Oh, I see you're working for the firm I have been trying to get into. Maybe you can help me. I will call you soon."

She was happy to help if she could, as she of course wanted to see him again and thought that something in his body language and tone suggested that he wanted to see her too. While she respected his being honest about his status, she also detected that he wasn't maybe so thrilled with his marriage or his life. Maybe because of her own emotions and self-interest she simply imagined his discontent and continuing attraction to her. When she got back home she went into the bathroom and climbed in her hot tub, letting the jets satisfy her screaming urges.

Several days later she received a phone call from him at her work inviting her to dinner.

"Sure, sounds good."

"How about the Ol' Steak House?"

"It sounds yummy."

"See you at seven."

"Seven it is, bye for now." She stared at the receiver, lost in her thoughts. The day dragged as she did her work, looking up at the clock every hour or so. Finally it was five and she raced home, her heart beating in anticipation of meeting him. She jumped in the shower, dressed, rubbed scented lotion all over her body, massaging her breasts and down between her legs. Then she looked at her resemblance to her father in the full-length mirror, with the dark hair, haunting blue eyes, and five-foot-eight frame, her long legs now donning black nylons, knee-high boots, and her black dress covering her voluptuous body, just showing enough cleavage to entice Deacon. She grabbed her shawl and out the door she flew.

It seemed like her black Beemer was in slow motion, but soon she spotted a parking place in front of the frame shop two buildings away from the steakhouse. She stopped and picked up the valentine. "This is gorgeous," she said, looking at the brushed gold frame and black background of the framed valentine. She walked to the steakhouse. She entered the lobby, where Deacon was waiting for her. Her stomach felt like it held a million butterflies and her knees felt weak. He slid his arm around her waist and escorted her to their booth. She slid in across from him. He touched her hand and she melted. They sat and ordered a glass of wine. "You'll never guess where I just came from." She smiled as she waited for an answer.

"No, I don't think I can." She reached into her purse and pulled out a brown-paper-wrapped package. She untied it and showed the framed valentine to him. "Oh, I forgot about this. You kept it all this time?" he said as he smiled and traced the card with his fingers, his mind traveling someplace back in time. A nervous smile came across his face. She watched him for a few minutes, not wanting to spoil his journey. "We had a wonderful two days, didn't we? My family still owns the cabin. Maybe one day we can visit it again—would you like that?"

She looked at him. "I have one question for you, Deacon. You're married—what do you want with me?"

His eyes dropped as he fidgeted with his napkin. "London, I made a terrible mistake a few years ago. I should have married you. I don't know what happened, but I thought I was in love with her, and our families were pushing us and before I knew it I was married. I am not happy, my marriage is falling apart, I have never been able to get you out of my mind, and when I saw you I saw the hope that someday I might be happy again. I know what I am about to ask you seems unreasonable, but I would love to get to know you again and see where it goes. I am not sure what I can offer you in exchange, except sincere friendship and passion beyond your wildest dreams."

Pleasure without pressure.

The Catherinism circled through her mind as she smiled and picked up her glass of wine, sipping a small amount, enough to wet her dry mouth. She smiled and said with her voice quivering. "Let's see, no promises . . . only time will tell." She looked at the menu. Her eyes blurred with passion as she searched for something delicious to eat. Not finding it on the menu, she knew what she needed to fill this ravenous appetite. "Would you like to come over to my house and have dinner?" She flashed her white teeth as she looped her finger around his and slowly stroked it up and down. He winked at her, knowing what she wanted, which matched his desire perfectly. He watched her squirm in her seat and he welcomed the challenge to fill her delights and satisfy his bulging desire.

They left the steakhouse in separate cars. Looking back in the rearview mirror, her heart sang as she knew she would soon be in his arms again. The gates seemed to move more slowly than usual. She was anxious. Once she was finally parked inside the garage, Deacon pulled alongside her and swiftly came around to open her car door and extend his hand.

The intensity between them had her breathless. As she was fumbling for her house key he pressed against her. He moved his hips back and forth. She could feel the warmth of his body and his anxiety while playfully kissing the back of her neck. His breath drove her crazy while he nibbled at her ear. She finally unlocked the door to the château and he swept her up in his arms, kissing her. His lips, soft and warm, never left hers as he carried her up the steps into the family room on the main floor. He laid her on the bamboo love seat, kissing her and tantalizing her sensually, with his full lips and his magical fingers. He peeled away her clothing, piece by piece, replacing each garment with a tender kiss. "Oh, London," he whispered as his mouth found her passion zone and his ravenous tongue teased her. His mouth followed his fingers as he reached up and released the clip from her hair and stroked the silky strands as they cascaded over her shoulders. He fondled her breasts and teased her nipples until they stood proud against his eager tongue. His stubbly beard rubbing on her tender skin brought a sensation she'd never felt before. She wanted more of that later, but right now she wanted to please him.

He undressed and stood in front of her. She admired his handsome, sculpted body. He had developed into a Greek statue since she had last seen him, and now he was standing before her again, waiting. She stood to embrace him. His cologne was intoxicating and she was hungry for a taste of him again. She traced his neck and body with her hungry tongue plus little nibbles and kisses. She stopped at his nipples, gently tugging at them with her teeth and circling them on her way down to her favorite spot. His desire pulsed, her head spun, and her mouth watered as he sat down and she knelt before him in front of the love seat. She grasped his erection and teased his swollen head for a moment with her tongue before gradually sliding it in and out of her mouth. *He is delicious*, she thought. He smiled wickedly at her as he grabbed a handful of hair and tilted her head so she could take all of him in.

She felt him throbbing and wanted him to feel her wetness and show him how much she desired him, but right now she wanted him to come in her mouth, and her main thought was to gratify him as he had thrilled her several years before. He pulled her closer to him, his muscles tensing, moaning as his hardness went deeper and deeper into her throat, faster and harder, until she felt his warmth explode within her mouth. He moaned and she collapsed as he pulled her against him. He shuddered with her head on his chest, his arms tightly around her. She loved being with him and enjoyed the pleasure of satisfying him. She took a deep breath, her passions playing second to his. She knew her time was coming and that in itself was well worth waiting for.

"How 'bout some snacks?" She got up, slipped on a terry cloth robe, and handed one to him. She then went to the wet bar and got out some grapes, cheese, crackers, and a bottle of wine. He got up and uncorked the bottle for her as she retrieved the glasses. They sat on the bamboo stools, drinking wine and eating brie cheese and crackers.

London loved the château she had inherited from her grandmother. There were large rooms with lots of windows overlooking fields of trees, and a stream that complemented the large brick estate. Her off-white wainscoting walls, cran-berry and cream-colored tile floors that bled into the adjoining front room with the cream-colored carpet, burgundy love seats, large manteled cream fireplace, and a combination of Louis XV French furniture plus contemporary pieces com-plemented the room nicely. The curved staircase opposite the foyer separated the front room from her favorite place, the dining room with its Louis XV heavy crystal chandelier hung over the French walnut table, surrounded by sixteen chairs.

She smiled as she looked around, sipping on her cool glass of wine. Deacon fed her grapes, cheese, and crackers and kissed her after each bite. He was so romantic and attentive to her, and she felt a big moment getting close. He pulled her toward him and kissed her. She could taste the wine on his lips as his tongue swept over her lips and tugged at her tongue, and the sensation almost caused her to fall off the stool. He grinned as he steadied her, then he reached for her dainty hand and led her up the stairs to the master bedroom.

He turned down the cream satin comforter and scooped

her up. She wrapped her legs around him as he placed her in the middle of the bed. He opened her robe while he slid his weight on top of her. His body was so hot and smooth, it felt wonderful on her. She gasped in anticipation of what would come next. Her stomach muscles clenched with longing, and the agonizing wait was almost over. He grabbed her hips and pulled her to him, his hardness lying between them. She tried to wiggle her body so his sex would drop down and rest between her legs, but he pushed down firmly on her tummy, flashing a devilish grin. He enjoyed watching her squirm as he reached down to tease and fondle her wetness with his talented hands.

He toyed with her sex, tenderly at first, and then more firmly and quickly as she felt her pulse begin to race. He stopped and moved down to the end of the bed, pulling her with him as she moaned and pleaded. He separated her legs and eased his face down between them to kiss her thighs. He ran his tongue gradually up and down, first along her right thigh, then brushed by her button. She gasped, wishing he would stay there, and then along her left thigh, while his unshaved face brushed against her skin once more with antagonizing sensations. He worked his way up to her slit, then to her button, her most sensitive part, where his light touch and warm lips were welcomed. He took her into his mouth, drinking her in, tonguing her, nibbling tiny bites and sucking hard. She moaned and her hips began to sway and shift in time with his motions. She was panting, burning to feel him deep inside, but part of her enjoyed this torturous foreplay, as she lived in the realm of fervor. He inserted his tongue deep inside her as she whispered, "Deacon, don't stop," begging for more. She wanted him so badly now as his tantalizing prolonged her agony. She was crazy with desire and aching to feel him. She was blazing hot and she knew this would be a good ride. She was ready for him to enter her, but only when he had decided it was the right time for both of them.

He kissed her tummy, her breast, her neck, all over her body, until she didn't know where he was, still withholding his hardness from her. Then, with one swift move, he placed her legs on his shoulders and plunged deep inside her wet juicy walls. She screamed his name, clenched him with her muscles, grabbed onto the sheets, and smiled as she closed her eyes, feeling the hardness as he filled her and pushed to the end of her. He rode her wild, her walls so wet as she clung to him. Not wanting to come too fast, he stopped and pulled out of her, watching her eyes open wide with a facial expression of what are you doing?

"Oh my God! Don't stop now!" London begged.

He grinned, holding on to his hardness with his hand. She reached down to touch herself, determined to finish what he had started. He let his hardness go as it searched for her. He grabbed her hands, holding them above her head, and watched her wiggle like a snake toward him, trying to reach him with her legs, her wetness shining like the morning dew. His maleness pointed straight at her mouth. He smiled, knowing she would get it only when he decided to give it to her. She looked at him, her eyes pleading for her passions to be fulfilled. "Deacon, please!"

He kissed her one last time before he flipped her over and dragged her to the edge of the bed. He stood over her and thrusted into her deep and hard. She closed her eyes as he crashed into her world of desire and passion. He ravished her as she screamed his name. He melted into her as she climaxed, carrying him with her in a wave of passion. Her body fell limp and relaxed as he pushed her up on the satin sheets and gathered her into his arms to hold her. They were both spent and peaceful as her mind drifted away. She smiled and closed her eyes, clinging to him as their bodies intertwined.

They met several times a month at the château for months; then one day he looked deep into her eyes. "There is something I need to tell you," Deacon hesitantly whispered as he brushed her hair away from her face and kissed her lightly.

London could sense the seriousness of his tone and felt her throat tighten.

"I have been given a wonderful opportunity. I have been made a partner in the law firm where I work. I am required to move to England and will be leaving next week. I was going to tell you when I got here, but when I see you, I forget everything else, and, really, this worked out better."

Worked out better? she thought, a tear already forming in her eyes.

She rubbed it away before looking up at him. She wanted to be okay with this, but she just had a sinking feeling.

He held her close and continued, "You're so special, sweetie. Never forget that. We can email and IM each other and visit by webcam. I don't want to lose you again."

"I don't want to lose you either. This webcam thing sounds like fun," she said, trying to lighten up her own mood. "I think we could get really creative with that. We will just have to see how it goes. You're special to me and I cherish these moments."

London stayed wrapped in his arms for as long as she could, until he finally had to go. She didn't get up to walk him to the door. It was all she could do to watch him leave before she buried her face in her pillow. He was gone, it seemed as quickly as he appeared, and her grandmother's words again appeared in her mind. *Real love never leaves.* She smiled, feeling he would be back.

Chapter 2

A SUNTANNED BEACH SNACK

Memorial Day weekend plans included going to decorate her parents' and grandmother's graves. Then she would celebrate. London was feeling flirtatious and in need of a suntan, so what better place to go than to the beach so she could enjoy people and water. She threw on the racy black string bikini that accentuated her small waist and firm breasts and added a black sheer sarong, covering it all with a patio dress proper for the cemetery. She placed flowers on the grave sites as she reflected on the day she was told about the car accident that took her parents and led to her moving in with Grams. She felt grateful that her great loss was balanced by great blessings in the aftermath. She knew she had been loved, at least by her grandmother, and dedicated herself to embracing a spirit of joy. Alone or not, she was off to frolic on the beach.

The white sandy beach at Greenwich Point, also known as Tod's Point Beach, in Old Greenwich, Connecticut, was a popular spot among the young. The half-hour drive in her convertible Beemer felt great, clearing her mind so she was ready for lying out on the beach and slathering on suntan oil and sunscreen—for soaking up some rays. She found a spot that had just enough people around to make it interesting, not too many, though, to disturb her peace. The breeze was soothing, and the sound of the waves surging against the shoreline was invigorating. The afternoon quickly passed as she enjoyed watching a game of beach volleyball. Hunks with chiseled muscle and tanned skin were running everywhere around her, bending over and picking up the ball for another shot. An occasional ball came her way, allowing her to engage with other beach lovers.

One dark-haired guy in white shorts came so close to her and looked so good that he actually made her sex tingle. *I could pull him over and take him right here*. She giggled to herself. She lowered her dark shades and drank him in, smiling as he retrieved the ball beside her. He had olive skin, and although his eyes were hidden by sunglasses, she was sure they were the type she loved . . . dark and mysterious, with eyebrows close set to his deep-set eyes, just like Deacon's. His muscular chest glistened like golden hills in the sunset. She was mesmerized as she watched his toned muscles flexing, filling her imagination with wild desires.

She put her sunglasses back on as well as her headphones. She pretended to ignore him as "Rude Boy" by Rihanna resonated in her ears. She couldn't take her eyes off of him, but he never even looked her way! She thought this captivating college boy was too young for her, so she disregarded him and picked up her book to read. She tried to focus, but the distraction was simply too much. She couldn't take her mind off his beautiful body for long. Peeking over her book, she studied his physique once more, tingling again and just wanting to grab, perhaps a part of him.

Maybe it wasn't such a good idea to come to the beach today, she thought in retrospect. After all, a private pool may have offered a more inviting atmosphere. She wasn't used to having a guy ignore her and it made her feel old and invisible. She decided to leave. She got up, grabbed her chair, towel, and beach bag, slipped on her flip flops and headed for the car. Then a hand from behind touched her shoulder. She felt like she'd been hit by lightning. She turned around, and it was him, her appetizing college boy. He had removed his shades and his eyes were even better than she'd imagined. They were the darkest brown eyes she'd ever seen and she wanted to surrender to them. She coyly looked up at him. "Hello." Her voice quivered.

"You dropped your book," he said, handing it to her with a grin.

Her cheeks flushed as she tilted her head and meekly replied, "Thank you." She reached for the book, but he didn't let it go.

"And you forgot me too," he said. He took the chair from her hand and walked her to the car. He opened the door for her and bent down to kiss her so she offered her cheek. "I'd love to see you sometime. My name's Todd."

"It's nice to meet you, I'm London. What a coincidence, meeting Todd at Tod's Point Beach." She was surprised at her own quavering voice. "Sure," she responded, extending her hand. "When?"

Her stomach clenched as he captured her in a steamy gaze. "Well, I'm free right now if you're not busy?"

"I'm famished," London said as she regained her composure. "I'm just going home to change and eat dinner if you'd care to join me?"

"Sure, I'll follow you. He paused for a second and looked down at himself as if to remember. "I'm all sandy from the beach, though."

She smiled. "You can shower at my place."

He climbed into a 1953 red Corvette, lowered the white

convertible top, and fell in line behind her. London studied him in the rearview, remembering when Deacon had followed her home. Her heart fluttered, but she shook off Deacon's image and diverted her attention back to Todd. He was gorgeous, the wind whipping through his dark hair. A feeling of insatiability increased between her legs. As they approached the estate, she pushed the button to open the gates.

Todd followed her through the entrance and down the driveway to the back of the house. She got out of her car and he followed her up the steps to the door as he took in the manicured grounds of the Château d'Amour.

"Wow, this really is some place! It's beautiful," he said.

"Thanks. I love it here. You'll find a bathroom downstairs. I'll wait up here for you. I hope you like grilled ham and cheese sandwiches." She smiled as she pointed toward the stairway.

He grinned and followed her directions. She went to the kitchen and organized the food. Moments later, she felt a hand on her back. She jumped, startled, and then smiled as she was assured that the hand belonged to Todd. Her body quivered as she felt his face alongside hers, his breath hot on her neck, and heard him whisper, "Come join me." His hands traveled down to her butt, lifting it up toward him, causing a wonderful sexual sensation between her legs. She turned toward him and he grabbed her behind her neck, placing his lips hard on hers.

His hands cupped her face, kissing her deeper and stronger than the first time as she stepped in closer to him. "There's more room in my upstairs shower." He went downstairs first to shut off the water, then he ran back and stroked his finger up and down the back of her thighs as they walked up the stairs.

They entered her bathroom, a chamber of Italian marble, adorned with fine gold-toned fixtures that accented the walk-in shower. Stopping at the shower door, he kissed her shoulders and turned her around, moving to her face and neck, all the while undoing her top. He let it fall to the floor and proceeded to tug the string to release her bikini bottom from her hips. He reached to turn on the water and twenty-four jets shot across the shower stall. He felt the temperature and adjusted it to warm.

She watched him and grew more aroused as the steam rose and his gaze turned more aggressive. He kissed her as his hands cupped her breasts. He pulled her to him, holding her tight, his lips pressing down on hers in a passionate kiss. His tongue teased hers as they both entered the mist together. He took the perfumed bath oil from the shelf, poured it on the natural sponge, and started to rub her with it. The loofah was rough on her sun-kissed skin, but the sensation awakened her pores and her senses.

He slowly rubbed her body with the soapy sponge. He held her steady with one hand while washing and caressing her breasts with the other. As the lather foamed, the sensual fragrance fueled her desire. She placed her hands on his chest, moving them in circles and marveling at how firm and smooth he was. He fondled her breasts, as their tongues played tag with each other. She felt her breasts swell at his touch. His fingers slowly trailed down her body as he let his nails touch her skin. She trembled.

She savored his patience and finesse—*not bad for a young guy*, she thought. Finally his fingers touched her spot. She gasped as she opened her legs. Her arousal zone swelled at his touch. She arched her body as he teased her, moving toward his hand and begging for more. She wanted his fingers inside her, but held back from saying so.

Finally, in one swift motion, he grabbed her legs, hoisted

her with ease, pressed her against the shower wall, and entered her hard. She was enthralled by his strength and lovemaking talents. She wrapped her arms around his broad shoulders, with one hand entwined in his thick, dark hair, and the other on his back, clinging to his flesh with her fingernails. He slammed in and out then he slowed to prolong the ecstasy. As he did, she moaned and bit at his ear, his neck, his shoulder, enticing him to continue.

She loved the way he felt inside of her, so full and satisfying. With her eyes closed, he could have been Deacon for a moment. Todd resumed his aggressive pace again, bringing her back to reality, pounding into her with amazing force as her nails dug deeper into his back. Her eyes met his, and they came together, melting into each other as the mist consumed them.

Her head fell on his shoulder as he turned off the water, still embracing her. He opened the door and eased her down to stand before him. He grabbed her robe, draped it around her shoulders, and helped himself to a robe as they walked lazily to her bedroom. He pulled back the cream satin comforter and laid her down. He then slid in next to her and held her close as they both nodded off.

London awoke in Todd's embrace, surprised to find that they both had drifted off to sleep. He stirred, pressing his body to hers, and she could feel his maleness throbbing against her behind, hungry for more. He kissed her ear then sat up, resting on his elbow, and rubbed her body with his artistic fingers, circling her nipples till they were all hard and pointed. Then he placed his warm lips on them and sucked them while his hand moved down toward her wetness. He touched her there, rubbing her button with his thumb while his other fingers went in her slow and deep.

"You're ready for me again, aren't you?" he asked. She moaned, kissing him with her warm, soft lips, their tongues playing tag with each other. Part of her wanted him so badly, yet she stopped. She slipped out of bed and walked over to the fireplace. She lit it to warm the chill in the air. The weather had taken a cool dip at the end of the day. She proceeded to light some candles and kept studying him as she moved across the room.

They lay together in front of the fire and talked. He confirmed that he was younger than her, and then told her how he preferred mature women. He'd had enough of the fluttery girls. He wanted someone more stable. "You know, as soon as I saw you I wanted you, but was afraid that you would not want me." He looked over at her and liked her hair, still damp, cascading across the satin pillow, her face glimmering in the candlelight. She was incredible to him and he began to wish he wasn't attending a school so far away and that he didn't have to tell her that he'd soon be gone.

Chapter 3

JULY FOURTH HOT BUFFET

London took Todd's news—that distance would keep them from continuing—in stride. Pleasure without pressure, she reminded herself. He had been there when she needed. She'd move on to the next one or the next thing. She longed for Deacon and logged on to the internet, hoping to connect with him, but had to settle for interesting conversations with other online friends since Deacon was too busy to chat. The others would tantalize her with sexy, suggestive remarks, but they only made her crave Deacon even more. She longed for his touch and especially his warm kisses.

She heard a video call chime in over her laptop, just as she was daydreaming about him. Deacon! She quickly checked her own image on the screen, fluffing her hair and pursing her lips before clicking to answer his call. She melted at the sight of him, lounging in his black leather chair, smiling back at her. Behind him, she could see glossy teakwood office furniture and a breathtaking view of the cityscape through the wall-to-wall windows of his corner office in Europe. He wore a white silk shirt and black tie. She wanted to reach right through the computer and grab him in a delicious embrace.

"Hey, my baby, want to play?" he asked, eyes glistening.

She gave him that come-hither look as she sauntered over to the bed, carrying the laptop with her. She stood back and untied her black satin robe, letting it flow to the floor, revealing her new black-and-white lace teddy. She stroked the tops of her black thigh-high stockings and snapped her garter belt as she spun around, giving him a tantalizing show. He gasped in approval. She slithered onto the bed, turning the laptop so he could follow her, and she reached into the nightstand to select a toy. She smiled as she got her vibrator out.

"I am so ready for you."

The satin sheets caressed her skin and she swayed, gently rubbing herself with her toy. Deacon penetrated her with his eyes and his commands, all of which she complied with.

"Oh, baby, I'm so hard for you," he said as he eased back farther in his chair. She could see his rising manhood in his hand.

"I'm rubbing myself as I think of your wetness and how tight you are. I so long to be inside of you again, to feel your wetness on me, with your silky walls hugging me . . ." His voice faded into a groan.

"Yes, I feel you . . . oh my God, Deacon, you feel so good, so hard . . . fuck me hard! I need you so!" She closed her eyes and listened to his moaning. She felt her body tighten up to grip him, riding her toy hard as the vibrator rubbed her clit. Her body wanted his as badly as her mind relived their past interludes. He made them come alive again and she opened her eyes to watch his motion intensifying, his hand moving faster up and down his shaft, moving in time with her toy as it moved in and out, vibrating and making her so hot.

She was amazed at how in tune she still was with his body. His voice urged her on, "Come for me, baby, now . . . now!" Her body trembled as she felt her climax start. Her legs began to shake as she heard his breathing speed up, and soon she exploded as her juices flowed out of her. Deacon yelled, "Oh my God . . . fuck!" as he leaned forward in his chair and finally came.

London sighed and smiled shyly at him as he reclined again, exhausted, zipping up his pants. Even far away, they were still fine-tuned, and she relished the moment. Suddenly, Deacon sat up abruptly, reaching for the mouse.

"Talk with you later, hon! I've got to run. Bye for now." And he was gone in a click from the screen.

The summer was full of surprises as London prepared for the July 4th celebrations. It was a nice night for fireworks, she thought, as she dressed to go to her favorite spot to watch the vibrant booms and bangs.

She and Todd had stayed in touch since their recent excursion, but he had gone up north with buddies and she was feeling lonely. She was thrilled at the thought of being at her favorite place in Tarrytown, the Fisherman's Cove, with its spectacular view of the Hudson River. If nothing else happened, just to be on the grounds of her special spot excited her, and always had since she was a child.

She dressed in a short navy blue skirt, high wedges, and a white, low-cut V-neck T-shirt with a red burst of fireworks on the front. She also took a navy blue sweater, tied around her shoulders, for nighttime. She got in her Beemer and off she went, headed for the shoreline celebration.

The Fisherman's Cove restaurant was open for dinner; it was where folks could have a sit-down meal and stay inside for the fireworks, or go outside to the amphitheater and listen to the wonderful music. Once inside, she received a warm welcome from her favorite hostess, who gave her a big hug and a smile. London loved the whole ambience of the night.

The dinner tables were all decorated red, white, and blue, with cloth napkins sticking out of crystal goblets like a flame. The centerpieces had small American flags surrounded by imitation sparklers and glittery red, white, and blue shattered plastic pieces in the form of sprays. It was all so festive and the place was packed.

After being seated at the table, among other people, she felt lonely, more so as she noticed that most patrons had partners. An attractive waiter startled her as she was lost in thought. He was delivering her plate of succulent prime rib, fresh asparagus, and mashed potatoes. The meal looked and smelled excellent, but London only picked and nibbled at it as she was craving other culinary delights.

She pushed away from the table and joined the other guests at the four large picture windows overlooking the river and waited for the fireworks show to begin. She occupied herself by people-watching and noticed one gentleman who seemed to be alone too.

He was tall, dark, and good-looking. She moved closer to him when the chair next to him became available. He smiled a consenting glance at her.

"My name's Antonio."

"Hi, I'm London."

When the fireworks started she moved up closer to the window, and he followed. He stood close. She gave him an approving half smile. He touched her hand. A few minutes later as a burst of light exploded in the sky, he held her hand tighter. She didn't resist. So he pulled her closer. His hand was soft and warm. She felt good and was assured she'd made a good choice. They oohed and aahed at the fireworks and sent each other signals with their eyes and body language. He put his arm around her waist and she felt that familiar tingling in her tummy.

The sky lit up with bursts of color and lots of noise. She loved July 4th and the excitement that came with it. Antonio whispered in her ear.

"This is fun. Would you like to continue and go to a special spot near here that I love?"

She nodded. He escorted her outside to a nearby gazebo, where they sat together. He only held her hands at first. Then he moved closer, touching her face with his fingers, stroking along her jawline and over her lower lip. She opened her mouth and nibbled on his fingers. He smiled and kissed the palm of her hand, tonguing the inside of her fingers.

He pulled her to her feet and held her close as he swept her hair back and kissed her neck, her earlobes, and then her lips. They embraced as the radiant night sky burst with colors that seemed to mimic the emotions filling her heart. He turned and pulled her backward toward him. She could feel the intensity of his excitement and she grinned. He held her hand, rubbed her arms, and kissed the back of her neck while gently tugging at her long, beautiful locks.

The short stubble of his beard tingled against her neck and awakened her senses even more. She wanted to have him right now. He turned to her and they embraced more passionately. He rubbed her back and as he went lower, his hands cupped her butt, lifting her up a little. When he touched her breasts, she grabbed his arm and whispered.

"Let's go someplace more private. Please take me. I want you so."

His breath quickened as he took her hand and pulled her into the bushes. He lifted up her skirt and gasped in surprise when he discovered she wasn't wearing any panties. He touched her sex with his fingers, sliding them deep inside her as she moaned softly in his ear. He reached in his pocket for his protection, pulling out the package. He opened it with his teeth, placed it on, and then pulled her up in the air. Her legs surrounded him as he slid deep into her. They both moaned with pleasure. Her wetness helped him slide deeper and deeper as she gasped. She grabbed onto his shoulders, lifting herself and crashing down into him as she rode him wildly. Their climaxes were rapidly approaching and she wanted to scream, but she had to restrain herself as there were far too many people nearby. Instead, she clenched him tightly with every muscle and muffled her moans into his neck as they exploded together. She laid her head down on his shoulder, trembling as he held her close, kissing her tenderly on the neck, face, and ears.

"I don't want to put you down," he whispered in her ear.

She looked at him and smiled as the fireworks kept on booming, the lights from the sky flashing. Finally, she lowered herself down and reached into her pocket for a small silky cloth that she used to wipe herself dry. She offered it to him and he wiped himself as well.

They returned to the gazebo, cuddling like teenagers and giggling in awe together at the fireworks. When the show was over, she followed him to his place. She lounged on an oversized couch with him, enjoying a glass of wine. He turned on some music and led her to the hot tub in his modern bachelor pad. She enticed him with a slow striptease. His pleasure rod grew rock hard and he grabbed at her. She stepped into the water, laughing, and melted into its steamy warmth.

He explored her nude body with his firm hands and kissed her. He pulled her up on the seat and went down to kiss and explore her further. She lay back, enjoying his mouth on her, the roughness of his short beard scratching her thighs, his tongue tracing her sex as he sucked all her hot spots with tender kisses. He put his finger inside her and she squealed with delight, then he pulled her to him and entered her, taking her even higher and filling her with rampant desire one more time.

Antonio soon realized that London was insatiable. He'd met his match and together they went deeper in exploration of sex . . . and many more times than he had thought possible on any given night.

The fling with Antonio didn't last long though. His career took him out to the West Coast. London was beginning to wonder if she had become like a stepping-stone for men leaving town, since her last three lovers had each done just that. Antonio was gone, Todd was away at school, and Deacon was still overseas and out of touch. What's a woman to do but fill in the gap with a new experience? She continued to video chat with Deacon occasionally, but the calls and emails became few and far between. Moments with him had become brief and always ended too abruptly. He seemed to have lost interest across the miles and she felt completely abandoned. Not one to stay in the dumps for too long, she thought a sport might be a healthy distraction and decided upon golf.

She skimmed through the newspaper and noticed several ads for golf schools. *Why not*, she thought. So she went to her closet, pondered what to wear to learn golf, and came up with a sassy white skirt, a short-sleeved light blue top, and a cable-knit sweater with light blue trim. She grabbed her handbag and went off to the Walnut Brook Country Club, her school of choice.

She loved driving her Beemer with the top down, especially on a beautiful summer day like today. She felt the excitement and loved the feel of controlling the road, hugging the curves, and downshifting. Her mood was lifting. If she decided to join the country club, this would be a trip she would enjoy daily. In the distance she could see the club, which was a historical mansion that had been restored. Its towering peaks showed through the treetops. The club was renowned as one of the most desired golf courses and training schools in New York State. She found a parking space reserved for guests and left her car.

She walked into the impressive cathedral foyer and approached the female desk clerk. "Hi. My name is London Shelby and I'd like to inquire about golf lessons."

The girl beckoned someone. She called him Steve. London looked through the window out to the deck and saw a handsome man put down his coffee and rise from the table. As she watched him come through the doors, she found herself already admiring his confidence and ease. Before he even spoke, his demeanor commanded her respect.

"Yes, Kelly?" the man grinned as he ran his eyes up and down London's body.

"Steve, this is London Shelby, and she's interested in learning the game of golf."

London's heart just about stopped. As fate would have it, he was handsome with dark hair, a golden tan, and deep-set eyes, all her preferred features. She glanced at his left hand . . . *No ring, but that doesn't mean anything anymore,* she thought. *No tan lines on that finger either.*

"Ms. Shelby, have you ever played golf before?" Steve asked.

"No. Is that a good thing?"

"Yes." He grinned. "Because then we have no bad habits to break." He winked as he threw her a dazzling smile.

He led her to the driving range. He handed her a club and showed her the grip. She tried interlacing her fingers as he showed her; his body touched hers. She suddenly felt uncomfortable as she stood there, her hands around the shaft of the club and facing toward the distant green marker. He showed her a stance and a practice swing and then came close behind her again. He put his arms around her, holding on to her arms, and showed her the swing, again and again. He moved away as he put a ball on the ground and asked her to watch him, which she did. Then he came back behind her, putting his arms around her again and putting the balls on the ground. She swung.

"Not bad," he said.

He gave her another ball as he came back behind her again, but this time he was closer. She could feel his breath on her neck and a stirring deep inside her that she tried to ignore. He held her close as they swung together.

"The swing is very important, plus you have to keep your eye on the ball."

Her mind was not on the ball, but rather imagined the shaft of this instructor who was having such a positive effect on her. He smelled so good, and the heat from his body being pressed against hers was a definite turn-on. His cheek was so close to hers that she almost dropped the club. He held her tightly, feeling her body move with his, his arms holding on to her.

After numerous attempts at swinging the club, she was relieved to finally stop and take a break. He offered to take her for a ride around the grounds. She enjoyed the tour and the cool breeze as they rode on the golf cart. He inquired about her "intentions concerning golf," but he seemed to be implying something else.

"I'm not quite sure, but right now, I think I will just enjoy learning the game. I might consider joining a league later. I would, however, be interested in looking at a set of clubs . . . and more lessons." She grinned.

He smiled at her as they strolled into the clubhouse. He

signed her up for private lessons and fitted her for some clubs. She bought a golf bag, shoes, and a couple of cool outfits. She had spent more than a thousand dollars in just a few minutes.

As she drove home, her mind was still racing and she was feeling good about her experience, especially the effects that her teacher had on her. When she pulled into the driveway of the château, she noticed a car following her through the gate and down the drive. It was her instructor, Steve.

He jumped out and said in a somewhat scolding manner, "Miss Shelby! You forgot your golf clubs!" Then he laughed as she blushed at the idea. She was so rattle-headed that she'd left her purchase behind and never noticed him trailing her. He took the clubs out of his Jeep and carried them down to her.

"Thanks so much, Steve. Would you like to come in for a margarita? It was mighty hot out there."

"Yes, sounds good, since I'm done for the day." He smiled as he set the clubs down and followed her into the house. She mixed up two margaritas and led him out onto the deck. He pulled her chair out for her and as she turned, he surprised her with a kiss on the lips. She clung to him, embracing him and tracing his tongue with hers. He kissed her neck and down to her breasts. He licked the salty sweat from her body, loving every bit of her. They quickly abandoned their drinks with a quick sip and headed back into the house together. She led him into the family room, where he spun her around and kissed her neck again, cupping her breasts in his hands.

He looked into her eyes and said, "I'm going to fuck you soon, but we need to agree on something first. I am in control of you at all times when we're together, here, as well as on the golf course. You are mine to do with as I please. I will call you tonight and see how well you can follow my commands."

London was shocked. She never had someone say something like that to her but she felt a strong desire for him and simply wrote it off as role-playing, like she did with Deacon.

That night she received a phone call from Steve. "Hi, we are going to have phone sex and I want you to follow my instructions." London felt uncomfortable being told what to do, yet there was something about his voice that caused her to respond with a "Yes."

"What are you wearing?" he asked.

"Just a lounge outfit."

"Damn it, describe it to me," he said in a gruff voice that startled her.

"Black satin shorts and a short black-and-pink robe over a black lace bra," she said.

"That's my girl," he responded. "Now, take off your robe and bra and I want you to find some lotion and put that on your breasts. Rub them slow and all around, feeling the fullness of them. Pretend it is my fingers massaging them." She went and got some lotion and put it on her breasts, rubbing them slowly and feeling so turned on she thought she was talking with Deacon for a minute. "I am rubbing them," she said as she listened to him. "I am stroking my hardness, thinking of you this afternoon and how hot you were and how much I will enjoy fucking you." She smiled as she felt her hands slowly drift down to her tummy. She wiped the lotion off on a towel and made sure her hands were clean before she touched herself. "What are you doing now?" he asked.

"I just wiped my hands on a towel," she replied.

"Did I tell you to do that?" he voiced sternly.

"No."

"You don't do anything unless I tell you to, understand." She felt like a little girl who had been bad and she didn't like that feeling.

"Come here," he said as he pretended to be with her. "I am touching your head as you lay it on my chest, and kissing you. You're okay, don't be upset, you will get used to being my sex slave soon."

She felt her tummy churn at that comment and thought about what she could have done that made him think she would enjoy this role. Then she remembered how she acted around him and how fast she had adapted to his suggestions. She really didn't use any restraint at all. She would have to stop this before it got out of hand. "London?" his voice brought her back to this reality. "Yes," she replied hesitantly.

"I want you to take your fingers and go down farther, to your wetness, and rub yourself." She did.

"Now I want you to take your finger and fuck yourself, listening to my voice and the speed I am using."

"I have a toy; may I use that?" she asked.

"Yes, but only when I tell you to, not any other time." She reached in her nightstand and took out her toy. "I have it, may I use it now?" she asked again.

"Yes." She placed it on her button and let it vibrate there for a minute and then inserted it deep into her. "Ohhhhhh-hhhh," she moaned as she let the vibration take her into the darkness of sex. She took it in and out of her body, feeling the sensation of the toy plus the voice that dictated her every move. "Do you feel me? Tell me how good it feels." She told him how wonderful it was and that she was coming. "Good, darling. Come for me," he said over the phone. "Come for Steve." She started breathing faster and faster, her body moving around the bed, her hips gyrating back and forth as she felt the impending climax. "I am coming," she yelled into the receiver. "Good," he said. "Come, baby." She moaned and felt the juice flow out of her as she quieted down. "You did good.

I will see you tomorrow at 10:00 a.m. for your first golf lesson. Sleep well, baby." The hum of the phone brought her back to reality. She rolled over and fell asleep, her toy in her hands.

The alarm ringing woke her up. She stretched a little and felt something hard under her. It was her toy. She smiled, remembering the phone call last night. She got up, went to the bathroom, and washed her toy, then plugged it in to recharge it. She took a fast shower, dressed in a white bra and panties with a short white skirt and shirt with a sweater, grabbed some yogurt and coffee, and off to golf school she went.

The wind in her hair felt good as it brought some sense to her. This thing with her golf teacher had to stop. She didn't want any more of the phone calls or the control. She had been independent and wanted to stay that way. Nobody was going to tell her what to do. Even though it was sort of a turn-on, she thought she had better put a stop to it early. She pulled into the parking lot of the country club and got out with her clubs and loaded them into the golf cart. She drove to his school area. Area one was for new clients. London was supposed to go to area two. She saw him with another woman in area one, his hands around her waist and his lips on her neck. London stayed behind the wall, watching him make his move on this new conquest. She drove to area two and got out, doing some practice swings. Soon she felt his hands around her waist as he moved his body behind her suggestively. She smiled to herself as she said, "Good morning, Steve."

"Good morning, London, how was your night?"

"Interesting," she replied as she continued doing practice swings. He kept watching her as she tried to avoid his eyes. In doing so, she walked toward her golf bag and tripped over its handle. "London!" Steve yelled as she landed on her knee. "Ouch," she cried. He helped her up and took her over to a chair for her to sit down. She had a nasty scratch and grass burn on her knee. "Let me take you to my locker and clean this up," he said as she hopped on one foot to his room. When she entered the room she sat down as he opened his locker, and she saw six pictures of girls. He went into the washroom to get a damp cloth and she hopped over to the locker to read the inscriptions on the pictures. *Steve, thanks for the whole in one. Betty.* Another one read, *Steve, you're the best, oh yeah your golfing instructions are great also. Susie.* London hopped back to her seat, just as he came through the door with some Betadine and a Band-Aid. He washed her knee and kissed it and then put some medicine on it with the Band-Aid. She smiled and said, "I think I will go home. I am feeling a little queasy right now."

"Okay, I will call you tonight to see how you're feeling."

She got in the car, drove to the front of the building, and talked with the receptionist about quitting the classes. She told her that she just got a job and she would not be able to attend the golf school. "Perhaps next summer." She limped out of the lobby, got in her car, and drove home. She had only been home a few minutes when the phone rang. It was Steve.

"Hey, what's with the quitting the golf lessons? I know you do not have a job."

"I know, but Steve, this is not going to work out between us. I can't do this and I need you to understand. I thought I could but being controlled by you or anybody is not for me. I am free and want to stay that way, do you understand?"

"Sure, baby, I understand. It was fun, see you around." He hung up and she looked at the receiver.

A few minutes later she heard a knock at her door. It was Steve. She limped to the door and opened it. He took her by the wrists and pulled her over to the love seat, where he bent her over his knee. He twisted her hair with one hand, pulling tightly to hold her in place, while he traced his other hand slowly up her thigh and under her tiny white skirt. He choked on his own breath when he felt her slightly wet panties underneath. She had mixed feelings of fear, but not enough to stop him.

"You are a naughty girl, aren't you? You do need to be punished! You tried to quit my golf class and that's being bad." He flipped her skirt up and spanked her hard with one swift smack. She gasped at the sting!

"That's for not listening to me." She had to laugh a little.

He hit her again, this time harder, and she winced and moaned.

"Stand up!" he ordered her.

She felt funny and even a bit scared, but she did as she was told. This role-playing was a new kind of excitement for her.

"Now, take off your clothes, slowly!" he said in a stern voice.

She eased off her top, then her bra, letting them fall to the floor. She slid her skirt and panties down, letting them drop. She stood naked and feeling very vulnerable before him as he rubbed his hands up and down his zipper.

"Kneel," he said. And she did.

"See this?" he pointed to his hardness behind the closed fly.

"Yes," she replied in an innocent voice. She licked her lips in anticipation, surprised to find her mouth salivating to taste him.

"Take it out and suck on it!" he commanded.

She crawled over to him, opened his belt, and undid his zipper, staring up into his dark gaze that seemed to hold her with such presence and power. Feeling his hardness inside, she reached down into his shorts and stroked his maleness.

His erection flew up in total freedom, and what a fabulous specimen he was.

"Suck on it!" he yelled.

She slid her wet lips over his throbbing head as it disappeared with force deep into her mouth. He moaned as she sucked it, in and out, his hands yanking her hair, pulling her head toward him hard, forcing her to comply with the rhythm he demanded. She felt torn and confused by her strong desire to please him, in spite of his offensive behavior. He was so big she almost choked, but she loved the sensation and the feelings that were building up inside of her . . . burning wetness, longing to feel him as she strained and fought to breathe. Finally, he backed away, dropping out of her mouth as she gasped for a deep breath of fresh air.

"That's enough! I'm going to fuck the hell out of you now!" he growled as he pulled her up and pushed her over the chair. She waited there as he put on protection, awkwardly bent over and panting. She was feeling a bit degraded, but thrilled and anxious to be so furiously fucked by him at the same time. She squealed as he smacked her ass again, then slid deep inside. She moaned as his manhood filled her emptiness, which ached for him. He slowly pumped into her, then went harder and deeper, raging with fury, her body reacting to each and every invasion with a rush of pleasure. She could feel her orgasm building as he reached around and rubbed her sex hard. He pounded and thrusted until they finally exploded together. Breathless once again, her body quivered.

He withdrew, pulled her up, and spun her around, seizing her tightly.

"That was amazing, baby."

She felt somewhat humiliated and totally exhausted.

"You now belong to me."

She felt good about the way he made her feel sexually, but she liked her freedom. For a split second, she felt torn between desire and freedom.

"Wait, what do you mean, I *belong* to you?"

"My dear, you are now mine."

"Oh no, I'm not! I don't belong to anybody. I told you on the phone."

He looked like she had slapped him. "Excuse me?" He looked threateningly into her eyes.

"I do not belong to anyone! Not now, not ever!" she announced.

"But baby, you just let me have you. You let me fuck you! Doesn't that mean anything to you? You really mean we are done?"

"Yes, it meant we had a moment of passion and that's it! If you want control, I suggest you control yourself and kindly remove yourself from my home!" she replied in exasperation, still confused by these twisted feelings she had for him.

He shook his head back and forth, eyeing her while he threw his clothes back on. On the way out the door, he looked back at her. "Does this also mean you're really not taking golf lessons with me anymore?" She felt a surge of confidence fill her as she replied, "You got it, pal! I'm all done, golf lessons and all." She shoved him out the door and yelled after him, "Grab those damn clubs too. I'm returning everything right now! It's over!" Her heart was beating so fast she thought it would jump out of her chest.

He left in a hurry, loading the clubs back into his car while mumbling to himself, "She's crazy!"

She pressed the button to open the gates and laughed to herself as she watched him speed off. *Looks like I taught the instructor a lesson or two!* She realized that as a result of her afternoon adventures she'd worked up quite an appetite. She decided to have something delectable delivered this evening as she didn't feel much like going out. Her thoughts drifted back to the last delivery boy who had brought her dinner and she bit her bottom lip, grinning.

Chapter 4

HOT DEVIL'S FOOD CAKE

London sipped on her dark Brazilian coffee sweetened with a splash of French vanilla creme, lounging on the deck all bundled in her robe, enjoying the morning sun. The leaves rustled and she watched a few fall from the trees, gracefully drifting to the ground. The cool breeze smelled of autumn already and she reflected on how quickly this summer had slipped away. She was glad that she'd decided to take a couple days off. She had been inundated for months, working long hours assisting the attorneys with a landmark case. When she could grab just a little time for herself here and there, she had taken long walks through her favorite park, did some swimming, and had conversations with Deacon at least weekly, but he was swamped at work too. Now that the relentless litigation at her firm was finally over, and the verdict was a huge win for the firm, she could breathe a sigh of relief. She was determined to spend some extra time focusing on herself again before the dreaded winter months arrived, and with them, more grueling hours at the office occupying most of her time.

She had attempted to call Deacon to video chat this morning, but he was unavailable, again. She had so enjoyed their webcam encounters, and even his rather unusual demands like touching her button or taking her toy and sliding it deep inside her while using another toy to massage her. Their remote fantasy world had become the highlight of her weeks. But during the past month, he had now missed two out of three of their online "dates" and she was becoming concerned about the distance between them withering away at their connection. The last time they'd spoken, she sensed a coolness about him that left her feeling confused.

She shook off her uneasy thoughts of her lover and went inside to warm up with a hot shower. She decided to dress somewhat casually for once in blue jeans, a sexy, low-cut lacy white top with a ruffled black cardigan sweater, silky scarf, and black boots. She swept some of her long dark locks back with a hair clip, allowing just a few unruly wisps to escape and curl back down around her face, accenting her dangly diamond earrings. Feeling frisky, she tried to reach Deacon one more time. No answer.

She took the long stroll across the estate to check the mail. Among the junk mail was a letter from her doctor reminding her to schedule her mammogram. This time of year always made her feel helpless and emotional as she thought back to losing her grandmother. Grams had procrastinated about her mammogram for a few years and she paid the ultimate price for her indiscretion. When the doctor discovered that she had breast cancer, it was too late and there was nothing they could do to save her. Grams was gone just six months later. London felt a chill and her heart ached all over again with the devastation of knowing that Grams might have been around for at least a few more years had they caught it earlier.

She swept away the tears streaming down her cheeks and marched back into the house. She immediately picked up the phone and called to schedule her appointment. To her surprise, the receptionist said they had just received a cancellation for that afternoon, so they could get her right in at 1:00 p.m. She grabbed a whipped chocolate yogurt for a quick snack and headed out.

She decided not to put the convertible top down today. She drove solemnly to the appointment, feeling vulnerable as she listened to sad love songs and pondered her own mortality. The traffic was very light so she arrived at the hospital more than half an hour early. She sat in the car, reading emails on her phone and filing her fingernails to pass the time. She felt eyes upon her and looked out the window to see a handsome young man nearby, pacing beside his car, talking on his cell phone and eyeing her with a predatory stare. She pretended not to see him as she looked down and continued sanding away at her nails, but she could feel his eyes penetrating her. He seemed so familiar that she had to look again. As she turned her head back up to take another peek, she was startled to find him right outside of her window. She jumped, then blushed as she rolled down the window a little.

"Hi, can I help you with something?" she said in an anxious tone.

"I never thought I would see you again." He gasped, stumbling over his words.

"And who are you?" London asked.

"Hi, I'm Rick. I've seen you before, at the Fisherman's Cove on the Fourth of July. I wanted to meet you then, but you were with someone."

She wondered just how much he had seen that evening, but he seemed harmless enough and she eased her window down farther. She extended her hand, "Hi, I'm London." He took her hand in his and leaned down to kiss it. She blushed again as she tingled all over. His forwardness was a little awkward, yet very enticing at the same time.

"It's a pleasure to finally meet you, London. What a co-incidence seeing you again. What are you doing here at the hospital today?" he asked, his voice still a bit nervous.

"Oh, I have a mammogram appointment, which I should be getting along to now, I suppose," she replied.

"Well, I could escort you in if you don't mind, and we can chat on the way."

"Sure," she answered, feeling her heart lift a little and her tummy tighten with that familiar ache.

She closed the window and grabbed her handbag. He opened her door and helped her out of the car. Lost in idle chitchat, they strolled together across the parking lot and through the garden terrace entrance into the hospital. She could feel the intensity between them as they stepped into the elevator together, alone. She pushed the button for the fourth floor, and the doors closed as she turned to ask him which floor he needed. To her surprise, he was right behind her when she turned around. He'd startled her again, and she stepped back as he pressed up against her and held her tight to the wall.

He looked deep into her eyes, then kissed her fervently with a passion she'd been longing for. For a feverish moment, she accepted his advances, returning the favor deeply and intensely as she ran her fingers through his dark hair. She wanted to stop the elevator and take him right there, but she pulled away, breathless and feeling uncertain about this mysterious stranger. She stared into his eyes, trying to read what was really going on behind them as she felt the elevator easing to a halt. *Ding.* The doors slid open at the fourth floor. He released her from his hold and she practically darted from the elevator into the hall. His face looked troubled as he watched her escape.

"London, wait. Will I see you again?"

"I'm not sure, Rick. I-I have to get to my appointment. I don't want to be late," she stuttered, then hurried away and disappeared down the hall. She felt relieved as she walked, yet she was puzzled by her own uneasiness. Rick was a sweet guy, very handsome, and yes, he was forward, but that hadn't really bothered her before. *So why does it bother me now*? she wondered.

Still heated after her steamy encounter, she stepped into the imaging center's waiting room. She checked in and walked over to the table to select a magazine that looked interesting. She chose a seat in the corner and sat down, admiring the soft colors of the room. They were calming and reassuring. The light shade of gray walls and the beautiful pictures hanging with portraits of whimsical girls, ladies, and flower gardens accented by dark purple frames. The chrome bucket-shaped chairs had richly upholstered seats and backs in the same dark purple color. Comforted by her surroundings, she relaxed again and lost herself in the magazine stories. She mused over the title of one article, WHAT MARRIED GUYS REALLY WANT. *A mistress, of course.* She chuckled to herself.

She was pleased when the nurse called her in promptly at 1:00, and she was even happier to escape the office for another year when it was over. Afterward, she was craving chocolate again and decided to treat herself to some coffee and sweets in the cafeteria. She chose a large slice of sinful-looking devil's food cake from the dessert display and mixed her coffee sweet and creamy, just the way she loved it. She found a table by the window and began indulging herself as her thoughts drifted back to Rick and their elevator encounter. Her tummy tightened again and her breath caught as she relived his passionate embrace. She felt silly now for rushing off so rudely. And just as she was wishing for another chance to talk to him, he walked right up to her table.

"You sure make that cake look delicious," he said.

She devoured the last bite and licked the fork clean seductively before responding. "Hi again, Rick, please have a seat," she said with a grin.

He slid into the bench seat beside her. "Thank you. Look, I have to apologize for being so forward earlier." His words were fast and nervous as he continued to explain. "I just find you so . . . well, irresistible. And seeing you again here today, it just seemed like fate and I didn't want to let the chance pass me up again to show you how I feel." He paused, waiting for her to respond. She just smiled and eyed him curiously. Filling the silence, he asked, "So, how did your appointment go?"

Her breasts were still sensitive from the test. He sat close to her, his knee brushing against hers.

"I won't know the results for a week or so." She gazed out the window for a moment, pondering what to say next. Turning back to face him, she said, "Rick, your kiss was a surprise, I'll admit, but it wasn't unwanted. I'm sorry for running off the way I did. I just had a somewhat emotional morning, and I was not looking forward to coming here."

"I understand," he said. "How about we start over? Hi, I'm Rick Hudson," he said with a boyish grin as he extended his hand to her again.

She giggled and played along. "Hi, I'm London Shelby."

"Well, hello, London, I'm very happy to meet you," he said, feeling a little more at ease. "I didn't mean to come on to you, but if I may say, you're a very attractive lady and I just had to say hi. I hope I'm not offending you, but I was wondering if you might have dinner with me some night, if you're available."

She giggled again because he sounded like he was reciting a

well-rehearsed speech. She studied him for a moment and then responded, "I'm not married, if that's what you mean. And the answer is yes. I would like to have dinner with you." *Rick is hot*, she thought. He had great features, including a nice smile and dimples, not to mention a sense of humor. "My bad day seems to be getting better by the minute," she added.

Rick got up and wrote something on the back of his business card before handing it to her. It read: FANTASY MANOR 7:00 P.M., SEE YOU THERE.

She smiled and asked, "So you must live close to Tarry-town?"

He nodded and smiled, flashing those darn dimples one last time.

"Sounds good, I'll see you then," she confirmed.

She thought about him and cringed again for running off the way she did. It wasn't like her, but she realized that her recent bad experience with her dominant golf instructor had left her scared. Her guard was up, and she was feeling especially delicate and vulnerable today.

She left the hospital, ran a few errands, and headed home to relax before her date. She took a hot shower, dressed a bit conservatively in her black silky pantsuit with heels, and left to meet Rick at Fantasy Manor.

The drive from her house was a short one. She soon zipped into the parking lot. She could see Rick waiting for her at the entrance and felt a twinge in her tummy. She felt his eyes on her as she approached. She greeted him with a kiss and wrapped her arm through his. When they walked inside, there was a line of patrons waiting, a crowd gathered at the bar, and it appeared that every table was full. The place was so stylish and inviting, especially the warm glow of the embers in the stone fireplace. Rick took her by the hand and escorted her to the front of the line. A sophisticated lady stood at a podium, scanning the touch screen on her computer. She looked up and her face lit up when she saw Rick.

"Mr. Hudson," she said, trying to contain her excitement, "right this way, sir." She gave London a smile of approval before turning to guide them to a private corner table by the window that was magically awaiting their arrival.

London was impressed. Rick ordered wine for both of them, but she really didn't need it. She was already intoxicated by him. She took a sip of her water and smiled at him. Her eyes searched his face for an emotion, a sign that he felt the same way she did, but he was very cool. When the wine came, he proposed a toast. "To you, and tonight," he said with such assurance of how the evening would end. She smiled, but at the same time, she was beginning to feel uncomfortable. Even though she felt a strong desire to be with him, she had reservations. After her experience with the golf pro, she was not so anxious to hit the bed, so to speak, with just anyone. For a moment, she wasn't sure if she should have accepted his dinner invitation. She felt conflicted, but she couldn't put her finger on why.

He was charming. The conversation flowed smoothly and the evening was rather perfect. They dined on New York strip steak and it was divine. She sipped her wine and toyed with her meat, placing it slowly into her mouth, seducing him as she savored each bite. He was captivated by her. The evening went fast and Rick was a perfect gentleman. She began to reconsider her own doubts and insecurities about him.

Soon she was home, with a second date already scheduled for the following night with him. She was proud of herself that she had not slept with him that night. He called her several times the next day to tell her how much he'd enjoyed being with her. She was beginning to feel a little more comfortable about him and she was looking forward to dinner again this evening. He was taking her to a luxury restaurant with gourmet cuisine located in Midtown. She pampered herself with a hot bubble bath, then dressed in a short black swirl-skirt dress, black thigh-high stockings, and stiletto heels. She complemented the outfit with small freshwater pearls. They were just right for this special evening.

Rick called to say he was running a few minutes late, but that he was sending a car for her and he would meet her at the restaurant. *What a nice gesture*, she thought, then she pondered his reasoning. She was sure he wanted to take her home tonight, and without her car, there'd be no escaping him this time. She contemplated for a moment, then threw all caution to the wind and agreed. She opened the gates and awaited the arrival of her chariot. Before long, she saw the headlights approaching and went out to meet the driver as he circled in front of the château. An older, kind-looking gentleman leaped from the car and ran around to open her door. "Ms. Shelby, I presume?" he said with a smile.

"Yes, sir. And thank you," she smiled as she eased into the regal black luxury sedan.

They traveled into the city in silence, with only the soothing sounds of soft music playing. Her anticipation of the evening grew with each passing mile. As they got closer, she noticed the driver making a brief call on his cell phone.

As they drove up to the entrance, Rick was waiting on the sidewalk with a dozen roses and a big smile. She grinned at his dimples again. The driver must have let him know they would be arriving soon. She was flattered as Rick opened her door and extended his hand, helping her from the car.

"These are for you, my dear," he said with a smile as he handed her the roses.

"Thank you," she said and gave him a quick kiss.

He leaned in the passenger window of the car, paying the driver and thanking him. She thought, *I could get used to this special treatment.* London hooked her arm through Rick's and he escorted her inside. He had reserved a private corner booth. She eased into the seat, he slid in beside her, and she snuggled up to him. They enjoyed the view, the ambience, and the delicious cuisine. After dinner, they sipped their wine, chatting and flirting. Rick slipped his hand under the tablecloth and under her skirt, sliding his fingertips across the tops of her thigh-highs, occasionally working a finger under her stocking and then gently snapping it against her leg. He was tantalizing her and she was hot, wet, and wanting. He leaned in for a kiss and slid his hand farther up her thigh. He gasped as he touched her sex, pulling back from their kiss with a shocked and excited look on his face as he discovered she was not wearing panties. His eyes narrowed and he kissed her deeper, sliding a finger into her wetness.

She stopped him, nearly panting at this point. "Rick, this is no place to be making out like two teenagers," she said, trying her best to look serious, but failing and giggling instead.

"But baby, I want you so bad. Let's get outta here and head back to my place," he whispered, his breath hot on her ear. She was sure this evening would end in his bedroom. She took a long, cool drink of her wine to calm herself as she squirmed in her seat, when a tall good-looking guy approached the table.

"Hey, Rick, how ya doin'?"

Rick's face blushed. "Hi, Joe," he said, and turned reluctantly to London. "London, this is Joe, one of my business rivals," he said with distaste. London nodded; she was uncomfortable and unsure how to reply. Rick continued, "So, Joe, I'm fine. How are you?" he asked sarcastically.

"I'm doing just fine, and it sure looks like you are too." He looked at London and grinned. "So, Rick, how is that beautiful wife of yours? I heard she was ill. Is she doing any better now?"

Rick's face flushed darker now, with anger and humiliation combined. Choking on his reply, he said, "If you must know, she is not doing well. The treatments have failed and she's in the ICU. It's only a matter of time now. But Joe, this obviously isn't a good time."

Joe feigned a weak apology, despite his obvious intentions, and excused himself.

When Rick looked back at London, the color had drained from her face. She looked at him with disbelief and disappointment. Her heart ached and her head spun. Despite her reservations about him, she was just beginning to loosen up and enjoy his company. She was beyond astonished, and as much as she began to feel sympathy for this wretched soul, she was disgusted at the same time.

"London, I'm sorry. I-I was going to tell you, really. There just wasn't a good time," he stuttered nervously, pleading with her. "She's been sick for so long, and that's why I was at the hospital when I saw you that day. She slipped into a coma, and I've been so lonely and I just . . ."

"That's enough," London replied vehemently, her color now returning and blazing into a fiery red. "Please move so I can get out."

"London, please . . ."

"Now, Rick!" she ordered. He rose from his seat and she squirmed out. She dug through her purse and threw some cash on the table. She picked up the roses and tossed them, saying, "Here, take these to your wife. She needs them much more than I do." She turned and walked out of the restaurant on shaky legs, tears welling in her eyes. As she waved to hail a cab, she vowed never to be without her own transportation again.

When she arrived home, she undressed and took a hot bath. She cried silently as the steam penetrated her, soaking away her anxiety. As she recounted the events of the past few days, she wondered what was going on with her. *Have I lost my good judgment? Have I lost my mind?* She was exasperated, and the last thing she needed right now was another married man in her life, especially that scoundrel. She realized she had been ignoring her own intuition. Her instincts had her running from Rick the moment they kissed, and she never should have doubted herself.

She remembered another thing her grandmother used to say: *"London, there are two kinds of women in this world, those who men cheat on, and those who men cheat with. You just have to decide which one you're going to be."* She was beginning to understand this more every day, and although both choices seemed painful, she wondered why anyone would ever want to be a wife at all. She had resolved one thing, though: there was no replacing Deacon. There was nobody who could. After her bath, she crawled into bed, curled up around her pillow, and cried herself to sleep.

Chapter 5

JUCY FILET MIGNON

The season was changing, the air getting chillier and, thankfully, Deacon had resumed his virtual role in her life. His work pace had slowed down a bit and he had returned to heat up her nights with ever more intense sexual sessions via webcam. She was grateful and relieved. They were thriving on each other's company almost daily again. She longed for him to visit, but she kept those thoughts to herself.

But London's silent wish came true. Deacon called to tell her that he had to fly into New York on business the following week. He was overseeing a merger between a European and an American corporation. She was even more thrilled when she realized that her law firm represented the U.S. corporation's interest, so she would also be attending the same meeting. She immediately called La Fontaine Hotel, where the merger conference was being held to check on the availability of a suite. She spoke with Monique regarding reservations and she was informed that all of the rooms were booked, with the exception of the Imperial Suite, which was five thousand square feet of pure luxury.

"I'll take it!" She continued to arrange for early check-in so that she could take advantage of the amenities before Deacon's arrival that day.

London requested a few more days off from work for the weekend following the conference so that she could spend time with Deacon during his stay in New York. She busied herself preparing everything in advance for the merger to ensure that everything would go smoothly. She didn't want any disruptions getting in the way of reuniting with her lover.

Her talks with Deacon became more passionate over the next week as the day of the conference grew closer. She was overcome with anticipation. She felt as if she were weightless and floating when she thought about being in his arms again. Her skin tingled as she daydreamed of his touch.

Thursday morning arrived. The conference was scheduled for Friday morning, but Deacon was flying in that afternoon, so he would be free for the evening and he was all hers! She took a shower and tied her hair back in a quick ponytail. She packed two suitcases full of all her favorite garments and lingerie, just in case. She dressed and raced off to the hotel.

She enjoyed the drive into the city and looked forward to a therapeutic day of pampering at the hotel spa. She gave her keys to the valet and was greeted by her personal butler, a service included as part of the Imperial Suite package. He was young and cute, edible even, but London had her mind focused on the main course, Deacon. She wanted everything perfect for him. The butler introduced himself as Bruce. He had the bellboy deliver her luggage to the suite while he gave her a brief tour of the legendary hotel and introduced her to the concierge. They explained all of the amenities and excursions that La Fontaine had to offer. The hotel lobby was remarkable Louis XV décor with crystal chandeliers that made her feel right at home.

Bruce escorted her to her private elevator and up to the suite, then reviewed the wine choices he'd selected for her as he stocked the private bar. He proceeded to unpack and arrange all of her personal items as they reviewed her agenda for the day. She planned to indulge at the spa for a manicure, pedicure, waxing, facial, and various other therapeutic treatments, followed by a one-hour full-body massage. Afterward, Bruce would draw her bath and have her meal promptly delivered. With the details finalized, he informed the spa of her arrival.

She wandered through the magnificent four-bedroom suite and took in the spectacular view. The décor was exquisite, with sumptuous textiles and furnishings inspired by the ambience of the royal court of Louis XV. There was a grand piano in the living room, a den with a library that was stocked with a vast assortment of titles, an amazing kitchen, and a sophisticated dining room to entertain guests.

Once Bruce left her alone she ran into the inviting master bedroom and jumped onto the bed like a child, letting out a small cheer in anticipation. She rolled around in the luxurious linens, hugging a pillow and laughing at herself. She couldn't contain her excitement. Lustrous marble and granite surrounded her in the master bath, adorned by gleaming 24-karat-gold-plated fixtures. She looked forward to her relaxing spa time, but she also couldn't wait to get back to this room to soak in the alluring bathtub.

She took the private elevator back down to the lobby. She was guided to the spa, a lavish oasis where every inch of her body was pampered with opulent treatments, scrubs, wraps, and rituals. The finale of a full-body massage stripped away every bit of stress she felt.

She returned to the suite, refreshed and rejuvenated. Bruce had her bath-oiled tub water warm and ready, fragrant and bubbly. She soaked awhile, admiring her French pedicure and her own long, slender legs. Feeling glamorous, she closed her eyes and pictured Deacon's face. Just the thought of him made her wet and wanting. She eased her hand down and toyed with her sex, teasing herself as she dreamed of his touch. She stopped contemplating whether or not she should save herself for him. She decided there would be plenty of orgasms for him to savor, and she slipped her hand back under the bubbles to pleasure herself. She rubbed her button and eased a finger inside to stroke her hot silky walls. It took only a few minutes and she was panting, tingling, and moaning to her own delicious motions. She let out one soft whimper as she exploded into the bathwater. She smiled and sighed.

She wrapped herself in her fluffy white bathrobe and rang Bruce to deliver her brunch. She was famished after the morning's activities and she feasted on pancakes with maple syrup, bacon, and a fresh fruit platter. She savored each scrumptious bite as she counted down the minutes until she would see him again, all the while envisioning her mouth on his beautiful body. She hoped he would still feel the same way about her.

She primped and fussed all afternoon. She slipped into her silky thin-strapped black dress, black stockings, and stilettos. Although the shoes hurt her feet a little, looks were everything for a night out. She also hoped that after the business meeting tomorrow, she would be spending much more time in bed than on her feet.

Her tummy fluttered as she took the elevator to the main lobby and sat waiting for him to appear. She saw him enter the lobby and her heart skipped a beat. He was more handsome than ever. She stood up and walked toward him as their eyes met. He dropped his suitcase and hugged her tightly. She knew nothing had changed; she could feel it in his embrace.

Bruce greeted Deacon and took his luggage. He arranged to have it sent up to the suite as they headed for the dining room.

Deacon pulled out her chair for her and kissed her on the cheek, whispering, "Hi, baby." She smiled as she felt the tingles between her legs. He took his chair and sat down with an ear-to-ear smile—that damn smile. She bent over and kissed him, her low-cut dress showing peeks of her breasts, and they were longing for his magic touch.

"Been waiting long?" he asked as she caressed his hand. Her tummy tightened up as his skin sent shivers down her spine. "Since I saw you last," she replied, her desires evident in her hungry eyes. Her hand moved sensually across his hand, in between his fingers, along his wrist, and down to the end of his third finger, the one she wanted him to put inside of her so badly. She smiled and ordered a latté.

"It's been too long since we last saw each other, yet looking at you, it feels like I've never left," he said. "The webcam just doesn't do you justice, London. You're more beautiful than ever."

He smiled and grabbed the finger she'd been trailing along his hand. He cupped her hands in his and kissed them gently. She breathed in the fragrance of her freshly brewed latté, pulling it deep inside her, letting the fragrance fill her mouth with the warm aroma going right where she wanted him to be. She swallowed, her eyes never leaving his. She looked down at him as his arousal was beginning to show. She shared his anxiety, surrounded by so many watchful eyes.

"No need for us to sit here. Are you ready to go to our room?" she asked.

He nodded yes. He got up from his chair and slipped his arm around her waist as they headed to the private elevator. Approaching their room, he turned and pulled her face toward him. Her eyes looked up into his as he kissed her with that mouth that she had been dreaming of for nearly a year. She closed her eyes as their soft lips met, her tongue touched his, and the jolt was electrifying.

Heated and blinded with passion, they entered the suite. He pulled her toward him, kissing her neck and sliding her dress down over her shoulder. He worked his way across to the other shoulder and slid her dress down, letting it fall to the floor in a pool of silk. She took a few steps toward the master bedroom with her come-hither look, but he grabbed her again and unfastened her bra, which joined her dress in the trail of clothing that was forming on the floor. She breathed a sigh of relief. He kissed her nipples and tugged at them with his teeth. Her smell again affected him as she felt a hardness growing in front of her legs, and she felt stirrings deep within her. She pulled away, luring him into the luxurious lair she had waiting for him. She felt giddy, as if it were their first time all over again.

As he followed her, he stripped off his tie, adding it to the trail that led to the bedroom. He picked her up and she wrapped her legs around him as their kisses became deeper and wilder. He laid her down, kissing her hard as he slid her into the middle of the bed. His body brushed over hers, not pressing on her, not yet. Their magic was all in the foreplay, the wonderful foreplay—in person, not by way of a computer screen.

He paused to study her lying there waiting for him. Her body blending with the cream satin sheets, her hair spread like feathers on the satin.

"You are so gorgeous," he whispered in his husky voice. "I've missed you so much."

She could hear the pain of a loveless marriage in his voice

and she ached to hold him. He would be hers tonight and in her heart for the rest of her life. She watched him undress. She watched him with her pleading eyes, and when he took the last of his clothes off, she knew he would be hers once more. His maleness was unbelievably long, thick, and ready for mounting, which would take as long as he wanted it to. He slid on the bed and knelt beside her, his feet by her head, kissing her body with his warm lips. His mustache tickled her as it made trails down her body. She moved toward him but he pulled back. She would have to wait for him, as he waited for her.

His hands fondled her breasts, his lips kissing her neck and all the way down to her nipples, where he licked them to hardness and sucked on them till they were pointed and hard. He smiled down at her as he licked her, slowly moving lower on her body. He was almost where she wanted him to be and she squirmed and arched her back, urging him to speed up the process. He looked over at her and narrowed his eyes as he continued his way down.

The lower he went down on her, the closer his erection came to her face. She took her tongue and touched it. He moaned and moved over on top of her so she could access it fully. She wiggled between his legs so his sex hung over her face. She slowly slid her lips over his throbbing head as his fingers slid deep into the most intimate part of her, his thumb moving over her aroused button. He rubbed it as she moaned, moving her body and trying to help him. He ran his tongue teasingly over her sex, then sucked and nibbled. She swallowed his manhood, taking him deep into her throat, pulling him toward her, in and out. He moaned and nibbled at her thighs. She pulled back and teasingly nibbled at his thighs too. *Two can play at this game*, she thought. She licked and sucked all around his manhood, teasing him with her teeth, teasing his head with her tongue, then taking him deep into her throat again and again.

He was rock hard now and the intensity was more than he could stand. He was pulsing to be inside of her. He eased around her and came up to kiss her neck again. He was ravenous now, and with such lust in his eyes that they burned all the way down to the lower part of her body. He pulled her toward him and she knew that soon she would be his again. His body pressed tightly against her and her juices flowed more than ever before, but he pulled away once more.

He sat on the side of the bed to put on his protection. The package was not cooperating with him and he forgot it as he watched her, waiting for her to move. She was at his mercy. He smiled, knowing it was when he decided to take her, and only then would he release her from her sexual torment. Only he could do that, but she knew she had increased his anxiety a bit more this time.

He massaged her legs as he worked his way up, opening them to see the glistening spot he had created. He knelt before her, teasing her button with his hardness, sliding it up and down. He slid inside of her just a little, then pulled away, pressing his head against her sex and watching her beg for more. Finally, he slid deep inside her. She gasped, but he didn't move. He stared devilishly as she moved her hips, trying to satisfy herself, but he did nothing to help her. She was almost in a fit.

"Please," she moaned. "Please, take me! Don't make me wait! We can play more games later, but right now I need you, Deacon."

He smiled as he moved rhythmically inside her, slowly at first, then thrusting faster, forcing into the depths of her body until both of them were moving together, moaning and breathless. He rolled over, still inside of her, pulling her on top of him. She mounted him, screaming his name, their hands intertwined as she rode him like a wild stallion, crashing into him over and over.

"Oh God, London! Oh, baby!" Deacon cried out. Through her own cries, she heard his voice and the sound of her name on his lips. It was magical. She felt his fire shooting inside of her and she came all around him. They climaxed together with such a force that it took the air right out of their lungs. She collapsed on top of him, her hair falling over his glistening body, and breathed a sigh of relief. She had never climaxed like that before and he held her close, wondering what happened. What was this carnal desire they had now? How could he ever let her go again?

They lay in bed touching each other, kissing and snuggling, feeling the effects of their ravenous lovemaking and knowing that more was due to come. They gazed at each other, both knowing what the other was thinking. He continued to kiss and hug her as they talked small talk. Their desire was mutual, and so close, yet so far away.

London reluctantly slid out of the bed and headed into the shower to rinse off. To her surprise, Deacon joined her and lovingly caressed her as he gently washed her clean for the next round. She savored this steamy moment, his hands touching every part of her body, gliding over her silky skin as the bubbles foamed. When he was through, she smiled and lathered up her hands with the fragrant body wash to return the favor.

She massaged his shoulders as she rubbed down his back, slowly working her way to his front. She kissed his neck as she cleansed his chest, running her fingers through his hair and pressing her fingertips into each muscle as she glided slowly downward. She knelt before him, rubbing each leg up and down as he began to rise again, her eyes fixated on his, watching his yearning for her growing stronger with each gentle touch. She worked slowly up his thighs until she held his maleness in her hand. She stroked him gently at first, then tighter and quicker. He closed his eyes and leaned his head back as he groaned. She stopped abruptly, smirking with that come-hither look as they slowly stepped out of the shower and dried off. He followed closely behind.

They crawled back into the bed together and she snuggled deep into his arms, toying with his chest hair again. She never felt scared with Deacon in any way. She was so secure about her emotions with him. They had always been able to read each other's minds, but tonight, their souls were connecting more deeply than they ever had before. He rubbed her arms and nipples, which were already aroused again. Soon their mouths connected and they kissed deeply. He put his hand between her legs, slowly rubbing her.

He lifted her up and carried her to the dresser, placing her on the edge and opening her legs. He bent down and touched her tenderly with his lips, enjoying the pleasures she had waiting for him. She moaned softly at first, but soon she went wild as he quickened his pace. He took his masculinity and rubbed it against her, teasing her with it until she was begging for more. He entered her as she grabbed onto him, her arms around his neck and her wet silky walls holding him right where she wanted him. He took her slowly, deeply. He took his hardness back out and carried her to the bed, where he placed her legs on his shoulders and entered her again. She screamed at his talents, and his way of playing with her. She felt her insides building and soon the feeling was so powerful for her that she exploded into one orgasm after another, like she never had before, as he emptied himself inside her. He kissed her again as he gently let her legs drop onto the bed. He collapsed on her, his heart beating right on top of hers. It was delightful.

After several more hours of lovemaking, they were famished. They dressed and went down to the hotel's restaurant.

"I am only going to be here one more day," he said. "I would like to make dinner reservations for tomorrow night at Tom & Jerry's Steakhouse. They've been in business for years and they have the best steaks in the city. Or would you rather go someplace else?"

"That sounds like fun."

"I can make reservations for seven-ish if that's okay?" he suggested.

"Tom & Jerry's sounds great, and you know I love steak. Maybe after dinner we could take one of the carriage rides through Central Park that Bruce was telling me about," she asked, beaming and batting her lashes at him.

He smiled, enjoying a peek at London's rarely seen child-like nature. "That sounds perfect. Let's do it."

Although they had the conference tomorrow, their night would be free and they agreed that they would spend it out of bed.

The next morning they had breakfast in the room and then made love before the meeting. The merger went smoothly and soon they were heading back to the suite for a quickie before dinner.

To London's surprise, Deacon had arranged for a limo to take them to dinner. They sipped champagne and the chauffeur took them for a spin around Broadway and Midtown before delivering them to Tom & Jerry's.

The rooms at the restaurant were medium-sized and each

different. They sat in the room with the fireplace, enjoying succulent filet mignon served with asparagus spears, hollandaise sauce, and red wine. For her dessert she chose chocolate cake with vanilla ice cream and hot fudge sauce drizzled over all. This was the best food she'd ever tasted. After dinner, the limo was still waiting outside to transport them to Central Park for the carriage ride. She snuggled deep into Deacon's arms, lost in the intoxicating romance of the evening. The ambience of the park and the skyscrapers that surrounded them was enchanting, and even if only for a short time, he was her prince and she was his royal princess.

When they returned to the hotel, they made love again. Each time was better than the last, and every time they were together was the best she'd ever had. Her orgasm was so intense, so emotional, that she cried a bit when they were through. He was so tender and loving, but soon he would be gone again. She knew deep in her heart that they would be together again someday, but she wished he could just stay. She tried unsuccessfully to muffle her cries and stifle her emotions. She wondered if his wife would ever find out about them, and part of her wished she would. Then maybe she could finally have him all to herself.

She knew her feelings for him would last a lifetime, and no matter what happened, she had her memories of him that would last forever. That weekend, the world seemed to stand still as two friends became true lovers. London was convinced that Deacon was her soul mate, and Deacon was overcome by the powerful feelings they had renewed together.

Deacon left for England the next morning. Bruce packed her things and chatted briefly with her. He seemed to sense her loss and brought her a single white rose to cheer her up. Her heart ached, but she smiled at his gesture and appreciated his kindness. She tipped him generously and thanked him for all that he had done to make her stay so lavish and enjoyable. The valet brought her car around and she drove back to the château, her mind consumed by thoughts of Deacon. He was her most cherished lover. He always had been and always would be. She missed him already and she knew the cam sex simply wouldn't be enough anymore. She needed something to look forward to, something to take her mind off things. *A trip to England maybe*, she wondered as her smile returned. It was good to be home, even if she was alone. She settled in as her mind wandered, plotting her voyage overseas and hoping to see Deacon again very soon.

Chapter 6

TANTALIZING DELIGHTS

The Monday staff meeting felt especially long, in spite of the great report of a successful merger. She robotically made her presentation, sat down, and gazed out the window for the rest of the meeting, reflecting on La Fontaine and her weekend with Deacon. She daydreamed of crawling back into the warm bed beside him. She shook her head and redirected her thoughts to the tediousness of the meeting, as best she could.

She was relieved and famished when it was finally time for lunch. She tucked her laptop in its case, grabbed her purse, and hurried out. The sensation of cool, fresh air on her face brought her back to reality as she strutted down the main street looking for a bar and grill. She was in the mood to try something new today. The Rest Stop had intrigued her before and she decided to enter the dimly lit pub.

She selected a stool at a high-top table, perfect for displaying her sensuous, shapely legs and stylish stilettos. Her eyes swept the bar. Over in the opposite corner sitting in a booth alone was a man whose eyes were focused on her. He held up a goblet of wine and she nodded, holding up her glass of water.

Her heart skipped a beat as he signaled the waiter to bring her a glass of wine. She smiled and nodded at the stranger. She browsed the menu and ordered grilled shrimp. After several sips of wine, she slipped off her jacket, exposing her silvery blouse with the stand-up collar, a deep plunging button-down top that barely held her breasts in. Her cleavage was framed by a heart-shaped necklace with a diamond in the center, which glistened in the dark. His eyes were still fixated on her. She could feel his intense gaze and with it, she could almost feel his heated touch. Her moist lips lingered on the edge of the cold glass as she sipped her wine. She moved her legs back and forth, her muscles tightening to contain the desire that was already building between them.

London loved Deacon more than any other man, but she still loved men in general. She loved their smell, the way they tasted and felt next to her body, and their strength. The endurance of a man really appealed to her. She loved to be taken, controlled, and ravished by them. Her gaze traveled back to the room and along the table, assessing all of the men, these men who were so consumed and controlled by their jobs that they only glanced fleetingly at her, which was fine. She was certain that most of them were far too intimidated by her power to even approach her, and her palate was far too refined for any of them anyway. She had her Deacon, and of course, other provisions.

As her mind wandered, she thought about how she loved certain words and the moments that they signified: "*Connection*," when a guy's eyes met hers and she savored the feeling of that tingle in her tummy; the thrill of "*anticipation*" of his first touch and the taste of his first kiss; and "*penetration*," the moment when he filled her emptiness with sustenance and satisfied her voracious appetite.

The man in the pub never left his table, but he drank when she drank. His eyes pulled her toward him, taunting her, teasing her, playing with her as she played with him. She took her finger and slowly dipped it into the wine and then touched her lips with it. He did the same. Her wetness increased despite the ring she noticed glimmering on his left hand. Even if he was married, she wanted him and he knew it. She felt herself reverting to her old habits.

When her meal came, she was no longer in the mood for food, as she had a growing hunger for something else. She toyed with her shrimp, dipping it in the sauce and placing each piece into her mouth as if it were his hardness on her lips. She sucked on it, nibbled on it, took bites, and then dipped it again and again in the sauce, licking it clean every time. She tore off a piece of bread and buttered it. Placing it in her mouth, she chewed it slowly piece by piece, then back to the shrimp, dipping and sucking over and over again. She enjoyed this game.

She noticed him squirming and she smiled. She watched him take off his jacket and loosen his tie and collar on his off-white shirt. She smiled as he patted his forehead with his napkin. She touched her drink, stroking her fingers slowly down the condensation and around the fullness of the glass. She brought it to her lips, sipping and lightly skimming the rim with her tongue. He slid back in his booth, never taking his eyes off her. She smiled and finished her meal with bravado, slipped on her jacket, and paid the bill. She could see his anxiety rising as she headed for the door, his eyes ablaze and narrowing with a sinister infatuation.

She was headed for her car when she suddenly felt an arm pulling her into the alley. It was him. He pulled her to him.

"I'm going to fuck you right here," he whispered in a

husky voice, his hot breath panting on her neck. He slid her skirt up, pawing at her butt, her tummy, her slim waist. His kisses were long, deep, and slow. His lips were soft, warm, and lusting for her as she touched his tongue with hers and tasted the wine. His breathing was harder now against her skin as his lips followed all the way down as far as he could go, kissing the tops of her breasts. She heard him unzip his pants. He touched her bare sex with his fingers, massaged her, inserted his fingers deep inside her, and moved them in and out. He penetrated her with his hardness as a deep moan escaped from his throat, then he pulled out, zipped up his pants, and gave her a devious look. He kissed her again, tugging at her tongue with his teeth, then pulled away and handed her a card as he turned to leave. She stood there numb, feeling weightless and breathless. Looking at the card, she blinked, her dazed eyes adjusting to the light, and the wine, and the almost-sex. The card read, COME TO ME TONIGHT 7:30 AT THE YORK PALACE HOTEL, ROOM 703, MATTHEW.

She composed herself and went back to the office. The meetings resumed as her thoughts roamed again, this time thinking of Matthew . . . the feel of his fullness and how the void space between her legs would soon be full again. Her anticipation was overwhelming. The monotony of the meeting continued, but her mind never left the alley. She turned her head, leaning into her shoulder, and she could still smell his cologne on her blouse. Her tummy tingled. She ran her finger across her lip and nibbled at her fingernail, remembering the bar.

Soon the meeting was over and she left early, racing for home. Once she'd finally made it inside, she collapsed on the couch, opened her legs, and touched herself. Yes, she was ready for Matthew. She wondered if she should wait for him, or satisfy herself now. She scoffed as she opened the drawer and took out her toy. She rubbed it across herself as her body trembled and she released a sensual moan. It felt so good. Her tender part had been excited ever since this afternoon and needed taking care of.

She inserted her toy inside her hot, wet sex, one part touching her arousal zone as the other went deep inside. She trembled as it massaged her into a long and smoldering climax. Her body relaxed as her juices flowed. She touched them and took her toy up to her mouth, tasting herself and thinking about what was waiting for her tonight. She tidied up, undressed, and turned on the bathwater and music. Soon she was submerged amid the sudsy bubbles, relaxing and enjoying the music.

Revived, she stepped out of the tub and dried herself with a big fluffy white towel. She walked into her adjoining bedroom to select her outfit for the evening. She chose her black silk strapless dress with a full skirt, black thigh-highs, stilettos, and her silky wrap. She hustled out the door, hopped in the Beemer, and sped off toward the hotel.

Standing in front of the door to his room, her heart was suddenly beating out of her chest. She thought she might just have a heart attack right there as she knocked. After a moment, the door swung open and there he stood, wearing only casual pants that hung low, his broad shoulders and chiseled abs revealed and glistening. He was a decadent dessert waiting to be devoured. Her mouth watered and her mind was back in the alley again. Her pulse raced faster, and she was certain she could feel her blood turning into hot, liquefied caramel.

His eyes pulled at her, his arms embraced her without a word, and his lips found hers. They were warm and soft and so full of passion. She melted in his arms. He walked her over to the couch, his lips pressed against hers all the way, never losing touch. He sat her down, pulling her legs toward him, and reached under her skirt to find no panties. He smiled approvingly as he touched her, rubbing her gently, searching for her opening, her hot spots. After a few minutes he asked her to touch herself. She complied, placing her finger on her button and then inside.

"Fuck yourself," he said as he unzipped his pants and took out his hardness. She wanted it so badly as her fingers were working their magic on her hot spots. He tugged at her hand and licked her fingers. He grasped a handful of her hair as he pushed his sex toward her mouth. She took him in her other hand and eased him into her eager mouth. She sucked hard as he continued sucking on her fingers, nibbling and teasing. She lingered at the thick head of his hot member, lapping the precum. It was throbbing as she sucked it down to the base and back up. He reacted with low moans. He took his fingers and penetrated her, fucking her deeply as they both trembled and climaxed together. Her body shook, his maleness ejecting his juice into her mouth so fast she could hardly contain it. He looked at her adoringly, stroking her face and hair, and still yearning to be inside of her again.

She snuggled deep in his arms, his hands massaging her back and her breasts. He teased and sucked at her nipples, bringing them to hardness. She groaned as her body prepared for his. He kissed her neck, her throat, and then her lips. He backed away, touching her lips with his long, slim fingers. He smiled at her while his fingers outlined her full warm lips. Then he kissed her. Their tongues played with each other momentarily, then he licked his way to her sex. He pulled her legs apart and sucked on her sensitive parts. She was hot and ready for him. He was savoring the effect he had on her. He placed his mouth over her button and sucked hard. She moaned, begging for his sex, which was already thick and hard and ready for her again. She couldn't wait until he took her, to have him back inside of her again the way he was in the alleyway.

She whispered. "Please, hon, I need you so badly."

He smiled and responded, "Soon . . . very soon."

He continued to suck on her until she almost screamed, then he pointed his protected hardness between her legs and entered her. Her body swelled as they moaned together. He pumped into her slow, then faster and deeper into her wet, silky walls, which hugged him tightly. She relaxed her muscles as he penetrated her, then she tightened them as he pulled out, again and again until her whole body tightened up and she could feel the pending explosion about to happen. He flashed that sinister look at her again as he shot into her, her body convulsing around him. She smiled as he kissed her again and again, lying on top of her with his hands cupping her face and his mouth on her lips.

After the second round, Matthew explained that he was only in New York on business and he had to leave in the morning. He said that he would look her up again should he ever return to the city. He didn't ask her to stay, and she didn't want to. She knew he was married and didn't want to be there if his wife called.

London smiled as she headed home, satisfied with the night, even if she did feel slightly used and abused. She'd gotten what she needed and so had Matthew.

Chapter 7

SYRUP-DRIPPING FRENCH TOAST

Almost two months had passed after the magical weekend at La Fontaine Hotel with Deacon. She hadn't heard a word from him since he'd returned to England. It was late and her mind was consumed by thoughts of him as she tidied her desk and turned out the only remaining light in the building. As she made her way through the darkness and down to the parking lot, she thought of how the looming storm outside resembled her brooding emotions. She usually contained her feelings well, but the loneliness, coupled with the gloominess of the weather, was beginning to dampen her spirit and challenge her resilience.

As a security guard escorted her to her car, against torrential rain and winds gusting to fifty miles per hour, she made a feeble attempt with her umbrella. It flipped inside out as she scurried, cursing her high heels as she lunged through the puddles. *Why didn't I wear boots today?* she wondered.

"Good night, Ms. Shelby. Drive safely," the guard shouted over the wind and thunderous sounds booming overhead.

"Thanks, George," she replied with a smile as he closed the door on her black Cadillac Escalade, her winter car.

She felt safety and comfort in the big SUV, protected against the storm as the downpour continued, raging through the sky and pounding relentlessly against the rooftop with a force that was almost deafening. She was glad for the heater, which was beginning to warm and dry her legs and feet. She shuffled in her seat, kicking off her shoes to let them dry. She checked her image in the mirror, stalling as she hoped the rain would let up. Her mascara was smudged and her hair was drenched. She sighed as she flipped the visor back out of her face. She flicked on the radio, and it was as if the music had read her mind. Alison Krauss and John Waite belted out their duet of "Missing You." As the rain washed over the windshield, blurring the city lights, she finally released the tears that had been welling up over Deacon, letting them fall freely down her face.

She sniffled into a tissue as she sang along with the lyrics, trying to reassure herself. Regaining her composure and changing the station, she set off for home. She found a station with news, traffic, and weather to get an update on the storm that continued to hammer the city. She heard "Emergency alert!" followed by several beeps, and the newscaster warned of the severe thunderstorm. He reported lightning, gusting, damaging winds that had caused downed trees and power lines, and encouraged people to stay inside. She scoffed at the announcer. "Some of us have to get there first." The traffic report followed, informing her that the interstate was closed due to a jackknifed semi-trailer and the subsequent pileup. She was relieved to know beforehand so she could cut through East Irvington up to Tarrytown and avoid the traffic jam on the highway.

Up ahead, she caught a glimpse of a sea of red taillights and the flashers of the state troopers at the accident. She exited the freeway just in time and headed down her alternate route, a deserted stretch of road near the Taxter Ridge Park Preserve. The storm raged on as she slowly made her way through the darkness. Suddenly, she slammed on the brakes as a tree branch blew across the roadway in front of her. Startled, she crept ahead, noticing more blinking lights. As she approached, she could see the emergency flashers on a wrecked pickup truck that was blocking the right lane. She slowed almost to a stop as she proceeded into the left lane, where she could see that the truck had crashed. A large tree had fallen onto the shoulder of the roadway and the front right tire of the truck was lodged up onto the trunk of the tree: it looked as if the tree had swallowed up the truck. Branches had crashed through the windshield, and behind them she thought she could see the driver stirring to get out. London pulled off to the shoulder in front of the accident and grabbed her cell phone, dialing 911. The phone beeped and flashed NO SERVICE.

"Damn it!" she yelled in exasperation as she slipped her still-wet shoes back on. She hesitated, then jumped from her SUV to go out and check on the driver. He saw her coming and eased down the window. She climbed up onto the running board and eased into the window slightly, ducking out of the rain.

"Sir, are you okay?" she asked.

"Yes, I think so. I'm not sure," he stammered, disoriented from the collision and holding his head in his hands. "I tried calling for help, but . . ."

"I know, the storm has knocked out cell service." All she could think about was getting out of this rain. "I'll help you," she replied quickly. "Do you think you can walk?" she asked.

He stumbled and she guided him to the comfort of the SUV. Once inside, both dripping wet from the storm, London eyed this burly stranger in her passenger seat with caution and curiosity. He wore a long black trench coat and a black rib knit beanie hat, with a few wisps of his blond hair trying to escape from underneath. He was adorable. Then she noticed the blood on the side of his face, coming from a cut above his eye.

"I'm London. Are you sure you're okay? You have a cut on your face," she said, reaching over to gently stroke his cheek. He turned and looked at her, still bewildered, but smiling now.

"London?" He exclaimed as he removed his hat. "It's me, Max!"

"Oh my God, Max. I can't believe this."

She leaned over to embrace him. Max Callaghan was her old flame from high school, and she hadn't seen him since graduation, which was nine years ago. They had dated awhile and had gone to the senior prom together. She sat back to get a better look at him and assess his injuries.

"Max, you look great, but that's a nasty cut."

"You look fabulous, London. It's great to see you too, but what a way to meet."

"I've seen better days," she laughed. "I look like a drowned rat tonight."

Max chuckled and eased the visor down to look at his wound in the mirror.

"It's not that bad," he argued. "But my truck, well, that's another story."

"I'm taking you to the hospital. You have to get that checked out."

"No, I'll be okay. I just need to bandage this up and I'll be fine. Then get a hold of roadside assistance to tow my truck." He fished out a card from his wallet with the phone number and attempted to call out on his cell again with no luck.

"I can take you to my house. We can treat that cut, and you can use my home phone."

"That would be great." He proceeded to explain to her how the lightning had flashed and the tree had come crashing down right in front of his truck. He had no time to stop and ran his truck right up onto it. She drove extra carefully, as she was blinded by the frequent flashes of lightning that lit up the entire sky, and the darkness that fell between them. Some of the streetlights were out.

"I'm sure glad I didn't shut off my landline," she said, once they got to the house. "I haven't really used it much since my grandma passed many years ago. It comes in handy at times like this."

"Oh, you still live at the château? That's such a great place."

"Yes, Grams left it to me and I didn't have the heart to sell it. It's been my home for almost as long as I can remember. So what were you doing out in the storm tonight?"

"I was at my construction site. I own a contracting business, and I met my crew at the job so we could secure the cranes and other equipment before the storm. We were running late and just got caught up in it."

She hit the button and the gates swung open. She felt a sigh of relief to be home safely, and she was not alone. She unlocked the door and headed straight for the laundry room. He followed behind.

"We'll fix up that gash in just a minute. First, let's get out of these clothes." She peeled off her soaking-wet jacket and suit as he looked on. "You haven't changed a bit," he said as he flashed a complimentary grin. He caught himself and felt a tad bit guilty for thinking this way at this moment. He stripped away his wet garments too. He was built like a lumberjack, with broad shoulders and abs of steel, humbled only by his tousled, wavy blond hair that hung just above his piercing blue eyes. Even though he wasn't her usual delicacy, just the sight of him had her steamy already. Her flame was rekindled—just that quickly—and she recalled just what it was she had seen in him so many years ago. She tossed their clothes into the dryer and threw on a robe, handing one to him with his wallet and keys, and ordering him toward the bathroom with a smile.

She sat him down in the chair at the dressing table in the bathroom and retrieved her first-aid kit. She pulled up a chair in front of him and nursed his wound. He groaned and winced a bit. She giggled and teased him as he flinched, but she took her time, gently stroking as she cleansed the skin around his cut. He wriggled around at her touch, their robes sliding back and their bare legs brushing against each other's. His breathing became a little quicker, and his eyes sparkled at her. She applied the bandage with a little pressure and sealed the moment with a small peck of a kiss on his cheek. He smiled and she knew he was captivated all over again. So was she.

"Now that you're all patched up, how about some coffee?" she asked.

"Thank you, and yes, that sounds great."

They headed down to the basement to the soda bar. She giggled as she pointed to the reproduction rotary dial pay phone that hung from the wall.

"You can call from there while I make our drinks. You don't need coins for it. It only looks like a pay phone."

"Thanks." He chuckled back. He pulled up a stool and took out his wallet. He dialed each number and waited as the dial rotated, eyeing her with one eyebrow cocked and a smile. She fired up the espresso machine and began whipping up two hot caramel mocha lattés. As Max sat on hold with roadside assistance, he checked out the surroundings. The room had a 1950s theme, with red shiny seats on the stools that lined the old-fashioned soda shop counter. Three gooseneck chrome-plated handles for the soda bar shimmered, accenting the historical Coca-Cola signs and matching metal chairs adorned with the logo at four small round tables positioned around the center of the room. The floor was black-and-white checkered tile to complement the tiled backsplash on the wall behind the counter that outlined a huge mirror.

The entire room reflected in the mirror, and he could see numerous photos of classic cars hanging from the walls, and Betty Boop smiling down above him. Beside him was a vintage jukebox loaded with 45 rpm records offering a trip down memory lane with an assortment of melancholy music to choose from, mostly from Grams's musical archives. He leaned against the machine, making arrangements to have his truck towed.

"It's all set. They will get to it as soon as they can, but the driver said it could be a while as they've had a lot of calls tonight," he explained as he made his way over to the counter, watching her putting the finishing touches on their lattés. "They'll take my truck to a nearby garage about three miles away, and I can just get a cab home soon."

"Or you could stay, and call one in the morning after the storm clears," London said as she handed him his coffee.

He smiled. "Sure, that would be great. I just don't want to impose on you any more."

"Max, you're not imposing. It's great to have your company tonight."

They sat down to sip their coffee and chat at one of the small round tables. The conversation flowed as they caught up on the past nine years. They talked about the upcoming ten-year reunion and contemplated how much things had changed in such a short time. London got up and strolled over to the jukebox.

"Do you remember the contest we had our senior year to select the best nostalgic songs for our graduating class?" she inquired.

"I do. And I remember your song was one that was chosen." He hummed a few notes.

"I'll Be Seeing You," a song written by Sammy Fain and sung by Billie Holiday. The vinyl 45 slipped into the slot and filled the room with sound. Max grinned as he rose from the table, taking her by the hand and leading her out past the tables to an open area of the tiled floor to dance. He was an excellent ballroom dancer, something that was hard to find these days.

Her body relaxed as his breath brushed by her neck, sending chills up her spine. His breath was shortly replaced by his warm lips, on her neck, her ear, and the side of her face. Then he cupped her face, looked deep into her eyes, and kissed her wanting lips. His lips were soft and tender, surprising for such a rugged, brawny man.

After the song, she led him upstairs. She lit the fire and they curled up on the bamboo love seat, cuddling into the warmth and comfort, enjoying the port in a storm that they offered each other. She sipped at her coffee, feeling his eyes on her lips as they brushed the rim of the cup. Their words fell away as his eyes told her everything. She put their cups on the coffee table and leaned in, kissing him fully on the mouth. He grabbed her around the waist, pulling her onto his lap in one swift motion. She was right: he was all man. She was sitting on his lap, kissing him softly as he untied her robe, revealing her perky breasts. He breathed in her intoxicating fragrance.

"My God, you smell delicious," he said as he kissed her neck. His hands slid up to her shoulders and pushed her robe off, sliding it down her back. She tipped her head back as he worked his way down to her breasts, kissing and sucking until her nipples stood at attention. He was so gentle, and that familiar ache was burning deep within her. She had been so lonely for weeks and distraught over missing Deacon. The attention she had been longing for had finally arrived, and she savored the moment.

Suddenly, the wind outside whipped and howled, lightning flashed, and thunder boomed, followed by the long groaning sound of a transformer surging electricity through the wires, then everything fell silent as the power flickered and the room went dark. Except for the warm flickering of the fire, the house was eerily pitch-black.

"Oh, that was a horrible sound. The backup generator should have kicked on immediately," London said, wondering why it hadn't.

"Well, let me first take care of you, and then I'll be happy to check on your generator for you," he said in a husky voice, pulling her tighter to him.

"Sounds good to me," she replied with hunger lingering in her tone.

She could feel his growing lust. She sent her tongue searching for his and found it. Their tongues played tag as he massaged her back. He held her close and she felt their feelings beginning to merge, feelings that had been locked away long ago.

Once burned, she learned—but did she? Here she was, her passions flaring up again, thinking *I like this man*, as she studied him. Something about his look . . . his deep-set crystal blue eyes, shimmering blond hair, and mustache that made his soft lips even more inviting. He had captured her, and her heart surrendered, a bit anyway. She still belonged to Deacon. Max smiled as he studied her face, seemingly aware of the deep thoughts consuming her.

"Is something wrong?"

She shook her head and gave him a tiny smile, feeling almost shy for a moment as he seemed to peer into her mind. She kissed him again and again, on his face, his neck, his lips—those wonderful soft lips. He pulled her to him and cuddled her in his arms.

"I won't do anything you don't want me to, okay?" he said, kissing her on the forehead.

He held her in his strong arms, kissing her, rubbing her, overwhelming her, physically and emotionally. She shooed away the voice in her head reminding her that Max was not a date. He was simply here by circumstance as a result of the storm. She didn't care. He had captured her heart for a moment, and this moment was all she needed right now.

He laid her down and kissed her more passionately than before. His arms around her, pulling her into his center, she felt all of him . . . his chest and the wonder that was being born between his legs. She wanted him. He explored her, touching her places she hadn't thought about for quite a while. The neglect had taken its toll, and she was ravenous for him.

He kissed her tummy and worked his way down, carefully observing her reactions as he proceeded. She was comfortable, and he was gentle with her as he kissed her down there. She opened up her legs to him. He smiled as he kissed her tenderly, inciting so much emotion within her that she almost cried. He touched a part of her that needed attention, and she was aflame. He was skilled and she relaxed, enjoying every moment of his tongue, playing with her, taunting her, her body moving toward that mouth and the tongue that was holding her captive.

"Yes," she moaned as she felt passions flare up, her life juices flowing—opening up and allowing her to feel again.

"Please. I need you so badly . . . take me please." She felt slightly embarrassed as she heard the words coming out of her mouth. But she was hot and needed him now. In this moment, she didn't care about anything else but the feelings between her legs and that he had something she wanted. It was close to her mouth and she took her tongue and licked the end of it. He moaned. She moved closer, sliding her lips over the end. He moaned louder and took it out of her mouth. He came up and kissed her gently.

"Not this time, baby—you're going to come for me," he whispered as he slid her to the edge of the couch and she felt him enter her. She had almost forgotten how good having someone inside her could feel. He slid into her with one push and stayed right there, collecting himself as he was overwhelmed by the intensity. She wiggled her body for some action, but he was very much in control. She adjusted her body around him, moving herself into a comfortable position for the act.

He waited for her and kissed every inch of her that his lips could reach while holding his hardness in position. Then slowly, he withdrew and pushed back into her. She felt all of him, and he took her breath away. He was so hard and wonderful as he reached behind her, placing his hands on her buttocks to pull her even closer and tighter to him. She gasped as he entered, more deeply with each thrust. He took her slowly, holding on to her the whole time, penetrating deeper and deeper, pausing as she reveled in his manhood. His pace was so sensuous, his manliness so luscious and gratifying. She wrapped her arms around him as their pace quickened and she moaned, hugging him tightly as they came together, a long and wet climax that seemed to go on forever.

He reached over and pulled the comforter from the sofa.

He covered her as he held her securely in his arms, and they rested together in the silence. The storm had passed, in all its fury, and so had her internal whirlwind of emotion. She closed her eyes and recounted the moments of the evening. He was so wonderful. She snuggled deeper into the masculine spirit who now possessed her, and the world she knew changed again.

She awoke the next morning to the smell of breakfast and coffee. She found Max in the kitchen, cooking up French toast and bacon. He was a tangy dish of masculinity with a side of softness that warmed her heart. The aroma was intoxicating, and the food was delectable as she licked the syrup from her hand while eating the wonderful toast.

He let her know that he had fixed the generator, and reports on the news said that power should be restored to the area in just a few hours. His cab arrived and she walked him to the door. He kissed her long and passionately before they parted ways. He said he would call her soon. She wasn't so sure, and her heart ached as soon as the taxi drove out of sight.

A few weeks later, she still hadn't heard from Max or Deacon. She went to the computer to see if Deacon was logged on. He wasn't. She had not talked with him in such a long time, and she was getting worried. As she dressed for work, she thought about the trip to England that she had planned, but only in her mind. She wasn't sure that he would welcome a surprise visit. She was concerned that he might actually feel invaded by her unexpected presence. She slipped into a long, slim-fitting black pencil skirt with a tight-fitting black cashmere sweater, belted at the waist. She complemented the ensemble with a cottony plaid scarf and high-heeled black boots. She slipped into her long, black double-breasted trench coat and headed out for work, feeling sexy, cozy, and shielded from the elements of the pending wintry weather.

When she arrived at the office, the meeting room was ready and waiting. The silver refreshment cart was stocked with chilled bottled waters and various refreshments, along with a lavish display of scrumptious fresh fruits, luscious Danish pastries, and assorted delights. The conference table was set with tablet computers, along with notepads and pens for those who still preferred to write notes during the meetings. The agenda indicated that this was a special meeting to introduce a new partner to the law firm, and his identity had not yet been revealed. London snacked on mouthwatering berries and raspberry Danish as she selected a bold brew from the numerous flavored beverages in the carousel tower. She poured her daily cup of java and mixed it sweet and creamy, inhaling the heavenly aroma.

The door swung open and the suits marched in. She eyed them all. They looked like clones . . . all but one, that is. *Oh my God, what is he doing here?* she thought as Deacon sauntered into the room, looking stylish as ever in a black tailored suit with a thin white shirt and a gray and black hexagon-patterned tie. Mr. Jackson, senior law partner, stood proudly in front of his seat at the head of the table as he introduced Mr. Deacon Wayne and shared the news that he would now be assuming a role as partner handling international matters, a new branch of the firm.

The lawyers buzzed about, reaching over to extend congratulations and handshakes. Others stood and shuffled over to chat and get to know Deacon. Some of the gestures of support were sincere, others masked their annoyance with being introduced to a new partner as they were awaiting their own promotions. London went unnoticed, and none of them were aware that she was already acquainted with the new hire. The only new thing about Deacon to her was the absence of a ring on his finger. She wondered what the deal was. What had happened to his wife? And when had he moved back to the States? She discarded her remaining morsels, poured another cup of coffee, and headed for the table.

The massive oblong walnut table held twenty-four chairs. A rare few paralegals had earned a seat at this discriminating table, but London was well-respected for her litigation experience and proficiency. She claimed the seat she had earned with dignity, and she now had to make an effort to maintain that dignity when she really wanted to run over to him and flood him with questions and kisses. She casually glanced at him and he glanced back, suppressing a smile.

The flurry of excitement in the room faded, deferring to the business agenda and the partner who now had the floor. Deacon sat, pretending to be fully attentive to the speaker, but really had his mind on London, who was trying not to appear flustered. He toyed with his pen, holding it straight up on the table and slowly sliding his fingers down, flipping it over, and repeating the motion. She got the message, and fortunately others in the meeting didn't notice. She watched, but attempted not to do so in an obvious way. When she squirmed in her seat a bit, he took it as a reply signal and then put the pen up to his mouth, gripping the tip in his teeth.

She began to tingle between her legs. She hungered for him. She was hypnotized by his seductive charm. His every move was sensual, his features magnificent—his eyes, his fingers, even his pen. That darn pen! She remembered his hands on her that same way and she wanted them on her now. She wanted to be that pen, and she envied it. She wanted his hands to be on her, touching her hotness like he did that pen, touching her wetness, fondling her, feeling her. She was overcome by her extraordinary appetite as it took on a mind of its own.

She wanted to escape, finding it difficult to remain calm in his presence, here among the rigid suits.

The meeting drew to a close. As the attorneys funneled out of the room, Deacon stayed behind. London strolled over to the refreshment cart, lingering, as he did, mixing up another cup of coffee. A few stragglers remained, but London and Deacon patiently waited them out. She snatched a big, juicy strawberry from the fruit platter and sucked and nibbled on the end of it as he looked on. She wrapped her lips around it, slipped the entire thing in her mouth, then pulled it back out. *Who's squirming now?* she snickered to herself.

The last of the clones found their way out and they were finally alone. She strutted over to the door, turned her back to it, and twisted the lock into place. She eyed Deacon with a menacing stare as she walked over to him, her eyes never leaving his. She eased herself up onto the table, adjusting her skirt and hiking it up a bit so that the side slit fell open, revealing her silky black thigh-high stockings. He caught his breath as he rolled back slightly in his chair, making room for her to slide directly in front of him. He moved back up toward her, almost touching her, but not quite. She knew his mouth was watering for a taste just as much as hers was. Her cashmere sweater plunged perfectly at her cleavage and the shoulder was beginning to slide down, revealing even more luscious skin. She tilted her head inquisitively and flipped her dark, beautiful locks to one side.

"Deacon, are you still married?" she inquired in her sweetest voice.

"When I was here with you for the merger, she found my laptop. Well, I had forgotten to erase our conversations. When I returned she had left me a note that she was filing for divorce. Just like that, it happened. I was neither disappointed nor upset. But I rather wish I'd been brave enough to tell her the truth. I was shaken up and needed time to cope. I was overcome with guilt for breaking her heart and not taking care of our conversations, and for being with you. And even though our marriage had fallen apart, I did love her once." London felt a bit ashamed of herself. She should've waited and invited him over for dinner to have this talk, but her impatience got the best of her.

"I wish you would have told me. You shouldn't have had to go through this alone."

"I was in total shock. I blamed myself. I was lost in anguish and regret. I'm sorry for not letting you know, I just needed to be alone to have some time to think about the rest of my life."

It occurred to London that they should leave the conference room and see who was around before they attracted attention and questions. The morning hour was getting late, and it seemed that most of their colleagues had left. They made small talk as they walked through the office, making sure they were alone.

"Deacon, may I show you where I work?" London said as he played along. Once behind her closed door, she asked: "And what did you decide about *the rest of your life*?" She wasn't sure she wanted to hear the answer.

"I'm still not sure. I just know that I'm glad to be here with you right now, and there's no place in the world I'd rather be."

Her heart jumped and her skin tingled as his eyes smoldered again, drawing her in with their enchantment. He sat up as she leaned into a steamy kiss. He ran his hand up her thigh and rubbed the lacy tops of her thigh-highs, teasing the bare skin just above them. Her sex was aching for his hand to go just a bit farther, and she scooted toward him, but he eased his hand back. She saw that twinkle in his eye and knew the game had begun. She leaned in for a deeper, more intensely passionate kiss as his hands moved toward her breasts, tugging at the sweater that invited him in. This time, she pulled back, grinning devilishly as she stood up. He gasped and almost spoke, but she bent toward him teasingly, still looking in his eyes and whispered, "Shh."

She knelt before him, undid his belt, and unzipped his pants to release the bulge from its prison. Her taste buds still tingled from the strawberry and her lips were moist as she placed them on the tip, then slid them over his throbbing head. She licked it with such zest that his head fell back to rest against the chair and he let out a soft moan. She continued to suck and he almost erupted before he pulled her up and onto his lap. He was panting as she took hold of his erection and slid it inside her. She sat there for a moment, pushing all her weight onto him, straddling him with her wetness as she felt the tip go deep inside, then she rode him up and down. His hand massaged her button and she felt herself building up to an orgasm as he filled her with his hardness. Just as she was nearing her climax, he lifted her up anxiously.

She had him so hot that he displayed an aggression she hadn't seen in him before. He stood up abruptly, manhandling her as he turned her around toward the table. He was rapacious and almost barbaric as he hiked her skirt up to expose her fiery sex that awaited him. She was gasping as he bent her over, taking her from behind. She sprawled across the desk, her hair cascading over her as she bit her lip to keep from making a sound. He thrusted into her, his hands on her hips, and rode her hard and wild. They were restricted to silence, and it made them tremble harder than ever as they panted and struggled to refrain from screaming in ecstasy. She never wanted this feeling to end. She treasured the sensation just before an orgasm, and the risky promiscuity, right here in their offices, escalated the intensity of the moment. He pounded and crashed into her. Their bodies collided in scorching obsession as they moaned softly into a bittersweet climax together.

Deacon's gentle nature returned immediately and he helped her up from the desk and stroked her hair back from her face. He smiled and they both laughed as she quickly adjusted her skirt and her just-fucked hair. He zipped up his pants and straightened his tie. They were overwhelmed by the intensity that had overcome them. He grabbed her in a warm embrace and held her as she buried her face into his neck, breathing in his delightful scent.

"Wow, London . . . baby, you always amaze me."

"You beguile me, Deacon."

"So, Ms. Shelby, was there something you needed?" he asked with a sigh, his voice taking on airs of nonchalance again as he released her.

"I got what I wanted. Thank you, sir. And there's more where that came from," she retorted as she curtsied.

She hoped he would follow her up on the invitation as they made their way discreetly out of the building.

Chapter 8

SENSUAL FRENCH CUISINE

London was packing lightly for her first-class flight to France departing the following night on business for the firm. She was assigned to work on an international law agreement. She was proud of herself for not only being recognized for her skills but for representing her country at this conference.

She liked to travel, though it could be grueling at times. She grew tired of the monotony, lines for security, check-in and scanning, planning hotels, restaurants, bars, and mediocre food. She was now just plain tired. However, this time her mind was at least pacified by the delightful fact that she would be visiting France.

She was relieved to hear the announcement "Now boarding first-class passengers" for her flight. She went to her compartment and loaded her carry-on in the generous overhead space. She sat down in the window seat and waited for the other passengers to file through. She was a bit displeased as she would have preferred the aisle seat, but none were available. *At least there are fewer seats in first-class*, she thought, so she wouldn't have more than one passenger seated beside her.

She was excited to be flying on a new, state-of-the-art aircraft with all the high-tech bells and whistles. The attendant delivered a preflight glass of wine to relax her before takeoff. She toyed with her personal onboard touch screen, reviewing first-class menu choices, available movie selections, and games. She tilted back in her cozy chair and gazed out the window into the sunset, watching the luggage carts and airport vehicles racing here and there as her thoughts drifted to Deacon. She felt someone next to her and turned to see who. It was Deacon. He was popping up everywhere in her work life now.

"Well, hello there, handsome." She grinned. "Why didn't you tell me you were flying to France too?"

"Sorry, I didn't even know until late last night," he explained as he stowed his carry-on. She settled in to read a book and sip her wine. He opened his newspaper and leafed through it, occasionally peering over it at her and her perky breasts. She had dressed for the trip in her wrinkle-free black silk skirt suit with thigh-high black stockings, but she had to have the three-inch black suede pumps, comfortable or not, as they made her luscious legs simply irresistible. She was so glad she'd chosen them now that Deacon was here. She felt sexy and she knew his desire was growing as she crossed her legs and eased back in her seat.

She pretended to read but her excited breathing was a dead giveaway that he was beginning to affect her sexually. As the plane was clearing for takeoff, she had that feeling she loved in the pit of her tummy. She polished off her wine and continued to halfheartedly read. After a few minutes she felt his touch on her leg. She glanced over at him as he moved her skirt up higher on her leg. Still holding his newspaper skillfully with one hand for privacy, he eased the other between her legs and slid his fingers up to touch her wetness. She reclined farther in her seat, opening her legs to invite him in with full access. As the plane climbed toward the heavens, she was ascending from within to cloud nine.

"You naughty girl, wearing no panties," he whispered. "You should be punished."

"And you should be my punisher."

He moved the newspaper so that she could see the effect she was having on him. He was so hard he was ready to burst from his pants. She reached over to taunt him, touching his bulge.

"Mmm," she groaned.

As the plane finally leveled out at thirty thousand feet, the lights came on and the pilot informed passengers that they were free to move about the cabin.

"Why don't you visit the restroom," Deacon suggested. "I'll be along in a minute. I will knock once, pause, then knock twice so you know it's me."

She agreed and rose from her seat, adjusting her skirt back to its rightful place. The elevation, along with a bit of turbulence, alcohol, and steamy lust, had her head whirling. She held on to the backs of the seats to balance herself as she made her way to the restroom. In the bathroom, she freshened up as she awaited his arrival. Soon she heard a knock, then a pause, followed by another two knocks. She opened the door and eased back to let him in.

He stroked her hair and kissed her eyes deeply and ravenously. He picked her up, placing her on the small sink. As he moved down her neck to her breasts, she threw her head back. He took his time kissing and tonguing her all the way down, his warm, wet tongue leaving cool trails behind. He stood back a moment to drink her in and she hungrily reached for his belt and unbuckled it. His hardness popped out and her mouth watered to taste him. Panting, she tried to lean down to reach him, but it would have taken a contortionist in the confines of the tiny room, and he wouldn't even allow her to try. He restrained her, resumed his torturous kisses, working his way down to the tops of her thigh-highs, running his tongue along her thighs and finally reaching her button. He licked so hard that she almost came, but then he stopped abruptly.

"No, precious, you'll have to wait like I have to." He smiled as he turned around to use the toilet, and then he exited, leaving her discontented. She was stunned at his cruel and arrogant game. She jumped down from the sink, used the toilet, and wiped away the wetness he'd instigated. She was beyond frustrated as she left the bathroom.

When she returned to her seat, he was sitting by the window, so she sank into the aisle seat. She wanted to say so many things, but she bit her lip in exasperation and crossed her legs. He could see she was irate, and he leaned over to whisper in her ear.

"It's a long flight. We'll have plenty of chances," he said with a slight snicker in his voice. His whispering breath sent chills down to her wetness, but she shifted in her chair slightly away from him, her lips protruding in a petulant pout as she sulked. She grabbed her book and continued ignoring him.

Before long, he leaned over to the controls and clicked off the light. The sun had disappeared, and the darkness offered some comfort and privacy. He reached over and took her book away, replacing it with a section of his newspaper. He then reached under the paper and pulled her skirt up just enough for his hand to touch her hotness. His finger touched her, opening her lips up. He felt her wetness and smiled. His little finger massaged her, and for some reason his touch catapulted her back to the memory of when she was four years old. And when her uncle touched her there on top of her panties and filled her with feelings she was too young to understand. She shooed away the evil thoughts of her first sexual encounter and brought herself back to the reality of her sensuous moment.

She closed her eyes as Deacon continued to tease her this way, her mind, her thoughts, everything was between her legs. His touch was so intense and she moved a little so he would be right where she wanted him, but again, he pulled his hand away. He leaned over.

"Now it's time to use the bathroom again, and this time, I'll go first."

He left and she soon followed behind. She tapped on the door and he pulled her into the small cubicle. He had his hardness out in his hand, and with one swift move he placed her on the sink again and entered her wetness with it. She moaned.

"Please don't leave me until I come," she whispered. He smiled that innocuous smile of his and pushed hard into her while holding her with his arms to keep her from falling into the sink. She wrapped her legs around him as he continued to take her. As she felt her climax approaching, she kissed him. He held her close, as she tightened herself ready for the event and moaned softly, "I'm coming, I'm coming." He groaned, but then withdrew again. He placed her on the toilet, washed his hands, and left her there.

What kind of man does this? She wondered how he could bring her to the brink of desire and then leave her frustrated. She composed herself as best she could and left the bathroom. Upon arriving at her seat she walked in front of him and sat down at the window again. He handed her the newspaper again, but this time she threw it on the floor. She was furious. She wanted to come and she was tired of playing his ridiculous games. She moped as he flashed that tantalizing smile at her again. He patted her lap and continued to read, whispering in a melodic tone, "All in good time."

She squirmed in her seat for a few minutes, thinking over the situation, then got up from her seat and marched back to the bathroom. She sat on the toilet and placed her fingers on her button. She was in control, not him, massaging her sex and thinking of him and his hardness at the same time. She rubbed it until she felt the climax approaching. It felt so wonderful, just a few more rubs and she would be able to resist him . . . but there was a tap on the door. Thinking it was someone who had to use the toilet, she got up, flushed, and opened the door. Deacon pushed her back, turned her around and bent her over the sink, lifting her skirt with the same force he'd used in the conference room. He penetrated her fiercely, then took it out, reaching around to touch her swollen, aching button. He massaged her and filled her with his finger at the same time. Holding her tight, he pushed deep inside her again, filling her with his hardness. After a few slow and taunting pushes, he sped up and she exploded with such force, her whole body shook as he emptied himself inside her. He cleaned up, patted her on the butt, bent down and kissed her on the neck, and left. She couldn't move. She was numb, relaxed, and completely spaced out. *Did that really just happen?* She freshened up and left the room, amid the whispers of the other first-class passengers who by now had figured out what had just taken place. Chin held high, she waved them off with a smug flip of her hair as she found her way back to her seat.

Deacon continued to read the paper, never glancing up to look at her, but he did slip his hand into her lap. After a few minutes, he whispered in her ear.

"Nice one, thank you." He leaned over and kissed her, and the last remaining onlookers finally turned their heads. She felt her desire slowly rekindling. He smiled and went back to his paper. She opened up the book, but couldn't get him out of her mind. The way he teased and touched her, his smell, and the wonderful hardness that always left her wanting more . . . her mind refused to think about anything else. She tried to read but realized it was ridiculous. She couldn't focus on anything but him. She looked back over at him and he was sleeping.

She waited a short while, then slowly got up and went back to the bathroom, where his scent still lingered. She sat on the toilet and rubbed herself, trying to recapture the essence of the moments before. A tap on the door interrupted her. She got up and opened the door. It was Deacon again. He took her in his arms, kissing her, pulling her skirt up as he unzipped his pants and entered her once more. He held her tight in his arms as he moved her over to the sink, where he took possession of her without stopping. He kissed her passionately, moving his hands all over her body, sucking on her breasts, cupping her face, kissing her until she didn't know where she was. All she cared about was the moment. She felt herself getting ready to climax, she prayed, don't pull out . . . don't stop . . . and he didn't. They came together. He held her close, kissing her and whispering in her ear. She looked into his eyes, so warm and wonderful that she cherished the closeness they both felt.

After returning to their seats, they were parched and famished. They ordered some wine and snacks from the attendant as they chatted over what to do when they landed. Deacon suggested dinner in the hotel dining room. She agreed and tingled with delight as she imagined a wonderful night in Paris together.

Their hotel, Chez Vous, was beautifully decorated in Louis XVI style, including the large crystal chandelier hanging heavily in the lobby. After she checked in, she unpacked and carefully chose her outfit for the evening. It was early morning in Paris, so she took a hot bath, put on her fluffy terry robe, and slid into bed for some well-deserved rest. Her alarm rang about 6:00 p.m., and she got up feeling refreshed. She dressed in her short silky navy skirt, white clinging top, navy thigh-highs, and high navy boots, then left to meet the man of her dreams.

They met in the lobby as he escorted her to the restaurant, which was close to the hotel.

"I thought we were going to eat in the hotel's restaurant," she said as they left the building.

"I had another thought," he mused.

They had a wonderful meal, and he never even made a pass at her the entire time, much to her disappointment.

"Oh, I am so full," she said, pressing her hand to her mouth as she looked at him. "I think I'd like to walk off this wonderful dinner. Would you like to join me? I'm going to my favorite bridge, Pont Neuf."

He smiled and said, "No thanks, I have something else to take care of." He kissed her on the forehead, and before she knew it, he was gone. She swished around, holding her head high, and she walked out of the restaurant alone.

The night was breezy. She felt good about herself as her boot heels clicked along the cobblestone street. She caught a reflection of herself in the windows as she closed in on the bridge, her short navy silk skirt moving with her body, her mid-white top clinging to her large bosom, her hair flowing past her shoulders in the breeze. She felt spectacular on this perfect night. Soon she saw Pont Neuf in the distance and she was enamored. It was her favorite spot in Paris, the ideal place to watch boats and enjoy the scenery. She could linger for hours, admiring the vessels as they passed by, spreading her long legs just wide enough for the air to tickle her down there, stimulating her with chills that traveled across her warm body.

She placed her arms on the ledge and looked down at the

boats going under, wondering if the occupants could see up between her legs. She never wore panties, as they stopped her from feeling the air on her sex. She heard footsteps approaching to the left of her and then they stopped. Her heart also stopped when she smelled the cologne, a familiar fragrance, as it permeated the Parisian air with romance. She smiled as she felt one of his hands on her butt, and the other lifting up her skirt and rubbing between her legs casually. She felt the heat of his legs close to her and his hands on the middle of her back, a face next to hers and breath on her neck as she heard the sound of a zipper. She felt his hardness touching her ass and felt something between her legs. His foot moved her legs apart while his arms reached around her hips, arching her back. He fondled her pit of passion, then with one motion, slid deep inside her. He moved so slowly at first. She moaned at his size, his hardness, and the wonder of the whole dark night. He continued to take her. She threw her head back as he violated her this way. He rubbed her with his talented fingers and moved her as his foot pushed her feet farther apart so he could get into her deeper. His hardness rubbed itself inside her wetness, back and forth it went. Her heart was beating faster. Her head tilted backward but she could not see his face. He rubbed her clit as he took her from behind, touching her sensitive parts and her ass, rubbing her faster, speeding up his assault on her. She felt herself coming and heard his breathing quicken. Harder . . . deeper . . . he tilted her ass up for more penetration of his hardness, her space expanding, welcoming him in as he throbbed and pulsated. His cum hit her walls and ran down her legs. Her juice mixed with his as she felt her knees weaken. She held on to the railing, catching her breath. When she turned to look behind her, no one was there. He was gone. She took out a tissue and wiped her legs clean.

The next night she went back to the bridge, but nobody was there . . . her lover did not return. Deacon had checked out of the hotel and she had no idea where he was, but she smiled with fascination as she pondered their interludes and enjoyed the nautical atmosphere once again.

The time for playing was done, and now it was time for work, the whole purpose for her being in Paris in the first place. She looked polished in a three-piece pinstriped black suit with a pencil skirt, and refined with the addition of a triple strand of pearls, along with black stockings and two-inch knee-high black boots. Just one more meeting, and then she would venture off to Versailles.

The meeting room was gorgeous, all with gold gilded walls, wainscoting, and crystal chandeliers. She looked around the room at all the suits, still looking for Deacon. He was over by a wall, talking with another suit. She recalled their night on the bridge and felt a shiver. She felt all eyes upon her and she knew she was looking good. She participated in the discussion and charmed the group with her knowledge and veracity. After the meeting, she searched for Deacon, but he'd slipped away again.

She went to her room, packed her things, and took a cab to Versailles, where she settled in her new room. She wondered where he was and thought about him and their wonderful time together at the bridge. She knew it had been him . . . his cologne told her so. She smiled at the thought of him and hoped he would be on the return flight home, seated next to her, tempting her deliciously again.

Today, she would be visiting Le Château. She dressed in a black skirt, comfortable heels, and a clinging top. She looked and felt great. She had planned for this all of her life. Her dreams and research had drawn her here. Her hotel was within walking distance to Le Château, and the stroll was fun over the ageless bricks. She imagined the stories those bricks would tell, if only they could talk, from the building of this magnificent palace, to the many wars and the awful Revolution. When she saw the golden gate with the emblem of the Sun King, Louis XIV, on it, she smiled from ear to ear. She marveled at the majestic fortress, and for a few minutes, she forgot about her sexual hunger, until she heard footsteps behind her. There was the faint smell of that familiar cologne, causing tingles in the pit of her stomach. She didn't dare to turn around as she approached the entrance to the Château.

She stood in line, waiting for the door to open, and she sensed him behind her. She knew it was Deacon, and she smiled to herself as his body heat touched her. Her sex was aflame but she played along with him, keeping her eyes glued straight ahead. The door opened to the palace and they followed a guide up the queen's staircase to the rooms above. He never left her side. She felt him looking at her—wanting her, and she felt herself being pulled toward him like a magnet.

As they walked toward the queen's flowery bedroom, he grabbed her hand and pulled her behind the screen, cupped her face, and kissed her warmly on the lips, his hand fondling her between her legs.

"I thoroughly enjoyed you on the bridge," he whispered in her ear as his face touched her neck, his five-o'clock shadow rough on her skin. She felt his hands cupping her breasts, pinching the ends and pushing them hard toward her body. She looked deep into the dark, penetrating eyes of her predator, who now held her prisoner. She wanted him so much, she could feel her body ready for him. The juices flowed out of her as she fell prey to his magical fingers on her hot spots.

He opened the door behind the screen and moved her

with him into the tunnel that ran from the queen's room to the king's. The walls were gray and rough. He picked her up and put her legs around him, his hardness penetrating deep into her wetness. She felt him deep within her as he filled her emptiness. He pumped into her rhythmically, slowly, kissing her deeply, holding her close. She felt herself building up to an orgasm, her body tingling—trembling to a climax. She loved the feeling. Welcomed it—waited for it as she felt him grow within her, pulsating, pushing, and prodding her to move her body in circles, bumping and grinding against him. The rough plaster of the walls caused her to have feelings never experienced before. A mixture of pain and pleasure that was simply erotic. He held her close as he detonated within her and she erupted all around him.

He held her tighter, kissing her gently. She wrapped her arms around his neck, loving the closeness she felt. He placed her legs on the floor and offered her a tissue, which she gratefully accepted. They left the tunnel and merged discreetly into the crowd gathered in the queen's bedroom. He held her hand as they walked nonchalantly through the Hall of Mirrors, a room the length of a football field, lined with chandeliers that were now plastic replicas of the crystal originals. The windows in the room overlooked the gardens. They wandered through the rest of the palace.

On their way out, he asked her to meet him for dinner at the local café to spend an enjoyable evening together. She accepted with a smile as he bent down and kissed her tenderly. They parted ways, but she carried him within her heart as she walked away.

She bathed and put on a short black halter dress that flowed with her every movement, along with the usual black silky thigh-highs and stilettos. She grabbed her black silk wrap and dashed out to meet him. Her hair glistened in the moonlight and she inhaled the crisp night air. She walked quickly to the restaurant, her heels clicking on the sidewalk. She turned to the side and saw the Château, which looked ghostly in the night sky, its size overwhelming.

She was almost at the restaurant when suddenly someone grabbed her, pulling her into the alley, his mouth covering her with a kiss that stirred her desires. She knew it was him with that damn cologne, and it always had the same physical effect on her. She was ready to be mounted. She had a feeling this was going to be longer than just a quickie. His lips never left hers as he carried her up the steps to a room he had rented for the evening.

She was hypnotized by his kisses, the smell of him, and his masculinity. His strong arms laid her on the bed as he slid on top of her, cupping her face with his hands. His eyes never left her face while he untied her dress. He slipped it off her, kissing every inch of her body. He descended slowly into her passionate abyss, opening her legs to welcome his tongue. He licked her vulva up to her button and back down to her wet opening, sucking her until it swelled and she moaned.

"Please take me, I need you so badly," she pleaded. She unzipped his pants and slipped them off. He positioned himself at her disposal, kneeling over her as he worked his way back down to her awaiting sex. She eased underneath him to indulge herself in his bulge. Her lips slowly parted as they moved over his swollen head. She licked it, toyed with it, and sucked it till the precum started, her body shivering, moving from one side to the other in passion's play. She grabbed his ass, pulling it toward her, pulling him deeper and deeper into her throat, gagging slightly as she reached across the bed for her purse and pulled out her small vibrator. She stuck it in her mouth to wet it and then carefully reached up to his ass and touched his anus gently, moving the vibrator in circles around there. She inserted it into him. He sucked in a deep breath in shock as she turned it on.

"Oh my God!" he yelled. "What the hell are you doing?" He was straining to turn and look back at her as he squirmed. She smiled a naughty smile with a wink as she held it in place and swallowed all of his hardness. He shot a mouthful of cum into her, and she swallowed it as he continued consuming her wetness. She felt herself building as she continued to hold his cock in her mouth, toying with it as he trembled, using her tongue to torture him further. She came slowly and with much relief.

They both collapsed on the bed. He moved up by her, cuddled her in his arms, kissing her as he continued. She returned his kisses on his chest, mouth, and eyelids. She had conquered him once again, or so she thought, beating him at his own game of surprises and leaving him starving for more. He put his fingers inside her, massaging her, taunting her, taking them out and touching her tenderness, then rubbing her some more. He went down and kissed her again and flicked his tongue back and forth across her arousal zone while she moaned with delight. She tried to get some rhythm out of him, some form or something inside her, moving her body so his hand would be next to her sex. The possible invasion of one finger was all she needed right now. She would do anything for pleasure and he was sure of it

He took her toy, washed it, and put it inside her as she screamed with delight, knowing that soon she would be reaching a full orgasm again. He left it there and flipped her over, using her black stockings to tie her to the bedposts. This she didn't like because she couldn't touch herself. He spanked her as she squirmed to free herself. He put lubricant on and rubbed his cock across her ass.

"My dear, you're going to be fucked like you've never been fucked before." He placed his member by the opening of her anus and slowly, gently entered her, much to her protest. She squirmed and moved as much as she could, but to no avail. He was entering a place never entered before and there was nothing she could do. The toy took care of one place as he pumped slowly into the other. He could feel the vibrations as he reveled at the position he had her in. He was relentless. He felt himself close to coming, but he held on until her body shook as she screamed into climax. He fell onto the bed, completely spent. He pulled the toy out of her and untied her so she could cuddle into his arms. She whimpered a little, but held on tight as her breathing returned to normal. He smiled as he touched her face and kissed her again and again.

Deacon had possessed her more than any man she knew, and she hoped he would never finish the game. To her, Paris was more than just the Eiffel Tower. She now knew it as the land of love and passion beyond her wildest dreams. She adored the way he made love to her. Like a tornado he whipped through her, taking her with him on a wildly passionate ride. She snuggled deep into his arms and fell asleep.

The next morning, she awoke to an empty bed, a red rose, and a note: YOU'RE BEAUTIFUL, SEE YOU SOON. He was gone. A plate of warm croissants waited for her beside a still-steaming cup of coffee. As she nibbled and sipped fervently, she daydreamed of encounters with her lover.

She freshened up, got dressed, and left the room, taking the rose with her. She felt uncomfortable waking down the street in the daylight with her evening attire on, but in Paris it seemed that anything goes.

Back in her hotel room, she took a bath and dressed in a denim skirt, a loosely fitting top that plunged off one shoulder, and crisp white tennis shoes. She was on a mission to a private house that held many art and Egyptian artifacts. She took the Metro, feeling great and excited about meeting up with her lover. She wasn't sure when or where, but she knew he was around somewhere. She kept searching for the intoxicating aroma of his cologne to warn her that sex was in the air. She exited the Metro and walked to the house, which loomed in the Paris sky. She knew the history of this wonderful place and was going to spend all day there. She walked for miles, viewing incredible historic pictures, statues, Egyptian mummies, and artifacts. They were the wonders of the world, all in one fantastic place. She was so impressed and awed by all the history that she did not notice the man approaching her. He touched her backside with tenderness and kissed her neck. She turned around to slap him, but of course it was her true love. He kissed her warmly and held her close.

"Miss me?" he whispered in her ear.

She smiled, "Yes, you left me alone this morning."

"Did you find the rose?"

"Yes, thank you."

"Then you were not alone, *oui*?"

She smiled at his reasoning. He scooped her up in his arms and kissed her passionately while others stared in envy at their romantic antics inside the Egyptian chambers.

"Would you like to be taken right here, right now?" he whispered in her ear. She blushed.

"Not in front of all these people."

He laughed. "Oh, you're suddenly so shy? Shame on you!"

He took her hand, leading her away to a room that was not part of the usual tour. He took her in his arms and kissed her, caressing her body, her face, her back, and her neck down to her perky breasts. She escaped as the world fell away and, in place of it, had this wonderful feeling of passion. She didn't know where she was, and she didn't care. All that mattered was that she was with him.

He lifted her up onto a desk, spreading her legs open. He got on his knees to kiss and fondle her. Her head flew back as her arms spread wide on the desk. Books, papers, and pens leaped off the leather-topped desk. She tugged at his hair, messing it up. The faster he went, the wilder she became. He came up and kissed her, unbuttoning her blouse as he kissed her breasts and planted kisses all the way back down where he took her again.

"Don't stop . . . please don't stop!" she yelled as he threw her into a frenzy of multiple orgasms.

He smiled and held her in his arms for a few seconds, then unzipped his pants. His hardness popped out, aroused and almost jealous of what just took place without him. He pointed it at her opening and slowly slid it into her wet, silky walls. He raised her legs up over his shoulders and took her again with so much force and rapture that he came almost instantly, exploding twice against her as he hollered her name and sent it echoing through the chambers. He didn't care who heard him. He handed her a tissue and she wiped herself dry. He helped her down off the desk and showed her a private restroom where she could freshen up.

She returned to find him sitting behind the desk, rearranging the items that had spilled onto the floor during their fury.

"Whose office is this?" she asked.

"It's my uncle's. He's the curator of this place."

"How interesting. My minor was in history, and he's just who I've been looking for."

"And you, my dear, are exactly what I've been searching for."

He grinned and came over to hug her again. She nestled in

his arms as he walked her over to the Corinthian leather love seat and there they sat enjoying each other.

"Oh, by the way, his name is Dr. Jacques Manqué. Would you like to wait for him?"

"Of course," she replied.

Once Dr. Manqué arrived, the rest of the day quickly faded away as London fired off questions. The doctor happily obliged. Deacon sat quietly, admiring her.

They thanked Dr. Manqué and headed out for their last evening in Paris together. London was filled with exuberance, and it was a night full of exciting tours and a delicious meal, but best of all was the dessert, which was just being in Deacon's arms.

She awoke the next morning to find him lying beside her. She studied him, his thick brown lashes, his full lower lip in a half smile, and the faint five-o'clock shadow that showed off his dark beard, all of which accented his sex appeal. She smiled and snuggled back into the bedcovers, dreading the time when they would be back home and back to the daily grind at work. She hoped that at least the return flight might be as exciting as it was getting to France, full of passion, fun, and games.

On the plane, it was as if he'd read her mind somehow, and he certainly did not disappoint her. He took her twice in the restroom and toyed with her repeatedly under the blanket that he purchased from the flight attendant. But soon the plane landed and her old life resumed, working, wanting, and waiting for Deacon to call.

Chapter 9

TEMPTING ROCKY ROAD ICE CREAM

When London arrived back in the United States, she didn't see much of Deacon. He seemed to avoid her at work and didn't call in the evening. She had a hard time getting him out of her mind and found herself longing to feel him inside her body on a daily basis. To thwart him from consuming her mind, she found a mystery man on the internet who called himself "Bruce." As she chatted with him, she imagined him as "Bruce," the sweetheart butler from La Fontaine Hotel who had given her a rose and tended to her every whim. She and Bruce would chat often, but they did not exchange photos or video pictures. They played with themselves, exchanging savory details and coming separately, but to each other's joy.

Today she walked away from the computer, feeling tired and forlorn. Her lover had taken her several times in her mind, through the fantasy world they'd created, but she had never seen him in person. Her body ached for a human touch and she felt it reaching out to him. Her mouth cried out to be kissed. But it was a fantasy she knew would never come true.

She got out her toy and played with it. It felt so good on

her hotness as she inserted it deep inside herself, thinking of Deacon as his face continued to loom before her. She felt the passion build into a full climax and she let it flow. After a few minutes she bathed herself, carefully put her toy away, and snuggled into bed. She turned over on her side, sliding the pillow between her legs to cradle it, and drifted off to sleep.

Her mind did not shut off. Her passion passed over the lines into her dream world . . . a world she loved and waited for every night. *Deacon was there waiting for her. He took her in his arms and kissed her deeply. She loved him and loved being with him. He fondled her breasts and skimmed his rough shadow of a beard across her nipples, nibbling and kissing. She melted into his arms as his tongue playing with hers, his hands moving over her body with sensitivity and firmness. He toyed with her and rubbed her body with his, moving her into positions he knew she loved. This dream lover of hers was taking her to places she never thought possible in the real world. His hardness was full of precum. She licked it. She loved it. She loved how it made her feel. He had it so stiff and hot for her. She sucked it, feeling the hard swollen end with her tongue. She licked the shaft all the way down to the end and up again, making it wetter and harder than ever before. He took charge of the situation by pulling away from her hot, wet mouth. He was not going to let this be a wham, bam, thank you ma'am situation. He was going to thoroughly enjoy this love feast and she was the main course. He cupped her face in his hands as he kissed her again and again, her mouth wet with his juice, his smell—his taste, his touch took her to a new world. He went down to her passion pit and licked it wildly, then back to her clitoris, where he spent time sucking it, licking it, and going to the entrance, where he tongued her deeply, watching her move, her passions growing, her hips swaying to his rhythm, his movements, his commands. He knew she was ready and so was he.*

He placed her on her knees and entered her from behind. The walls of her vagina awakened to his fullness. She felt him at the end, all her nerves awake and ready for him. He felt her body, her wonderful passion parts that he massaged so well. He pumped into her gently at first, then sped up as she coached him, her body moving rhythmically back and forth, sideways, her hips swaying to the rhythm set by him. She reached underneath and played with his hard, filled testes, moving them, squeezing them. Then she touched herself, wetting her toy before she inserted it inside his ass, gently. He moaned and she screamed as he went deeper into her. It felt incredible.

She felt him speed up and felt his hardness grow larger, filling her insides, her mind, her body, all in one passionate spot. He lifted her up higher and went deeper yet as he groaned her name passionately and came with such a force that it made him fall on her chest, her body shaking as she also came. He took her in his arms, holding on to her as he brushed her hair from her face, kissing her tenderly while wiping the love sweat from her lovely face. He kissed her again and again while he held on to her.

When she awoke to the darkness, she felt as if he'd really been there. She even thought she could almost sense his fragrance lingering. She was on her tummy, her rear was in the air . . . and her sheets were wet. She lay back down, thinking about her dream lover. She smiled then and drifted off into a peaceful sleep.

She awoke the next morning, remembering the dream she had. It felt so real she had to touch herself again. She mentally pictured Deacon as he was in the dream, his face, his expressions, his smile, the dark hair, and his deep-set eyes with the dark eyebrows protecting and shielding them. "Hunting eyes," her father used to call them. Everything about him tantalized her. She closed her eyes and pictured him again, walking right up to her, grabbing her around the waist, and kissing her with his strong and demanding mouth. She melted and her heart ached for him as she wondered to herself, *Why has he been so distant at work? Why hasn't he called after work?* There had been no connections at all since their Paris trip, no texts, no emails, nothing. She decided she would confront him as soon as she saw him at work. She would corner him in an office or even a closet if she had to, wherever she could grab a moment with him. But right now, she was sexually hungover. She touched her passion part and it was still stimulated from the darn dream. She was wet like she had just come, but she was so hot that she knew she hadn't. She reached for her toy and placed it inside herself. It felt so good. She moaned and knew that she needed this. As a matter of fact, she was going to need a lot of this before the feelings would go away.

It had been a long time since she had been with a man, since France, she thought. She loved being with men, especially Deacon. She closed her eyes for a moment and could almost feel him there with her again. She rubbed her breasts till her nipples were hard, pinching them, making them hurt . . . a good hurt. Her passion pit was tingling, waiting, and wanting. Her toy was not doing the job. She got her other toy and it massaged her well as it vibrated. She rubbed herself with it, wanting a man badly. She felt like dressing and going out to find one. She inserted the toy inside her, turned it on, and felt herself float away on a cloud of passion and wonder.

Before her eyes, Deacon appeared. His lips touched hers and his hand replaced the vibrator. She felt her climax soon approaching and she enjoyed the fantasy immensely. Afterward, she tidied up and got ready for work.

She arrived at work on a mission to track him down. She found him in the kitchenette.

"You've been naughty," he said to her, his eyes hard.

"Yes, want to help next time?" she asked timidly with a smile.

"Of course, but first you must tell me about your night. I want details of what you did and how."

London sat down, whispering discreetly as she explained her sexual cravings for him, how he stimulated her thoughts and desires, how she'd dreamed about him loving her, their bodies and souls becoming one together. He smiled at her animated stories and kissed her tenderly. She melted at his touch. She knew he could take her and she wanted him desperately, but not here. *Not at work, not again*, she told herself as she attempted to restrain her animalistic hunger for him.

"Can we meet later?" she asked in a low, steamy voice, batting her lashes innocently.

"Sure." He agreed and invited her to his place.

She was delighted as she floated through the remainder of her day.

After work, she raced home to indulge in a luxurious bubble bath. As she soaked, she pondered why Deacon had been avoiding her at work, and why he was all get-up-and-go now. Tonight she was determined to get some answers. She dressed in black lace lingerie, silky stockings and stilettos, covering her bedroom attire with only a heavy black trench coat and a scarf. She felt fabulous and couldn't wait to be with him.

As she stood before his door, memories of their first time together came flooding back. She smiled as the chills and tingles returned, overwhelming her. He opened the door and she untied the sash on her coat, revealing her lacy teddy, which barely hid the fact that she had no panties on. He was astonished and pleasantly surprised as he pulled her inside. He kissed her again and again. She actually felt suspended in midair. Her own world dissipated and in place of it was the one man who had completely captured her heart.

She smiled and spoke boldly in a low, sexy voice. "Are you going to fuck me or what?"

"No. You're going to fuck me," he said sternly with that sinister smile. He sat down on the love seat, his pride emerging as he stroked it.

"You want this? You're going to have to earn it," he said with a grin. She walked away and over to his sound system, flipping through his musical selections and choosing some sexy dancing songs. She loved to dance. She had taken classes with her friends long ago and had the hang of the erotic moves that strippers use. She discovered it was a great way to get in shape and harder to do that it looked.

She danced all around him, using her scarf to touch and tease him, peeling off her stockings as she bent over, her sex in full view, then taking off her teddy and placing it under his nose before pulling it away. She watched his maleness hardening and she could see precum forming at the end. She approached him and put her legs on each side of him, easing in slowly for a lap dance where she could take him inside of her. But to her surprise, he pushed her off.

"Not just yet, my darling. You must sit in front of me first and masturbate."

She blushed.

"Oh, now you're getting bashful? Okay," he said as he got up and started to put his hardness back into his pants.

"No, No," she pleaded. "I will."

She took her toy out of her purse and licked it for a moment, staring deep into his eyes before placing it by her clit. It was already waiting for her to release the emotion. She inserted it in her hot spot and got it wetter. She moved it back and forth as he sat watching, his hardness mimicking her motions . . . watching, waiting for its turn and the thrill that it was temporarily being denied. She kept her eyes on him, watching him massage himself up and down. He went in rhythm with her and she felt her passion building stronger and stronger. She moaned and moved, wanting him to invade her. With her eyes she invited him to fuck her, but he let her take herself as he watched. They both came together, separated only by the awkward empty space.

He smiled as he walked over to her and kissed her strongly on the mouth. He touched her wetness with his hands full of cum. He rubbed them on her already wet spots. She moved away from him teasingly, feeling slightly exploited. He pulled her back and continued to kiss her.

"Oh, baby, you have no idea how that turns me on."

He played with her toy, putting it inside her, taking it out, and touching her clit with it, watching her get turned on yet again.

"Please take me again," she begged.

He placed his fingers on her lips. "Sh . . . ," he whispered as he kissed her again and again.

She felt him come alive, his maleness hardening again as they kissed. He put his finger inside her, massaging her, taunting her, taking it out, and touching her tenderness, rubbing it. He went down, kissing the most sensitive part of her and flicking his tongue back and forth across it. She moaned with delight, trying to get some rhythm out of him, some form or something inside her, moving her body so his hand would be next to hers, urging him to invade her with his one finger again. It was all she would need right now for her to enjoy another huge climax. But no, he held her at bay while she slowly lost her mind, crossing over to the dark side again. She would do anything for pleasure and he was sure of it.

He took her toy in and out, turning the vibrator on and off. She screamed with delight, knowing she would soon be reaching her orgasm again. He left it there as he flipped her over and reached for her stockings, which he used to tie her hands to the bedposts. She wasn't thrilled about this, but she remembered her French trip and what a turn-on it was. She hated that she could no longer touch herself.

She reminisced about how wonderful it had felt, the mix of pain and pleasure, but she still didn't like the restraints. He put lubricant on himself and rubbed it across her ass.

"My dear, you're going to be fucked harder than when I took you in Paris."

He placed it by the opening of her anus and slowly entered her, despite her pleading "No"s. She squirmed and tried to avoid it as much as she could, but it was no use. He was determined to enter her there and he did so slowly, turning on the vibrator and enjoying the feeling at the end of his swollen hardness. She groaned as he pushed inside, deeper and harder, and still she resisted within herself as he pressed on. Finally, she relaxed, welcoming his fullness. As she did, her body shook into climax and they exploded together. She sank into the bed, completely exhausted. He pulled out of her and untied her arms and held her tight against his chest. She snuggled deep in his arms. He smiled as he touched her face and kissed her. She realized that she trusted him to the depths of her soul, and she knew he was the one for her, now and forever.

She did not want to wear out her welcome, so she decided to head home. She bundled back up in her black trench coat as he scolded her for traipsing around half-naked in the cold. She giggled as she kissed him good night.

On the way home she decided to stop for a latté at the local diner, despite her attire. *No one knows what I'm wearing under this coat*, she mused to herself. She placed her order and searched around for a place to sit.

"Want to join me?" said a man as he eased his newspaper down to look at her.

She almost dropped her cup. It was Deacon. She put her latté down on the table as she pulled out her chair. She couldn't take her eyes off him. He smiled and touched her hand and she felt a certain warmth and peace come over her. How he had beaten her to the diner she did not know, but she had more important questions bugging her and now was the time for answers.

"Why have you been avoiding me at work?" she asked.

"I've been trying to make a good impression with the other members of the firm, and not get into trouble. You do know how you affect me, London."

"But I have missed you and our special times together."

"You've still been chatting with me, you know," he said with a smile.

Her mouth dropped open and she gaped at him in shock and surprise.

"You're Bruce, my mystery man?"

"Yes. You didn't know it was me?" He raised an eyebrow at her. "Do you chat naughty with all the men?"

"No, b-but . . . ," she stammered, regaining her composure. "I didn't know you were Bruce," she replied with a hint of sarcasm. "I just missed you and I was bored. I never thought much about who it really was and I didn't care." She paused before continuing, carefully changing the subject.

"By the way, there's something I need to tell you. I gave my two-week notice at work. I am retiring and today was my last day. I kept it quiet as I didn't want anyone to make a fuss over my leaving. They're all a bunch of stuffy suits anyway."

Deacon looked surprised at her decision, but he smiled. "This doesn't have anything to do with me, does it?"

"No, it's just time for me to enjoy life."

Now that she understood his recent distant behavior, she felt better already about their relationship.

The next morning, London looked out the window into the snowy yard. The birds were eating and the heated birdbath was getting plenty of use. She relaxed, snuggled in her fluffy robe, sipping her coffee, happily watching the birds bathe. She was lucky to have bluebirds that stayed around all year and nested nearby. The phone rang, distracting her from the blissfully peaceful moment.

"Hey, baby, whatcha doing?" It was Deacon.

"Nothing, just watching the birds bathe. It's as if they're having a party in their own private hot tub." She snickered as he laughed.

"I'd like to watch you bathe," he replied.

"Mmm . . . ," she said as she twirled her hair, melting at the thought.

"Hey, I know it's cold out, but I've got a craving for something sweet. Would you like to meet me later at our ice cream parlor?" he asked.

"Sure, what time?"

"How about six o'clock?"

"Okay, but only if you'll play a game with me."

"What kind of game?" he inquired.

"It's a game of seduction."

"Sounds good. I'll see you there."

She could tell by his voice that he was smiling. The day flew by and soon she was sitting in the ice cream parlor, talking with her friend Paris, who worked there. Paris was working her way through college still and refused to let London help her with tuition. She enjoyed working and especially waiting on the little children as their faces lit up over all the delicious sweet treats to choose from. They chatted about men and work as Paris served up a hand-dipped, double-scoop cone of Rocky Road ice cream. London smiled like a little girl as she thanked her. Paris moved on to the next customer when London noticed Deacon enter the parlor. He quickly sat down across the room. She made eye contact with him as she licked her cone, watching him squirm in his seat. She nibbled off the top, watching him and feeling the want of sex in her tummy. She continued to lick the melting ice cream cone, around and around she went, her tongue lapping the cold cream with dark chunks of chocolate, her mouth going over the top all the way to the cone part. When she took a bite off the top, Deacon left the building. She quickly finished her cone and threw the napkins in the container.

"Gotta run! See you soon, Paris!" she shouted behind her as she hurried out the door.

Approaching her car, she noticed Deacon's Lexus parked beside her. He was sitting inside, wiping his forehead. She loved that she'd made such an impact on him. He was so good-looking her heart flipped, and she felt a stirring inside her again. He looked at her like he was pleading with her but in a distant way. She thought about him and how she could take him home and enjoy him for the afternoon. She walked over to his car and looked inside. She immediately noticed his arousal as he gazed at her with a pathetic look. She smiled and walked over to the passenger door. She slid in beside him and kissed him warmly on the mouth. He grabbed her and held her close . . . so close she could hardly breathe.

She whispered in his ear, "I am sorry for my little game. I didn't mean to cause such a problem."

"It's all right. I haven't been able to get you out of my mind since last night," he said, which surprised her.

He had become the envy of every stalking secretary at work. He was the office catch, whom no one had been able to land, and his name had been on the gossiping lips of many eligible bachelorettes more than once. She treasured him and wanted to be very careful as to how she treated him. He belonged to her and she didn't want to lose him.

"Let's go to my place. I think we can have some fun."

He nodded with a smile. "I'll follow you."

As they drove to her château, London's mind drifted. She thought fondly about her grandmother and how she had believed in all kinds of love. To her, love and passion were the only things worth living for. She had money and she didn't have to work or worry about anything. She wanted the same for her granddaughter, to live and enjoy life, and especially love. London had definitely inherited her charms and lust for life and passion but above all . . . love. Now she was ready to settle down and her choice for life was Deacon.

The gates opened and both cars went deep onto the estate grounds. As they walked inside together, she said a special thanks in her mind to her granny for her excellent taste, especially the beauty and openness of the rooms. She felt so free, so safe and comfortable here, and Deacon made it complete. She fixed him a cup of coffee and they sat in the breakfast room, sipping and talking.

"I remember our trip to Paris, and how surprised I was to see you next to me on the plane."

"I knew I was going, but wanted it to be a surprise."

"Now we are members of the mile-high club. You just about drove me nuts, the way you teased me, and then the wonderful orgasm I had was worth every minute I had to wait."

"You know, London, I have never found anybody like you, we are very good together."

"I think so." She smiled and drank some of her hot brew. "I will never forget the sex we had on the bridge in Paris, I knew it was you . . . the aftershave gave you away."

"Hum, maybe I should change my aftershave."

"Don't you dare." She kissed him on the cheek. "I also so enjoyed our encounter at the Château in Versailles. I wonder if Marie Antoinette had sex in the tunnels behind her room?" Deacon smiled. "Well, we have great memories, and they are only beginning." London felt so close to him, closer than she had ever let herself feel about any man. He reached across the table and touched her hand and she felt chills go up her spine in a new and tender way. She touched his hand and placed her fingers on top of his, feeling his warmth. She touched in between his fingers as he smiled and did the same to her. She felt a stirring as she got up, took his hand, and led him to the family room.

"May I?" he asked, pointing to the fireplace.

She nodded as he knelt down to light it. The entire wall in front of the fireplace was glass windows that overlooked the backyard and the secluded wooded acreage behind it. She enjoyed her privacy and even demanded it. It was part of who she was.

She was sitting on the bamboo love seat in the family room when he came over to her. He stood in front of her and pulled her to her feet. He put his arms around her, touching her face as he pulled her close. He rubbed her back and worked his way around to her front, where the rise and fall of her breasts competed with his deep breathing. He kissed her on the mouth so softly, then all of a sudden he pulled her to him tighter, holding her so close she could hardly breathe. He clung to her this way for a few minutes, catching his breath. She heard whimpers come from deep within his throat. Sounds of passion—his and her needs and wants. She danced him over to the stereo system and pushed a button. The house filled with the romantic sounds of Frank Sinatra. He held her close as they swayed to the music, his lips finding hers as they exchanged kisses and nibbles. They looked out the windows and watched the snow falling silently on the deck that overlooked the yard.

He was so tender and intimate with her now, a quality that he had never shown her before during other sexual interactions. He pulled off her sweater and began kissing her bare spots, holding her close, nibbling on her ear. When her bra finally fell to the floor, he kissed her nipples, cupping them in his hands. He kept his eyes closed the whole time, as if his mind were elsewhere and he was reliving a moment from the past. The hardness of her nipples filled his mouth, as her head moved back in awe of his talents and the wonder of this magic he worked on her. Her head spun as he laid her down on the sofa. His kisses were so full of longing and love that it took her to an unfamiliar place.

Normally the kisses she received were full of angry lust and desperate passion, but this time they were full of tenderness. She could feel his longing for a lost love. The thought made her shudder for a second and she choked back her tears, knowing that she had never had that kind of love. She had never allowed herself to feel that kind of intense feeling. In that moment, she finally began to realize the true difference between having sex and making love. She envied the relationship between this man and the woman he'd lost, and she hoped she could fill the emptiness he was feeling. She touched his hair, kissed his neck, and touched his lips with hers. He pulled her to him and kissed her so deeply it took her breath away. She felt feelings from her toes all the way to her nose. What a wonderful moment she was experiencing. She prayed he would not open up his eyes and see she was not the woman he thought he was making love to. For once in her life, she wanted to be her.

He finished undressing her and kissing her tenderly, touching her tummy, her softness, her passion place, and finally her sex. He inserted his finger into her as she moaned softly, then he took it out and touched her button, moving his mouth down to that spot and taking advantage of it. He opened her lips farther as he put his tongue deep inside her, searching for all the right places. He knew how to make great love and she was more than grateful for this moment in time. He felt her passion build as he took off his clothes and his hardness was right beside her. She wondered if it would shock him if she took it in her mouth. She had done this before successfully, but this type of lovemaking was different and foreign to her. He was reliving a memory and she wondered if the woman he was thinking of had done those types of things for him. *Would it be out of character for her to take him and suck on him?* She didn't want to spoil this moment for him. His eyes were still closed as he came closer to her.

"Take me," he asked.

She gladly licked his precum as he moaned and he slid beside her in her favorite position. They played with each other, his face buried in her sex and his hardness in her mouth. She enjoyed his hardness and the wonder of this man as he pulled himself out of her mouth and slid on top of her. He opened her legs wide for his deep penetration and pulled her down to him. She eased back onto the sofa as he entered her. Much to her surprise, he filled her and then some. He pumped into her slowly and then pulled her ass higher as he went deeper into her. She felt herself starting to come as he kept pumping into her, faster, deeper, and harder. She was no longer in this world but floating around in some incredible void, full of passion, with the feeling that she was about to climax at any moment.

"Oh God, I'm coming!" she yelled, and he dropped on top of her. His passion was spent and replaced by their juices flowing out of them onto the tiled floor. He pulled her to him and held her close as she lay in his arms. She closed her eyes and enjoyed his warmth and comfort.

After a few minutes, she leaned up on her elbow to look down at his face. His eyes were closed with his eyelashes resting on his cheekbones. She felt his warmness cover her body. She'd had many men, but never felt this way about any of them. Her heart fluttered something new . . . something more than before. Her body trembled and shivered as she was overcome by her love for this man. She snuggled back into his body, tugging a blanket over them from the back of the sofa. She watched the flames flickering and dancing across the walls, and the snow falling outside as she drifted off to sleep in his arms.

Chapter 10

DESIRABLE HOLIDAY TREATS

The next morning, she awoke on the sofa and Deacon was gone again. He did leave a note on the coffee table beside her: *TIME FOR WORK. I'LL BE MISSING YOU. SEE YOU SOON. LOVE, DEACON.* She smiled as she held the message and savored the scent of him that still lingered in the air and on her body. She knew he had to go out of town for a few days on business to finalize some legal matters before the holiday break on the weekend. The following Saturday was Christmas Eve and she hoped to celebrate with him. It was going to be a long week without him, but she planned to keep herself very busy somehow.

This being a Friday, she thought about how nice it would be to sleep in and not race to the office every morning. She had enjoyed applying her exceptional skills and knowledge each workday, but she was certain she would enjoy early retirement just as much, if not more. She knew her grandmother's estate would keep her comfortable for the rest of her life. She also understood that Deacon would continue to work for a living, not only for income but for the sake of his pride. He would never consider joining her in early retirement. Even though she could take care of him, she wouldn't even suggest the idea for fear of offending him, but she missed him and wished he could spend his days with her.

The day was terribly boring already, but her mind was working overtime to conjure up many tasks and activities to make her time without him eventful. She logged on to the laptop and started an agenda, a list of things she would accomplish before Deacon's return later next week: *haircut, manicure and pedicure, decorating, gift shopping, fun in the snow, time with friends.*

She logged on to see what some of her friends were doing today, and to see if they had holiday plans scheduled for the upcoming week. After her recent interlude with Max, she had joined a social network, and before she knew it she had linked up with hundreds of her old friends from high school and college. She chatted with a few girls whom she had been close to years ago, including her good friend Jen. Finally, Paris got online. Together, the group chatted and everyone seemed to be in the same rut of boredom, and they were lacking holiday cheer.

"Let's have a party!" Paris suggested.

"Yes, how about my place next Friday night at eight o'clock?" London offered. "And be sure to bring your significant others!"

Everyone agreed and she was suddenly overcome with excitement. She knew that despite their busy holiday schedules, her friends would never miss a gala event put on by London Shelby, as it would certainly give their holiday spirits a boost.

"Do you have someone special, London?" Paris inquired.

"I sure do!" London replied, smiling to herself as she thought of Deacon. She couldn't wait to show him off to her friends and hoped that he could make it. She typed a quick email inviting him to the party. She knew that he would check emails while he was away and she hoped he would reply soon.

She then jumped on the phone to call her personal friend Jon, a master chef and culinary artist who owned a classy catering company. She knew he would drop everything to accommodate her party, even if it was last-minute.

"London! It's so good to hear from you, darling!" Jon was bursting with excitement to hear her voice. "Oh! A party, a holiday party! I have a full staff for the upcoming week and we can certainly be there for you, my dear."

He was ecstatic and London could hear his fingers snapping as he called his staff to attention. He immediately lined up servers and a bartender, then reviewed menu choices with her. She selected grilled shrimp skewers, succulent lamb kebabs, roasted asparagus, vine-ripened tomatoes with pesto, along with a variety of other veggies, fruits, cheeses, snacks, and desserts. Jon had two large fondues that he offered to bring along, one for cheese for the appetizers and another for chocolate, which would be perfect with the fruits and desserts. He also suggested some fine aged wines from a local vineyard, along with eggnog and other warm, festive holiday drinks. He assured her that everything would be informal but classy, casual yet chic. She agreed to leave the rest up to his culinary expertise.

"Now, do you have a decorator helping you with the arrangements, London?" Jon asked.

"No, I was planning to handle that myself," she replied.

"Oh dear, well, I must come and help you this week. How about Tuesday? I'll bring a few suggestions and I can have a Christmas tree delivered that day. Nothing like the fresh scent of a real tree for the holiday!"

"That sounds great. I haven't had a real tree since . . ." Her voice caught. "Well, since Grams was still here."

"Oh, bless her soul, and yours. You're going to have a real

tree again this year, dear. It's going to be a fabulous holiday," he squealed, his exhilaration radiating through the phone.

"Thank you so much, Jon. I can always count on you. I can't wait to see you Tuesday."

London hung up and zipped around the house, tidying up, planning, and thinking about the decorations, the food, and Christmas. She loved Christmas, her favorite time of the year, which made her feel like a child again. Even at her age, she still listened for reindeer hooves on the rooftop until she fell asleep on Christmas Eve, and she visited Santa Claus every year. Normally, she would have done so the day after Thanksgiving, but she hadn't made it there yet this year. She made it a point to visit him by Christmas Eve next weekend at the latest.

The phone rang. London hoped for Deacon, but it was Paris.

"I know I'll be seeing you next weekend for the party, but I've got a couple days off this weekend. How about we spend some time together like the old days?" Paris proposed.

"That sounds like fun!" London went over her list with Paris and they were on the same page. They decided to spend the next morning cross-country skiing, followed by an afternoon at the spa, indulging themselves, and they would top the night off with cocktails and dancing at the club. Sunday, if they were up to it, they would enjoy some holiday shopping together.

Saturday was eventful and flew right by. London was thrilled to have Paris to pass the time with. It was Sunday already and their shopping excursion was delightful in the hustle and bustle of downtown. They focused on a few gifts, then splurged on sexy lingerie. They modeled for each other in the fitting rooms as they tried on each outfit. London finally decided upon the traditional red lace teddy for Christmas, and a racy black ensemble for New Year's Eve. She insisted on treating Paris to some lavish purchases, and Paris reluctantly gave in.

Tarrytown was alive with the sounds and smells of the season. Roasted almonds and Brazilian coffee permeated the air, luring them in for a snack. Bells were ringing on the street corners and storefronts. With each Santa Claus she encountered, London would discreetly slip them a hundred-dollar bill, much to their surprise. She couldn't wait to sit on Santa's lap at Midtown Mall. She was certain he was the real deal. But they couldn't make it there today as Paris had to get going. London still planned to return to finalize her shopping on Christmas Eve. She had a special gift in mind for Deacon.

Before she knew it, Tuesday arrived. The Christmas tree was delivered and set up on the stand by two handsome, burly, cheerful men whom she tipped generously on their way out. Jon arrived just after with bundles of linens, holiday décor, and big ideas to help London spruce up the château for the big party. He was such a whirlwind when he entered the room and she was delighted to finally see him again. They went up to the attic together to retrieve Grams's decorations for the tree. As they carried the boxes down, London found herself emotional, teary-eyed, and missing her grandmother. The fragrance of the real pine tree really took her back in time. Jon noticed she was misty and hurried to the threshold of the family room to hang the mistletoe, then dragged her over and gave her a peck on the cheek to cheer her up. She giggled and cheered up as she chuckled to herself. *We're both lucky that Jon's gay because he's so handsome and adorable that I might enjoy more than decorating with him.* She snickered at the thought.

The two of them spent the day decorating and chatting. Between hanging ribbons, bows, ornaments, and glittery décor, she told him all about Deacon. It felt so good to share her story with someone. Jon understood how London had been raised. He knew Grams well and knew of the wild lifestyles both women had led. He was glad to see London beginning to settle down with one man. Although he hadn't yet found his significant other, Jon was still playing the field.

Soon everything glistened with gold and silver everywhere. The decorations twinkled and warmth filled the house. They savored some divine chicken noodle soup and sandwiches together that Jon had brought along, and he whipped up some hot chocolate with whipped cream for a sweet treat afterward.

"Okay, young lady, bundle up, because we're heading outside to spice things up a little!" Jon said as he hustled London along. They started on the back deck, clearing snow from the outdoor stone fireplace and grill area, where he would be cooking for the party. Jon wanted the space to have some ambience, so he had brought along strings of white Christmas lights to drape around the deck and he planned to have the fires going inside and out that evening.

Then they made their way down into the yard, stringing more lights around several small pines scattered here and there, in front and back and up and down the driveway. When they were finally through they returned to the backyard, where Jon dropped into the snow and started making a snow angel. London laughed and joined in. After a few minutes, Jon got up and walked behind her, and to her surprise, a snowball landed on her chest, spraying snow into her face. She screamed and jumped up. The battle had begun as they packed snowballs and chased each other through the yard, dodging, throwing, and laughing until they both fell into the snow again, exhausted.

"Let's build a snowman before I go. Right here, where he will be visible from the deck," Jon suggested.

"How about you build the man, and I'll build the woman?" London replied.

"Sounds perfect." He grinned.

They set to work rolling and packing the snow, building their snow couple together as London reminisced. She told Jon a story of doing this very same thing with Grams back when she was just twelve years old. Grams built the snowman, and she built the snowwoman. Grams had been chatting about things unknown to London that afternoon, trying to explain the birds and the bees to her. When London turned around, she noticed that Grams had put male parts on her snowman. They laughed hysterically and proceeded to add the female parts to the snowwoman together.

"Let's keep our snow couple PG-rated today, okay, Jon?" London laughed.

"Or I was thinking we could just have two snowmen to be politically correct." Jon chuckled with one hand on his hip.

They finished off their snow couple with hats, scarves, buttons, carrot noses, a pipe for the snowman, and a red poinsettia flower for the snowwoman. They were masterpieces. They had such a great day together, and London was glad she'd had this time without Deacon to spend some time with friends. As evening set in and the sun was quickly fading, Jon said good-bye. London hugged him and thanked him for his help, not just with the decorations, but also with her spirits. Along with the house, he had brightened her soul with his lust for life and she looked forward to seeing him again at the party.

The rest of the week disappeared, and before she knew it, it was Friday. She had been up early and worked hard all day to finalize the details for the big event. She hadn't yet heard from Deacon, but remained hopeful that he would be able to make it to the party. The night was still young and she decided to take a short nap. It would be a long evening and she wanted to feel refreshed. She set her alarm, closed her eyes and drifted off to sleep.

Deacon appeared and he was at his cottage, where they first made love. He was standing by the railing on a deck, overlooking a stream and a vast forest. She walked over to him and their lips met. She felt warmth simmering inside her, taking over her body. The stillness of the trees, the crisp cool air, and the quiet moon and stars accentuated their heartbeats as he led her into the front room of the rustic log cabin.

Beep, beep, beep . . .

Damn, she thought as she awoke to her alarm. *I wanted to know what happened next.* She was groggy as she looked around the room. Shadows spilled over the back of the house as the moonlight lit up the rustling trees. *The party! And Deacon?* She ran to the computer and there was a message from him. SEE YOU AT 9:00. She was thrilled. She jumped into the shower, quickly toweled off, and dressed in a long black velvet skirt with a glittery silver belt and a white sheer blouse with stand-up collar and enlarged full long sleeves.

She welcomed Jon and the catering staff, and soon the place was buzzing with commotion to prepare for the guests. She sampled some wines with Jon and nibbled at the snack table, chatting with all the delicious servers Jon had arranged. They were all so young and handsome in their crisp white shirts and black ties, informal yet classy as he had promised. The intercom announced the arrival of the first guests as they parked in the circular drive in front of the château. London greeted Paris and her date at the door.

"Party time!" Paris declared as she shimmied around the room with a bottle of champagne that she had brought as a gift for London. Paris was stunning and elegant, model material at five-foot-eight with a svelte figure, haunting green eyes to match her emerald green velvet sheath dress, plus a golden tan and light auburn hair. She was such a fun friend and London loved her. They had been out of touch for a while and she had missed her. It was good to have her back, and no party would be fun without her.

Jen arrived, gorgeous as well in a red full-skirt dress. She had a Swedish kind of look with long blond hair, crystal blue eyes, a perfect complexion, full lips, and a toned, racy physique. Jen joined in, dancing around with Paris and dragging London in as well. Together, the three of them could have been the new *Charlie's Angels* girls.

Other cars started filing into the drive and soon the place was hopping with action. The fireplace blazed in the background while partiers drank as fast as the bartender could serve them. The music was jamming and had everyone in the room on their feet. Some people took the fun outside, gathering on the deck with Jon and another chef around the stone fireplace and grill, which did the dual service of cooking the kebabs and knocking the chill off those waiting to eat. Those who couldn't wait enjoyed roasting marshmallows and almonds and dipping them into the chocolate fondue.

London smiled as she gazed off into the backyard. Large snowflakes were falling to the snowy ground, covering it like a white blanket, the lights that she and Jon had hung were twinkling on the small pines, and the snowman and snowwoman were smiling up at everyone. Jon was amazing. She never could have pulled this off without him.

Her mind drifted back inside. Everyone had a date except her and she was beginning to feel awkward as she watched them taking turns kissing under the mistletoe, dancing, and cuddling with each other. It was 10:00 and he still had not arrived. She headed to her bedroom to check the mirror and use the bathroom. As she entered the room, someone shut the door behind her. To her surprise, it was Deacon.

"Did you think I wouldn't come?" he said as he pushed her to the wall with a kiss. He cupped her breasts, then pulled off her blouse and undid her bra. His mouth left hers and kissed her all the way down to her nipples, which already were hard and pointed. Her hot spot was so wet and wanting while his hands touched her. She was a little anxious about having so many people in the house and also had an urge to return to tend to her guests. She knew they would soon be missing her, but his mouth consumed her body and she couldn't resist. She gave in as she tried to get her mouth down on his hardness. He cupped her face.

"Not this time, precious, it's my turn."

She smiled as he unzipped his pants, letting them fall to his feet. He stepped out of them, took out his hardness, and rubbed her passion zone with it. He went between her legs, touching her wetness. She felt him circling around, teasing her with his hardness.

"Please take me now," she pleaded, feeling the passion. She grabbed on to his neck and wrapped her legs around him as he slid deep into her, taking her breath away. As he kept pushing, he held on to her ass and at the same time tilted her toward him. He carried her over to the bed and placed her on the edge where he laid her down, kissing her, holding on to her. He put her legs on his shoulders and penetrated even deeper.

Every time she had him, he felt bigger than before, always wonderful, hard, and throbbing. She felt herself relax as he pumped into her with slow, deep thrusts, sucking her breath out of her each time he partially pulled out. Her wetness increased; her vagina walls pulsed. She moaned and he groaned as he flipped her over and took her from behind, his hand touching her erogenous zone. He rubbed and made her come at the same time as him. He convulsed inside of her as the door suddenly opened. She and Deacon gasped before recognizing Paris. The three of them came to a standstill and stared, not knowing what next to do, until Paris smiled with approval.

"Sorry, sorry. I thought you were alone in here. I mean . . . ," she said, making a graceful exit.

Deacon and London giggled and got themselves together to rejoin the party.

"At least she had good timing,"

"Oh, Deacon, that was my friend Paris, by the way. So glad you two could finally meet since I didn't get to introduce you at the ice cream parlor."

He straightened his tie, then gave her a quick slap on her now-covered behind.

"Ms. Shelby, I do believe there is a party going on downstairs and it is rude for the hostess to not be there."

She fluffed her messy hair, touched up her lipstick, and stole one more kiss before they went downstairs. London thrived on introductions as everyone finally met her Deacon. The night was a huge success and a few taxis even had to be called for those who had overindulged in the spirits.

She awoke the next morning, hoping to find him beside her, but Deacon was gone as usual. She missed him more than ever and couldn't imagine that he would be working today. They'd been so busy with the party they hadn't had much time to discuss their weekend holiday plans, but she thought they would be together. She shook off her worries and reminded herself that it was Christmas Eve and time to finish shopping and visit Santa Claus.

She bundled up in her black wool coat, red scarf, and red gloves. She enjoyed the drive to the city in the snow in her SUV. Sounds of the season bellowed from the radio and she sang along, excited for her adventure. On her way, she decided to circle through the parking lot at the law firm offices to see if Deacon was actually at work on Christmas Eve. She thought she might pop in to pay him a visit and scold him, but his car was not there.

Her next stop was to pick up Deacon's gift, a Rolex engraved on the back: TO THE MAN WHO STOLE MY HEART, LOVE FOREVER, LONDON. Deacon deserved only the finest, which of course included her too. She couldn't wait to see him and stun him with her new red lace teddy, then with his new watch.

She proceeded on to the mall, where she found the long line to see Santa Claus. Just like the children, she wanted to see him too but was informed by an elf that she had about an hour to wait. *Oh well*, thought London, *that's the price I pay for procrastinating.* She waited with the others and drew the attention of some little children who noticed that she was not escorting someone their size and giggled at her. The elaborate decorations throughout the mall, including a toy train circling on its tracks through a wintry scenic town, were lovely and made her joyful. She hummed along to the tune of "Baby, It's Cold Outside" as her mind drifted to memories of Christmases past.

She remembered once asking Santa for a Sonja Henie ice-skating doll when she was seven years old. He had asked her why she didn't want something more modern. She explained that she wanted the antique doll because she loved to watch Ms. Henie's old black-and-white films with her grandma. London also told Santa that someday she would be an Olympic figure skater too, just like Ms. Henie. She recalled the joy she felt when she opened the box to find her doll, perfect in every way right down to the lace-up, genuine leather, white ice skates. She played with that doll for years to come and it still sat proudly on a shelf in her bedroom.

On a Christmas, not so many years ago, a good friend had surprised her with a diamond ring. She had returned it to him with a note, THANKS, BUT NO THANKS. She was a free spirit and enjoyed her independence very much. She wasn't ready to be tied down to any one man at that time. Now, as she was getting older, she was changing. The thought of having someone there at her side, through thick and thin, was starting to become inviting. She could see the benefit of marriage, if it were to someone whose love for her would match hers for him and would want her forever.

"Ma'am?" an elf called out to London. "Ma'am, it's your turn."

She walked toward Santa and her heart pounded a bit, just as it had when she was a kid. The man in his red velvet costume looked a bit surprised, then showed amusement that this grown lady was approaching. "May I, Santa?" She giggled as she sat lightly and gently on his lap, posing for a photo. A faint wisp of familiar cologne surrounded him. She whispered in his ear what she really wanted for Christmas. "Santa, I would love Deacon to be with me on Christmas Day." Then she gave him a quick kiss on the cheek. She picked up her photo, did a little more shopping, and headed home.

The newly fallen snow made driving a bit tricky. The plow trucks were zipping here and there, racing to keep up as the snow fell rapidly. Heavy or not, the snow was no match for London in her SUV. She pushed it into four-wheel drive and moved effortlessly through the storm, until she got home, where her tires slipped a little on the icy driveway. She maintained control and parked safely in the garage.

She wrapped her presents with care, including the special one for Deacon, and placed them under the miniature decorated pine tree covered in crystals that sat on her dresser, which was Jon's surprise for her. She watched as the sun shined through the crystals, causing the wall to fill with tiny rainbows from the prisms on the shimmering tree. She kept thinking about Santa and his eyes, his familiar scent and how she had felt so connected to him. He reminded her of Deacon. Every attractive man reminded her of Deacon. But she knew Santa was Deacon. That's why his car wasn't at work today, and why he wasn't here with her now. She smiled at the thought of him sitting there all day, patiently greeting each little child and making their holidays bright. It warmed her heart and filled her with more desire. She had mentioned to him that she had to go visit Santa and he never said a word.

Soon it was dark and the mini white lights glistened across the property outside on the tiny pine trees that lined her driveway all the way to the house. Her Christmas tree looked so beautiful she was almost sad that tomorrow was Christmas Day. She didn't want the holiday season to end, along with all its joyous spirit. She drank some hot chocolate and went to bed, wishing Deacon was beside her.

It was about 2:00 a.m. when she awoke. She thought she heard footsteps on the roof. She listened closely for a moment, grabbed her blanket, pulling it up to her neck as she sat up in bed. She heard the noise again, much louder this time. She got goose bumps and her hair stood on end. There was definitely someone up there. She slowly reached into her nightstand and retrieved her tiny 9mm Ruger. As she cocked it, she felt a wave of safety and self-confidence come over her. She was an excellent markswoman and was not worried. Among so many other things, Grams had taught her well to take down a target if she had to.

She made her way downstairs, armed and ready. She saw a shadowy figure outside the front door. He was tall and fat. She blinked her eyes to see if she was dreaming. From a distance, it appeared to be Santa Claus. She got closer and peeked out the window. It *was* Santa Claus. He looked like the same one she had visited at Midtown Mall. She was sure of it, and she was almost certain it was Deacon. He waved at her, and she turned off the alarm system and opened the door.

"Ho, ho, ho, Merry Christmas," he said in a deep, jolly voice. He smiled as he took a large bag of presents off his shoulders. He kissed her on the cheek, then walked over to the front room. He placed the presents under the tree, then spun around and grabbed her, kissing with his white beard tickling her face. She played along, still pretending not to know that it was him, but after a minute she tugged his beard off.

"Oh my, what a surprise," she shrieked, feigning astonishment. They laughed still in their embrace. He kissed her like he hadn't seen her in months.

"I am so happy to see you!" he said with a childlike tone that she hadn't heard in him before. He caressed her and held her tightly. He was the best Christmas present ever.

He picked her up and carried her up the curved staircase to her room, where he kissed her some more as he undid her silky robe. He covered her with kisses and hugs as he stroked and fondled her lacy lingerie hungrily. He peeled off his Santa suit, and they both laughed as the belly stuffing fell out onto the floor.

"Now, wait here and don't move. I have three surprises for you," he said.

He raced abruptly from the room, streaking through the house and down the stairs. She couldn't imagine what he could be up to, but she anxiously awaited his return. He finally came back, cradling a small bowl in his hands.

"Let's begin with your first surprise tonight, a hot oil massage."

London melted as his magic hands stroked and massaged slowly on every muscle. She wiggled with lust as he worked his way down her back to her thighs, stroking between them and teasing her with the warm oil. He rolled her over and caressed her front, teasing her again as he stroked her breasts, stimulated her nipples, and slipped his hands down to her sex.

Suddenly, he sat up on the bed. "And for the next surprise . . ."

He revealed a new toy—a vibrating ring that he slipped over his hardness. It would tickle her button as he eased in and out of her. She wanted to feel him now and she pleaded with him, squirming around on the satin sheets, still slippery from the oil, pulling him toward her with her eyes.

"Are you ready, precious?" he asked, kissing her as he lay down next to her, his mouth on hers. He licked her lips and toyed with her tongue, his fingers now inside her, moving them in circles. She breathed deeply and reached for the button to turn on his toy. He gasped and rolled over on top of her. She felt his fullness and the pending emotion, and finally the explosion that sent them both to the mattress. He pulled her to him, held on to her, coddled her in his arms, kissing her, pulling her hair back from her face as he kissed her again and again.

"Merry Christmas, baby," she whispered in his ear as she wrapped her arms around his neck. "That was exhilarating."

He looked at her and said, "I love you, London."

"I love you too, Deacon," she replied, surprised at the sound of her own words. "Let's go have some coffee by the fire together," she suggested. As she remembered the surprise she had for him she grabbed it off the dresser.

They slipped into their robes and went downstairs. She whipped up two espressos and they sipped and cuddled by the fire, chatting about his day at the mall. After a while, she got up to retrieve the special box from her pocket and handed it to Deacon.

"Open this."

"Shouldn't I wait until morning?" he asked.

"It is morning, silly," she retorted.

He grinned as he gently peeled away the wrap and opened the velvety box to reveal the gold Rolex. His face lit up and he gave her a kiss.

"It's very extravagant. Thank you, London."

"You deserve it. Now read the back," she urged.

He did as she ordered. "TO THE MAN WHO STOLE MY HEART, LOVE, LONDON."

He hugged her and kissed her.

"And now, for the woman who has stolen my heart . . . ," Deacon said as he smiled and handed her a gift. It was a very small box that he had tucked in the pocket of his robe.

I wonder when he put that there, she thought.

She looked at him with surprise as she pondered what the contents might be. She was sure it was jewelry of some sort, diamond earrings probably, or maybe a Pandora bracelet. The suspense was killing her, but at the same time she didn't want it to end, just like Christmas, and just the same way never wanted their time together to end. Every moment they spent apart felt like forever to her. There were so many times she went without receiving a phone call or a message from him, but she never gave up. He was so deep within her heart, and she cherished the time she had with him.

"Would you open it already?" Deacon insisted.

As she began to unwrap the paper, and just before she opened the box, Deacon got up off the couch and down on one knee. She looked at him nervously as she revealed the contents . . . a large white aquamarine gemstone glistened in the firelight as her eyes twinkled with the tears welled in her eyes.

"London, I have loved you from the moment we met, even though I couldn't do anything about it at the time. I believe that things were meant to be this way, and now that I am free, I have to be with you. That's why I came to live here in New York, because I had to be close to you. Please be mine forever. London, will you marry me?" Deacon pleaded.

"Yes! Yes, I will marry you, Deacon."

She cried as he hugged her with one arm, wiping away her tears with his free hand. He carried her back to the bedroom, snuggled in behind her, and tucked the blankets in around them.

"Merry Christmas, my love," he whispered in her ear.

"Merry Christmas, darling," she replied, and she smiled as she gazed at the sparkling ring on her hand. She finally had her prince, and she felt like the royal princess once again. It was by far the best Christmas she'd ever had.

Chapter 11

SINFUL CHOCOLATE ÉCLAIRS

Her days started earlier ever since Deacon had been staying overnight. He'd moved some of his belongings into the château on Christmas Day, since the lease on his condo was up, and he was looking for another place. She had been cherishing her mornings waking up beside him, and she would sneak into the kitchen to prepare breakfast. She enjoyed feeling domesticated and he was thrilled to awaken to the delicious smells wafting through the house. Today was Friday and she decided to bake chocolate chip muffins, a special recipe Jon had passed along to her. She chuckled as she read Jon's personal note he'd included on the recipe card: THE BEST WAY TO A MAN'S HEART IS THROUGH HIS STOMACH! As the muffins baked, the aroma traveled upstairs and she smiled as she heard Deacon stirring. He greeted her with a sniff. They chatted over coffee and warm muffins, oozing with melting chocolate. He looked handsome in his three-piece suit, and she snickered as she kissed him good-bye, wiping chocolate from his chin. She sat by the window watching him exit the driveway.

She felt wonderful as she looked at the sparkling ring on her left hand, lounging, warm and snuggly in her fleecy pajama outfit, a Christmas present from him that marked a change in her usual way of dressing. She smiled as she recalled him saying, "I want you to be comfortable, sweetheart. You're always sexy to me in anything, and even sexier when you wear nothing at all." She curled up by the blazing fireplace, and her mind was afire with thoughts of other attentive things that she could do for Deacon. She had never imagined wanting to please a man so much and she felt somewhat out of her realm.

She thought back to the conversation they'd had earlier this week. They were lying in bed, spent after three amazing rounds of lovemaking, but unable to sleep. London had talked about the loss of her parents in a car accident when she was ten and the passing of her grandmother later on. Deacon had opened up and shown immense compassion. "I am so sorry, hon, it must have been very difficult for you. I can't say I understand your loss, since I have both parents still alive, but I am sure you felt alone and very scared, especially when you lost your grandmother." He put his arms around her and held her while he kissed her cheeks. There was no doubt that they felt connected to each other physically and emotionally, but this deep outpouring of honesty began to link their souls on a much deeper level as they began to feel their own mortality together. That was when Deacon had confided in her and revealed more of his desires. "Not to change the subject, but have you ever heard of a 'bucket list'?"

"Yes, I saw that in a movie, but I don't have one. Do you?"

"As a matter of fact I do." He reached in his back pocket and took out this worn piece of paper. "I made this when I lived in England." He laughed as he unfolded the paper. "Here are some of my wishes. She looked at them, the first five were: *1. Move back to United States. 2. Try to recapture my life and find London.* She blushed and snuggled closer to him. *3. Get into a great law office, or 4. Open my own law firm. 5. A ménage à trois.* She never finished the paper as she folded it up, thinking about number five. Most men secretly wished for a ménage à trois, but she wasn't so sure he still wanted one now that he had proposed. "Do you still want this?" she asked as she pointed to number five.

"Yeah, I'm bad, I still want one."

London poked playfully as she tucked it in her memory. She sat contemplating what it might be like to make love with Deacon and another woman. She convinced herself that since they were engaged, she could relax and enjoy that type of an encounter.

She decided to ask her friend Jen if she would consider the idea. Although London had never been with a woman, she knew Jen was bisexual and had experience in this arena. She also knew she would be very comfortable with her, not to mention that Jen was very attractive. After Deacon left for work, she grabbed her cell phone and dialed the number. After three rings, she almost hung up, but then Jen answered.

They recalled the party and chatted about the great time they had that night and about Christmas.

"Deacon proposed to me on Christmas Eve," London replied excitedly as she told the story of her visit from Santa Claus.

"Oh my God! Congratulations. That is great news. Oh, I love weddings. Have you set a date yet?"

"No, we haven't, but I will certainly keep you posted. So how was your Christmas?"

"Same ol' stuff, ya know how that goes."

"Yep, I sure do. Hey, do you have time to stop over for a chat?"

"Sure, I can stop in on my way to work. I'll see ya in a few."

"Okay, see you soon," London replied.

London took a quick shower and tidied up the house. She put out Jen's favorite flavored coffee, café mocha, filled the coffee machine, and anxiously awaited her arrival. She opened the gates then snuggled back down on the sofa. She looked around at her home, still all decorated and full of Christmas spirit. Her heart was filled with love, warmth, happiness, and excitement.

Soon Jen knocked at the door.

"Hi, hon." She greeted London with a hug. Jen's perfume was wonderfully intoxicating.

"Thanks for coming," London smiled.

"So let me see that ring," exclaimed Jen.

London flashed her aquamarine gemstone proudly as she glowed with radiance.

"Oh my, that is beautiful. I'm so happy for you."

"Thank you. I've never been happier in my life."

They prepared their coffees and snuggled in on the sofa together.

"So what did you want to chat about?"

"I have something to ask of you."

London took her time approaching the sensitive subject by explaining the deep discussion that she and Deacon had recently had about mortality and the "bucket list," then finally blurted out the question as she felt herself beginning to blush.

"So, how would you like to be a part of our threesome?"

"With you and Deacon? It would be my pleasure, London. And when are you planning this surprise for him?"

"If you're available, I would love to get together for New Year's Eve."

"That's perfect as my plans were just canceled for that night. Wow, Deacon is so hot, girl. Are you absolutely sure you want to share him with someone else?"

"Yes. I know it will make him very happy and I would do anything for him. You're the only one I could trust to do this with us. It will be a wonderful belated Christmas present for him, and a memorable way to ring in the New Year."

"I'll say . . . as long as you're sure. By the way, you look fabulous, hon. You're glowing. Love looks good on you," said Jen as she touched London's thigh. London felt a chill go up her spine and between her legs, a real sexy tingle. . . .

"Thank you. So how about dinner at seven?" London suggested. Jen agreed and moved toward London. She gave her another hug and whispered in her ear.

"Don't worry, I will take good care of you both." She gave her a smile and raced off to work.

London was awed how easy that was. *Ask and you shall receive.*

She raced out to the store for groceries to prepare a simple yet elegant meal, followed by champagne, which would serve two purposes. She picked up some of Deacon's favorite lavish scotch. She was sure he was going to need it after what she had in mind for him. She also stopped by Jon's Catering & Delicacies Shop to discuss the table setting. Jon was busy preparing for another eventful holiday weekend, but he greeted her with open arms. He pulled out a set of black-and-gold place mats and an arrangement that would complement her dinner table. She thanked him and was tempted to let him in on what the special occasion was, but decided to keep it to herself.

The day flew by between running errands and cleaning the house. By the start of the evening, Deacon called to let her know that he was picking up a pizza on his way home from work. "You've been cooking too much," he said. And he wanted to relax and watch a movie with her. She was relieved to unwind for a while with him, but it was all she could do to contain herself and refrain from ruining the surprise she had lined up for him.

She simply mentioned that they would be having a special guest for dinner on New Year's Eve. He explained that he did have to go to the office again, even though it was Saturday and New Year's Eve, but he promised to be home in time. She scowled a bit about him working so much, but he dodged the subject by tickling her until she laughed uncontrollably, then he carried her up to the bedroom for another glorious night of lovemaking.

New Year's Eve morning, she sent him off with a full tummy, a smile, and a kiss. She spent the day preparing the guest bedroom for their evening interlude. She soaked for what seemed like hours in a bubble bath, refilling it several times to keep it warm, and massaged her body parts that were still a little tender from the night before. When she finally got out, she dried off and lathered perfumed lotion of the same divine fragrance over her entire body. She dressed in her short little black dress with her black thigh-high stockings, garters, lace bustier, and no panties.

She moved into the dining room, where she set the table with sheer black-and-gold place mats, gold chargers with round black plates, and goblets with gold trim. Gold silverware and black napkins with gold napkin rings added to the place settings. In the center of the table was an elongated gold vase with black, cream, and gold artificial flowers, matched at each end of the arrangement by a gold candleholder and a black candle. The house was immaculate and the table setting looked like something straight out of a magazine. Pleased with her accomplishments, she proceeded into the kitchen and slipped on an apron. She prepared a light meal of salad, baked chicken, baked potatoes, and fresh Italian bread with butter.

Just as she was finalizing the last-minute details, the gate buzzer lit up. She pushed the button to let Jen in, who had arrived early. She watched the car lights follow the curved driveway to the back of the house. London felt tightness in her tummy. She was a little nervous, but this would be something new, something to please Deacon. She welcomed Jen inside and they embraced warmly. Jen joined her in the kitchen to help with serving.

More car lights appeared. Deacon was right on time. She pushed the button to shut the gate and they were now secure. London's heart was beating fast as she greeted him at the door. She welcomed him with a warm kiss and handed him the bottle of champagne to uncork.

"Deacon, you remember Jen from the party, don't you?"

"Surprise," Jen said as she came out from the other room.

"Sure. Hi, Jen, of course I remember." He had a curious expression on his face.

Jen snickered as she watched the two of them, knowing the secret surprise London had in store for him. He joined them at the table and uncorked the bubbly. Jen and London giggled and squealed, "Happy New Year!" as the cork popped out and the champagne ran down the side of the bottle. Deacon filled their flutes and the three of them toasted the holiday. Their dinner flowed with conversations of work, travel, and holidays. Jen told a few wild stories about her and London's younger days together.

Afterward Jen helped London clear the dishes, the two of them taking turns, intentionally and dramatically, to bend over to reach across the table. The body language of the two made Deacon even more curious. He could sense anticipation in the atmosphere between them, but he wasn't sure what it was all about. He retired to the front room and poured a scotch, thanking London for remembering to pick it up for him. He flicked on the intercom for some soft music, but kept looking over his shoulder as he sipped his drink, watching the women together. He noticed Jen was very touchy with London, feeling her back, and that London responded with no hint of surprise. They drank the rest of the champagne as they finished cleaning up.

Once the dishwasher was loaded and everything was tidy, Jen took London's hand and led her to the guest bedroom. They strolled past Deacon, who was champing at the bit to know what was about to happen. They left the door open so that he had a full view of the room. He saw Jen pull London toward her, kissing her on the neck and lips. London took a deep breath and thought, *Here it goes.* She felt funny about this kiss with another woman. She noted how soft the lips of a woman are. Yet in some ways it was like any other kiss. Their breasts were brushing against each other's and that felt a bit odd too. She told herself to relax and began to train her mind on Deacon to be aware that he was watching. That made her hot and wet. He soon turned around and gave the women his full attention. A bulge in his pants was evidence that he liked what he saw. He gulped down his scotch and poured another. Jen noticed and took the occasion to slip from the room. London took her clothes off while Jen approached Deacon and took him by the hand. She pulled him close to her for a kiss, but his eyes were still fixated on London, and hers on him.

He was following the leader, but still held back a bit. The mystery in the air was exciting, but he wasn't in control and he was unused to that.

"This is a gift to you from London," Jen purred into his ear. "This is a new game, and you, my dear, are going to be the prize." She kissed him again, more aggressively this time, her tongue playing with his, her hands moving over him, touching him, prodding him to respond. He grabbed her ass and pulled her in closer, then walked her backward into the bedroom, where London was now lying on the bed waiting for them, her body glistening in the candlelight. He motioned for Jen to join London on the bed. She slipped off her dress and moved in beside London. He undressed, exposing his throbbing hardness, then sat in the chair to observe in amazement as he stroked himself for a few minutes.

He watched Jen fondling London. She rubbed her body against hers, kissing her, sucking at her nipples and working her way down to her thighs. London was breathless and moaning already. When Deacon could no longer wait, he came over and touched Jen with the tip of his hardness. He moved it over her nude body, then touched her ear, her neck, and her face, pushing with an eagerness to be inside of her mouth, then he rested it between Jen and London. He wanted to fall on both of them, taking them one by one, but Jen pushed him away teasingly and continued kissing and licking London between her legs. Her sex was so wet, she felt hotter than ever before, and she enjoyed watching Deacon get teased for once.

Jen motioned to Deacon to come back and be a part of the lovemaking. He threw himself between the two and fingered Jen. She moaned softly. He licked her and she licked London, as he got behind Jen and entered her. She moaned softly as he took her with hard, short strokes. London was still being fondled in her passion zone by Jen, who was getting so hot she almost bit London. Jen finally stopped for a moment to enjoy Deacon, who was riding her for all he was worth. He was hot and ready for both girls. London fingered herself as she watched them, her heart a little heavy. She was trying to go along, but now her feelings were mixed. She didn't quite know what to do or how to feel watching the man she loved take another woman. He continued stroking Jen. He then pulled out quickly to give his prize to London. She sucked it hard as Jen went down on her to finish her off. They lay in an embrace for a moment until the passions picked up again.

Deacon grabbed London and took her in his arms, kissing her. His erection returned harder than before, and he moved on top of her. He penetrated and filled her. He found her G-spot and took her on a wild ride. They were beautiful to Jen, who looked on as Deacon rode London's pussy. She then approached Deacon from behind and played with his ass, inserting her finger deep inside him. He moaned loudly as she felt him come again. London was soon to follow, her body shaking from the jolts of her orgasm. She looked up at Deacon in ecstasy as she came.

Deacon left London's body as Jen moved in, kissing her and fondling her, licking her into an encore orgasm. As Deacon watched, he wondered if London was doing this for him or for herself. He felt a slight pang of jealousy for a moment, but he relaxed and smiled, gratified with his woman, who gave him this gift.

Jen strapped on a dildo and went back to London, sticking it in her mouth and then rubbing it between her legs and all over her passion pit. As she was bending over London, Deacon's hardness returned and he moved over to the bed to rub Jen's buttocks. He moved his cock between her legs, got it wet, and inserted it deep inside her again. Jen slammed into London with the artificial cock as she was being fucked hard by Deacon. It was wild and wonderful for the three of them as they explored countless orgasms in a screaming rage.

The evening was winding down as the three of them went into the hot tub and soaked their sore spots away. The air outside was freezing but the water temperature was perfect. They sat low in the tub, before scurrying back into the house, being careful enough not to slip and fall.

Minutes from midnight, Deacon uncorked a second bottle of champagne and turned on the television to watch the ball drop in Times Square. They toasted the New Year together one last time as they counted down the seconds. They all enjoyed their bubbly and chatted as they relaxed. Deacon cuddled London closely and Jen saw her window to make a grand exit. She bundled up in her robe, thanked them for a great time, and said she would see herself out. She left London snuggling with Deacon's arms around her. He held her tightly, thanking her for the wonderful gift as he issued small kisses over her face and neck. She had given him a memory that would last a lifetime.

They spent most of New Year's Day in bed together, with Deacon leaving only to pick up Chinese takeout. They watched a marathon of classic romantic movies, eating with chopsticks from the pint-sized containers, lounging in their pajamas. They cuddled, joked, and laughed and made love just once in the afternoon, slowly and gently as they were still aching from the activities of the night before. London never wanted this intimate, peaceful day to end.

Monday arrived, gloomy and uninvited. She awoke to a note on her pillow from Deacon that he had to be in court early that morning. He was gone already and she hadn't even been able to enjoy breakfast with him. She lay in bed missing her fiancé as warmth and wonder filled her heart. The sun was trying to peek through the clouds outside and the light shined through the windows momentarily. She looked at her ring, reveling in the prisms dancing on the wall, created by the reflection of the passing sunlight. The colorful spectrum mimicked the love she felt radiating from her heart. She'd thrown all caution to the wind and she would do anything, be anything, just for Deacon, just to be with him forever.

She got up, dressed, and headed to the grocery store again. It felt good to be out of the house in the early morning. She wanted to pick up some special items and seasonings for more of the new recipes she planned to try this week. She was really enjoying her time in the kitchen lately, exploring her own unexpected culinary talents. Jon had given her quite a few recipes to choose from and she wanted each night to be a different exotic meal to tempt Deacon into coming home to her, instead of working so late.

On her way to the store, she noticed a silver Lexus that looked like the one Deacon drove parked alongside her favorite coffee shop. In her distraction, she swerved over the line, but her attention was quickly drawn back to the road by a honking horn. She straightened out the SUV as she wondered if it was him, why he wasn't in court. She decided to turn around so she wouldn't spend any more time just wondering. She circled back and parked behind the building. That's where she also then noticed Jen's car.

She had a sinking feeling as she walked toward the entrance. She stopped in her tracks for a moment. She spotted them, Deacon and Jen, right through the window in the corner booth. Jen was touching Deacon's hand and they were sitting very close together. She quickly turned before they saw her, ran back down the sidewalk to the parking lot. Tears sprang up in the corner of her eyes. She got into her car and headed home. She was driving through her emotional haze when she saw Jon's place. She pulled over and parked, wiping her eyes and trying to collect herself. Jon's shop didn't look as busy as it had been Friday before, so she decided to go inside. She needed something to ground her and shift the terrible feelings bubbling up. The quaint store had a warm and wonderful atmosphere that smelled of fresh baked goods and delightful spices. The counter was deserted and the place was very quiet. London strolled along, eyeing plastic cakes set up on small tables, inviting samples under ornate glass covers, and the display case that was crammed with cupcakes, cream puffs, and other colorful delicacies. She rang the bell on the showcase and was relieved to see Jon come out of the back room.

"London, darling, how wonderful to see you! You look simply . . . oh, my dear!" He put his hand up to his face. "What's wrong?" He noticed that she looked a bit ashen and disturbed. "Come sit down," he said, patting a stool and putting his hand on his hip as he leaned against the showcase.

"Oh, Jon." She fled into his arms, sobbing. She hadn't really expected to do that. He hugged her tightly, patting her head and stroking her hair. "What's the matter?" He tried to comfort her. "Who did this to you . . . I will go punch them tout de suite."

She held her hand up, showing him her engagement ring. He grabbed her hand and smiled as he kissed it. He looked closely at the gemstone gleaming. "Well, okay, good news. Congratulations. But why the sad look? Tell me." He was confused.

"Jon, Deacon proposed. I was so happy. I thought I'd give him a gift." She backed away to take a breath. "How stupid I was." Jon stepped back too, cocking his head to the side, thinking to himself the words *Come on, get it out already.* "I gave him a three-way, with Jen. I asked her to engage in a ménage à trois with us on New Year's Eve. And today, just now, I find the two of them meeting without me, together at the coffee shop." She looked at Jon's face now and tried to read his response.

"That bastard!" Jon growled out as he paced around the room, taking in a deep breath and sighing. "Shit. Now, London, there could be a very simple explanation to all of this. Please don't jump the gun. Give him a chance to explain and always give him the benefit of the doubt before jumping to conclusions." He was talking to himself as much as he was trying to convince London.

"Tonight when he is home from work, talk it over with him. I'm sure he can explain everything to you. But for now, get hold of yourself. Don't torture yourself. Have a latté with me and some chocolate éclairs. When the going gets tough . . . chocolate."

He set out their glass mugs, frothing with whipped cream and garnished with cinnamon sticks, then grabbed the whole bakery tray of mini éclairs and set it on the counter before them as he came around and sat beside her. The pastries were drenched in chocolate and generously overstuffed with vanilla custard. She put the scrumptious dessert to her lips and devoured one, and then another. Jon did the same. Thank God there's food when you're at a loss for words.

"For moral support, of course." He raised an éclair-filled hand in the air and issued a nervous laugh.

London was feeling stuffed but better and hugged Jon as she felt the need to get up and get home at last after stopping at the grocery store. She drove past, but tried not to look at the coffee shop again. She failed to fully avoid looking and did notice that Deacon's car was nowhere in sight. She stayed focused on her shopping goals and her dinner plans then headed home.

She unpacked her bags and settled in, lighting the fireplace to take off the chill. She walked around the house, admiring all the warm and wonderful Christmas decorations, which would soon be taken down and tucked away for another year. She dreaded January. Empty of decorations, the house would suddenly feel bare and cold—back to reality. She snuggled into her recliner next to the fire, watching the flames flicker and listening to the clock tick away. She didn't want to admit it to herself, but she was waiting for 5:00 p.m. to come—the end of the workday, when Deacon would be home. She needed Deacon to make this right. She trusted Deacon with her heart and she wanted to be sure he wouldn't do anything to hurt her, especially now.

She picked up a romance novel she had lying around and tried to get lost in the story, but her mind kept flashing back to the sight of Deacon and Jen . . . her hand on top of his. The image rewound and played over and over again in an end-less loop. She laid her head back as tears formed in her eyes again. She closed them and drifted off to sleep.

The shadows lengthened as they darkened to a close. She opened her eyes from her nap to see the time—7:00, and he still wasn't home. She stood up, marched to the bathroom to freshen up, then drove away from the château on a mission to track him down.

The roads were clear and she looked out her rearview mirror at her home as the gates closed behind her. She remembered what Jon had said about "benefit of the doubt," and she calmed herself as she drove, knowing there could still be a reasonable explanation for his actions and whereabouts.

Twenty minutes later she was in Tarrytown at Deacon's workplace. London drove by and didn't see his Lexus. *Hmm,* she thought. She sat a moment and then decided to drive by Jen's place as it wasn't far out of her way.

As she approached Jen's apartment, she saw Deacon's Lexus parked next to Jen's car in the carport. Her adrenaline surged as she pulled into a guest parking space and made her way up-stairs to the door. She knocked, but there was no answer. She turned the doorknob and the door was unlocked. She entered, calling Jen's name. No answer. She noticed a trail of clothing on the floor in the hallway that led up the steps. A blouse and a shirt mixed with male and female shoes, a pair of pants and a skirt, a bra and lace panties, boxers and socks that marked the end of the line at the next closed door. She stopped dead in her tracks. Her heart was beating so fast she could hardly breathe. She knocked lightly as she heard voices and commotion. Still in utter disbelief, she pushed the door open to find Deacon and Jen in bed together. A painful-sounding, involuntary noise escaped from London's mouth: "Ohhhhhhhhh!" It was all she could mutter as she ran down the steps, Deacon's voice trailing behind her. He stood in the doorway, calling her name as she got in her SUV and laid rubber in a cloud of smoke as she burned up the asphalt with her rage. Tears flowed as she tried to calm down so she could drive home safely. Her cell phone rang. She reached over and declined the calls, even the one from Jon, who she knew was calling to make sure she was okay tonight. She wanted to throw the phone out the window.

The twinkling lights of her home took on a new aura. She felt like they were laughing at her now, mocking her for being naïve. She was furious and wanted to rip them from the trees, tearing them down along with all the other decorations. She wanted everything stripped down and back to normal, cold, naked, lonely, and dark, just like the vengefully dark place she felt herself slipping back into. Her heart was broken. *Why didn't I just leave well enough . . .* She wanted to slap herself.

As she walked into the house, her cell phone was buzzing frantically from inside her purse to alert her of all the voicemail messages. Once inside, she noticed the answering machine was also blinking. She ignored them as she poured herself a double of Deacon's favorite scotch and toasted the end of Deacon.

She took off her ring and put it in the ring box on the dresser. There were no words that could ever wipe away the vision that had blinded her. No words . . . nothing . . . ever. She collapsed onto the bed and gulped down her scotch, trying to drown her sorrows. She hugged her pillow and cried, "Oh, Grams, I need you so badly now." She sobbed uncontrollably. She scanned the walls, holding on to her pillow, looking for answers. She looked at her grandmother's picture and the journal of *Life Lessons.* She got up and reached for the book, then sat down, leafing though the pages for help. On one page the words "IF YOU'RE FEELING SAD AND BLUE FIND SOMEONE WORSE OFF THAN YOU." Next page, "NOTHING STARTS WRONG AND ENDS RIGHT."

"Right," she said, as she continued to leaf though the pages, looking for the magic cure for heartache. On page five Grams said, "LOVE IS NOT BASED ON SEX ALONE." *Hmm,* she thought. Every relationship that she could remember was based on sex, she mused. Was that why they went bad? She fell back into the pillows, crying and holding the book close to her heart.

She tossed and turned as she crossed over into darkness, nightmares filling her with dread as she was yanked back in time to horrible experiences from her childhood.

London's mother was there, towering over her and screaming into her tiny face as she scolded her for being naughty. London trembled, holding her blanket, embarrassed and ashamed, cowering and confused. Her mother spanked her repeatedly with a wooden spoon and took away all of her stuffed animals. She warned her never to touch herself there again as she stormed out of the room. Little London cried herself to sleep, missing her fuzzy friends, who always comforted her at night.

Then she awoke, rolled over, and drifted off to another nightmare of her uncle rubbing and touching her there. London asked him why it was okay for him to touch her, when Mother would whip her for touching herself there. He told her that her mother knew what they were doing and it was only okay when he did it. He opened her legs and moved his finger on her sex spot, whispering in her ear that it was okay, because he was her favorite uncle. . . .

London awoke and ran for the bathroom, barely making it to the toilet as she vomited. She gasped for air and stood to rinse her mouth with water. The nausea lingered, so she brushed her teeth and rinsed with mouthwash. She crawled back into bed, still nauseous and feeling defeated as she recalled her fuzzy nightmare. She lay there, blinking up at the ceiling, watching moonlight and shadows dance across the room, thinking about her life and what made her who she was.

Ever since she was a little girl she had been told she was naughty. The first moment was when her mother had caught her masturbating at eight years old. London recalled how confusing it all was and it took her years before she realized that her mother didn't know anything about what her uncle had done. He had touched her from the age of four and continued up until she was too old to sit on his knee anymore. It made her ill to think of him. She curled up in a tight ball around her pillow and cried herself back to sleep.

She awoke again after a few hours of restful sleep. She felt dazed and confused, but she knew she needed to feel that sensation again. If she was going to be naughty, she might as well enjoy it. She remembered her grandmother, who told her not to give her heart away, because men would only abuse it. She was right! As she touched herself down there, she enjoyed the feeling immensely. She tried to push Deacon out of her heart and mind. She got out her pleasure toy and positioned herself for a treat.

Her mind envisioned different men, but still kept coming

back to Deacon. She brushed him out as she picked up her favorite juicy book. *Oh dear*, she thought, *what am I going to do? Not even my vibrator can turn me on. I need some stimulation and nothing is working, but I can't get my mind off of sex!* Her body was aching for action and her toy couldn't give her the pleasure she so badly needed.

She went to her computer, where she had a naughty site she enjoyed. She zoomed in there for fun and games. She watched the girls and guys playing naughty. She touched herself as she watched four different men, but nothing happened. She clicked over to watch some live action on streaming hot sex cams. She finally stumbled across something that really turned her on and she reached for a toy, letting it go to work. Her body shook in anticipation as she watched the kinky wildness between various couples. She focused in on one guy who was simply yummy. He was handsome, yet savage. His deeds were barbaric, but London found herself longing for him to spank her. She was naughty and deserved to be punished too. She reached for her other toy and placed it inside as she watched his action and copied his motions. She closed her eyes and fantasized, his cock deep in her sex and thrusting into her as if she had crossed over into the porn site with him. She wished she was there with him, on the screen right now with others watching him punish her. She homed in on him and felt the explosion building up inside her. She trembled and moaned as her eyes rolled back. She welcomed the feeling and finally relaxed.

Exhausted, she crawled back into bed as the sun began to rise. Although it was out of character for her, she thought she might sulk for a while longer in bed today. She promised herself that she would go shopping tomorrow, as that was always the remedy for any ailment.

Chapter 12

HOT STICKY CINNAMON ROLLS

ondon arrived at the mall just after it opened in the early morning hour. It was quiet with the exception of a few shoppers still making returns and exchanges of poor-choice gifts they'd received during the holiday season. As she strolled along, the irresistible aroma of fresh-baked pastries drew her in. She followed the scent to the bakery where she and Grams used to go when they shopped together. She ordered a colossal-sized cinnamon roll, smothered in rich, melting icing that ran down the sides of the warm roll and pooled on the plate. She chuckled to herself that she almost needed a bib to devour this delicious treat. She battled with her conscience as she gorged, thinking, *This probably contains enough fat and calories for two whole days.* She licked the icing from her fingers and justified her indulgence: at least she hadn't stayed in bed all day again today.

She had gotten out of the house and on with her life today. She washed the gooey snack down with an espresso, disposed of her dish, and headed to the restroom to wash her sticky hands.

Now she was sugared up and ready for some power shopping.

She strolled a bit more, eyeing the store window displays and the vendors along the midway. She was amazed at how quickly the retailers moved on to the next fashion, the next season, the next holiday. Christmas decorations had already been whisked away and replaced with hearts and cupids for Valentine's Day, which of course made her think of Deacon. She frowned as she thought of her own Christmas decorations that she needed to go home and take down, alone. Her heart suddenly sank and she cringed, choking back tears.

She turned her attention to another dazzling and cheerful store window display that was already promoting attire for spring break. Sun and beach cutouts covered the walls of the store with lively images. The mannequins were staged in vibrant string bikinis with matching sarongs, or colorful shorts and capri pants with sexy summery tops, posed amid sand and seashells, beach towels and chairs, with backdrops of panoramic ocean views. London perked up with the liveliness of the displays and thought a tropical vacation would be in order very soon indeed.

As she headed for the store, she had an eerie feeling of eyes upon her. She looked around the corridor of the mall but didn't notice anyone paying particular attention to her. She brushed off the intuition and carried on. As she entered yet another shop, her senses were overwhelmed by party music and the fragrance of coconut oil. Her body moved to the beat as she whirled through the store, loading up her arms with bright sundresses, skirts, swimsuits, and an assortment of shorts, tops, pants, and accessories. She headed for the fitting rooms.

She emerged from the dressing room with a few things: shorts, capris, and matching shirts. At the register, she picked up more, sucked in as she was by the point-of-sale displays. She selected coordinating sunglasses, nail polish, lip gloss, and a beach bag. She swiped her card, feeling the rush of spending rejuvenate and empower her emotionally. She gathered her bags and headed out toward her favorite department store. Once there, she told herself she would focus on more realistic purchases for the current season. The weather was still bitterly cold out, and she hoped to find a new outfit to bundle up in as she braved the elements.

She felt eyes upon her once again, that uncomfortable feeling of being followed. This time she did notice a guy trailing not far behind. She sought out her personal shopping assistant in the store, a woman named Krystal, first thing. She greeted the woman, didn't say anything about feeling stalked, but rather gave her packages to Krystal behind the counter while she shopped, then Krystal led her over to women's apparel, where she offered suggestions and paired garments for her to choose from. After they'd chatted awhile and looked at garments Krystal pulled for her to consider, London saw the suspicious man enter the store and then confided that she felt she was being stalked. Krystal subtly looked around to check the man's behavior and agreed that he was acting a bit strange. She silently alerted security by pressing a button on her radio. They would now be monitoring her location by video and sending officers to the area.

London and Krystal continued shopping, and the creeper remained in the area, but someone from security had arrived, according to Krystal. Minutes later while Krystal walked away to pull more clothes for London, she felt herself being jerked backward. The strap of her bag caught in the crook of her arm. London turned, screamed, and pulled back, holding on to her purse despite the pain. She also kicked at the man and aimed to bury her two-and-a-half-inch boot heel into his groin. Her move worked. The purse snatcher fell back to the floor. The security guy was next to them by then, putting the guy in a hold. Another security person from the store appeared.

"Are you okay, ma'am?" asked one of the officers.

"I'm fine, thank you," replied London. The stalker was up on his feet and handcuffed. The security officer took a breath, looked at her, and said, "That was impressive." The other officer smiled.

"Thank you. My kickboxing classes finally paid off, I guess." She chuckled as she flipped her hair back over her shoulder and grinned. Krystal was standing at London's side looking at her customer with an expression of awe.

"Wow, London. You'll have to share your trainer's name with me," said Krystal, smiling at her.

London was a bit shaken up, but she and Krystal had a mission to complete. Krystal brought her a bottle of water and sat her down to look at the great outfits they collected, including snug-fitting black leggings paired with a long charcoal and silvery gray cashmere sweater that plunged into a V-neck to accentuate her cleavage. The sweater was accessorized with a black elastic belt that sat high on her figure, emphasizing her tiny waist. To top it off, she chose three-inch platform black zippered over-the-knee boots.

"Now that's an outfit to kick some ass in, London." They both laughed. Krystal was still energized by all the excitement as she gathered up all of London's purchases. Since there was still almost three months left of winter, she also suggested a new black leather midlength trench coat with a faux-fur neckline, stylish hats, scarves, and gloves to accompany London's practical wintry selections. London also made some lavish jewelry purchases to help her cope with the nakedness she was feeling on her left hand. She paid at the register, surprised to find that many of her clothing purchases were discounted at clearance pricing, and she thanked Krystal graciously with a thirty percent tip for her services. She felt empowered as she sauntered out of the store, toting her new wardrobe collections with an assortment of fashions suitable for every season.

As the brisk air hit her face outside the mall, she felt revived. She had taken charge of her emotions through a therapeutic shopping trip. She had fought off an attacker without getting hurt. She wouldn't want to have to do it again, but she was proud of herself. London had grown tired of being pushed around and taken advantage of by men, and the attacker had picked the perfect moment to mess with her. Maybe she had been helped by the early morning sugar high of that cinnamon roll. She patted her stomach and smiled.

She loaded her purchases and climbed into the SUV and noticed that her cell phone was on the car charger. She was surprised that she hadn't even missed having the phone on her, but then again she wasn't looking forward to anyone's phone calls right now. She checked it and saw that she had several voicemails from Deacon. She only partially listened to the messages, each one a repeat of the last with him begging for forgiveness, begging to see her. She deleted them all, shrugged it off, and tossed her phone into her purse. She felt rejuvenated and happy to still have so much time left in the day. She wouldn't let anything stand in her way. She was now determined to head home and take down the Christmas decorations. Her adrenaline raced through her body as she drove and she felt the need to burn off some more pent-up aggression in a productive manner.

She put away her purchases at home and noticed the light blinking on the answering machine. She listened this time to each message, all from Deacon. She gazed out the window watching the new afternoon snow falling to the ground in a fresh blanket of white. Inspired for her own fresh start to a brand-new year, she bundled up and headed out to the yard to take down the decorations. Those twinkling lights had continued to mock her as she thought about her future.

As she untangled the strands of lights from the trees, her mind wandered, seeking guidance on how to straighten out her own life and make sense of what would come next. She boxed up the lights and set them in the garage, then made her way up to retrieve a few letters from the mailbox before heading back inside, her skin chilled from the bitter wind.

She brewed a fresh cup of java, fuel for a second wind so she could continue her tasks indoors. She warmed up by the fire, sipping her coffee as she boxed up the décor from the Christmas tree. She fondled the ornaments gently as she placed them into the container, each one drifting her thoughts back to special memories of Christmases with Grams. She thought about the real meaning of her grandmother's lessons and realized she had really never paid any attention to them.

London had made herself available to dozens of men without compunction or personal values. She had hidden her feelings, not wanting to think about what she was doing. She just did it. Now, she faced the failures in her personal life. She wasn't too proud of her shortcomings and vowed she would no longer be that person and that she would start right now. Her value had to come from within, not without. . . . Men could use her only if she let them, and that would stop. She was almost as bad as a prostitute. She didn't charge money— she had her own—but that was the only difference. She was taught—and knew—that she was worthy of love and a good man. Where had she gone wrong? She was being guided by lust, not love, and it was not right. She knew there could never be another Deacon in her future and that saddened her very much. She also knew life was just beginning for her and she was young enough to start all over again. She hauled the boxes up to the attic, bidding them a fond farewell until next Christmas, when she hoped things would be different. With each decoration that she took down she felt like she replaced it with a positive thought. No more fast sex. No more letting herself be used only for pleasure. She sighed at that one. She always enjoyed the thrill of a man's touch. She would miss that so much, but the heartbreak that came from that touch was not worth the pain. There would be some pressure on the man of her choice, and that pressure would be that he would have to respect her first. *Next time I won't allow my need to please someone get me into a situation such as a three-way that leads to a broken heart. I'll never get involved with a married man. I'm paying for the bad karma I created by being with one.* She spied her grandmother's *Life Lessons* book again and opened it to page one. "REMEMBER, DEAR GRANDDAUGHTER, 'NOTHING STARTS WRONG AND ENDS RIGHT.'" "Oh, Grams," she said out loud. "You were so right." She sipped her coffee and thought about her grandmother. One thought that entered her mind was the advice of *pleasure without pressure*. It worked great for her grandmother since she had already been married and had the security of being loved in her life before she was so promiscuous. However, London didn't have that love, and in searching for it, she lost a part of herself, a valuable part . . . her self-respect. She must rebuild and her thoughts from this day would help her.

She worked up an appetite while tidying the house, but had no desire to cook. So she popped a frozen dinner into the microwave and sat down at the table to read through her mail. She opened an annual bank statement showing savings and interest on one of many accounts her grandmother had left to her. This aggressive account had incurred a large sum of interest, more than four hundred thousand dollars, in the past year. London basically lived off the interest on all of the funds from her inheritance. Her expenses were covered and she rarely ever had to tap into the principal investments except for an occasional very large purchase. And now she had an unexpected windfall to spend.

The good news perked up her spirits. The microwave beeped, she sat to nibble at her turkey medallions and mashed potatoes, and contemplated what to do next. She poured a large glass of white wine to celebrate and made a toast. *"To Grandma, thank you for this gift and the bright future I have ahead of me. I will once again make you proud as I manage the wealth and knowledge you've passed on to me."* She finished her dinner and made her way up to bed, feeling satisfied with the day's accomplishments, yet mentally exhausted. She fell into a deep sleep and a very inspirational dream.

London found herself in Le Château de Versailles, back in the Hall of Mirrors. She was surprised at her own reflection as if she were Queen Marie Antoinette, smiling proudly back at herself. She was surrounded by unknown masked men lurking in the shadows as she looked into the mirrors, but when she spun around, they disappeared. She strolled along, admiring herself and her royal attire, exploring the castle with a newfound freedom. A guide suddenly appeared before her, another masked man wearing a tuxedo. He didn't speak, but he led her through a secret passageway behind one of the mirrors to hidden rooms she never knew existed. She floated through each room, amazed with appreciation as he unveiled treasures, magnificent heirlooms, and regal furnishings. She felt a passion running through her, but this was a different type of romance. It wasn't about men or sex. It was her love for the French style, her curiosity for the era and its old-world charm. She found herself in the queen's grand apartment, enchanted by the crystal chandelier overhead and the bright gold accents that surrounded her. Her masked man took her by the hand and swept her off her feet as they danced through the exquisite chambers. When the song was through, he kissed her gently and laid her down on the bed, leaving her breathless in the silence. She reclined, taking delight in the luxurious fabric as she stared up at the awe-inspiring ceiling painted by the great rococo artist François Boucher.

London awoke and sat up as chills ran over her body. The dream had been so vivid. It was still dark outside, and she snuggled farther into the covers and pondered the meaning of the dream she just had, the details becoming clearer now as she stirred, unable to go back to sleep. The masked men seemed obvious. But what were the treasures in the castle's hidden rooms . . . they filled her with a new and wondrous childlike curiosity. She wished she could fall back to sleep and return to the castle. She had felt safe and powerful there, surrounded by extravagance and protected from harm.

Suddenly, she had an idea. Use the four hundred thousand dollars to open a shop—an antique store. She would create her very own miniature French palace, filled with exquisite treasures so others could enjoy what she had seen. She'd buy the building in downtown Tarrytown that had once belonged to her grandmother. She had seen a For Sale sign in front of the building. She turned on her laptop at 4:30 a.m. to search for commercial property listings.

She couldn't sleep anyway. The property was listed. She clicked to email the real estate agent, Brandon Thomas, sending a message to contact her.

She showered and thawed out some cinnamon rolls she had bought yesterday and made a cappuccino, daydreaming of her new future. When the phone rang she looked at the clock. It was 8:00 a.m. and the name that showed on the phone was Brandon Thomas. His office was a block away from the store. He could meet her there as soon as she wanted. She fired up the SUV and raced into town to find him waiting out front. "Mr. Thomas?" He smiled and shook her hand.

"I knew your grandmother and worked with her real estate investments, including this building. She was a wonderful woman. I believe I even met you here when you were very young." London smiled at this older man who made her feel so comfortable.

The building hadn't changed much since she had been a little girl. A jewelry store occupied the space when she was visiting with her grandmother's tenants.

As London walked through the rooms, she could feel her grandmother's hand like a breeze through the window. She began making mental notes of what she wanted and where. The ceiling was still painted in scenes depicting love in the Renaissance days, with cherubs touching each other fondly—this was straight out of the previous night's dream and the royal bedchambers. The leaded glass windows showered rainbows all over the walls. She couldn't wait to begin transforming the interior. Although the exterior was a simple brick façade, the entry was impressive and the ornate French tiled roof added stylish sophistication. There was even a full basement to accommodate a massive storage for her inventory.

The space was perfect. She would have an inspection done and she agreed to the asking price. She wrote him a check for the down payment and he let her know he would have purchase documents ready to sign the next morning, pending the results of the inspection. Mr. Thomas gave her the keys and headed back to his office to draft the papers. She called Max. Even though they hadn't spoken since the fall, when he'd crashed his truck, she knew that he was the best contractor for the job and would give her an honest assessment of the building's potential. Max's business was slow during the winter season. Lucky for London, he was willing to help her and had the time. She paced the floors as she awaited his arrival, visualizing the different pieces of furniture she would place in various corners of the rooms. She was a perfectionist and wanted only the best. Research would be important in getting prime French antiques. There was a gorgeous fireplace on one wall with bricks laid in an arch formation around the opening. She could picture a blazing fire with two Louis XV chairs on either side. Those would not be for sale, but for her and her guests to relax in and enjoy the ambience of the store.

Her mind raced with thoughts of inventory, orders, expenses, and income. She felt exhilarated and empowered thanks to her grandmother, who had given her the financial leg up. She would and could accomplish this on her own. She would fulfill herself. No man was involved in bringing her this joyful sensation. She had something to be passionate about . . . besides passion itself.

She named her new venture Le Magasin d'Antiquités, French for "The Antique Shop." The sound of Max's diesel truck pulling up to the side of the building pulled London from her thoughts.

He took a look at the exterior before coming in. He was as adorable as ever, London thought, with his piercing blue eyes and defiant wispy blond hair. He wore a tan Carhartt work coat, khaki cargo workpants, and dirty steel-toed boots. Yes, London felt herself tingle, but she stifled the feelings, turning her attention back to the matter at hand.

Max stomped his snowy boots off on the cobblestone walkway and entered the shop.

"Hi, London." He greeted her warmly with a gentle hug and a peck on the cheek. "I was so glad to hear from you. I'm sorry I haven't been in touch since I saw you a few months ago. We were so swamped working eighteen-hour days trying to finalize our jobs before the first snowfall, and before I knew it, too much time had passed. I had good intentions about getting back with you, but it felt awkward after so long, if you know what I mean. So, how have you been?"

"I'm doing well, thank you," London replied with a grin. "And it is a modern world. I suppose I could have called you too, and I'm sorry I didn't."

Max looked at London inquisitively. "I heard you got engaged. I ran into Paris on New Year's Eve at a party and she said you were getting married."

"I was, yes, but it was quite possibly the shortest engagement ever. Look, I don't really want to talk about it, but . . . I found my fiancé in bed with Jen." London felt herself blush in embarrassment as she divulged so freely to Max. "We had a threesome and . . . well, afterward he made his choice. I suppose it's as simple as that, so now I'm just trying to move on."

Max tried but didn't succeed in hiding his astonishment. She immediately regretted revealing that part of the story.

"Oh, London. I'm so sorry. I was happy to hear that you'd finally found someone special, but you deserve so much better." Max was kind, gentle, and caring, in direct contrast with his rugged exterior. The sincerity in his voice reassured her and she was no longer bothered by the fact that he hadn't called. She understood what it was like to be busy at work and lost in daily responsibilities. Her heart was very forgiving of him and despite all of the men who had let her down in life, Max was still unique, genuine, and honest.

"So, let's take a look around the inside and see what you've got going on here," Max finally said, breaking the silence as he proceeded to inspect the structure. She gave him a tour of the building, explained her remodeling ideas, and shared her budget allowance for renovations. He explored the basement and the upstairs, then went back outside to conduct further careful inspection of the foundation and the roof. She tagged along, following him down the cobblestone beside the tall and narrow building, watching him kicking at the brick façade and examining the mortar joints. She cringed as he climbed up the fire escape on the back of the building to the rooftop. The roof was icy and snowy and he slipped just a bit as he ascended.

When he came down, he explained that the slate French roof tiles would need some minor repairs. But the foundation appeared to be in sturdy, stable condition.

"You've got yourself a great place here," he said upon re-entering the store with her. "I'd really enjoy working on the renovations with you. Would you like me to work up a quote?"

"Yes, as long as we stay within a budget. How soon can you start?"

She walked him through her thoughts in more detail as he took careful notes of her suggestions. He shared his own ideas as they brainstormed. She hadn't realized before just how experienced and knowledgeable he was in his profession. Together, they reconstructed the main archetype theme for the building. He recommended that the second floor over the back half of the shop be made into a loft space. She thought that was a great idea and she hoped that she could rent it out, preferably to someone who would work at the store and help her manage the place.

On the way out, she hugged and thanked Max. As she stepped back, their eyes met, their faces so close they almost touched. She could feel electricity surging between them, but she refrained from kissing him and he respectfully followed her lead.

Max let her know that he could begin work as soon as the papers were signed. She called to schedule an appointment with the sign man for the following day. She knew the building would be hers and she wanted to get the ball rolling.

She decided to stop in at Jon's place and invite him to a late lunch. She hadn't talked to him since she'd found Deacon and Jen together at the coffee shop. She hadn't even told him yet about finding them in bed together. She didn't want to burden him with her troubles, but it seemed only right to tell him the rest of a story he participated in.

Jon was delighted to see her as always and thrilled to escape the monotony of his day in the hot kitchen. They enjoyed pasta, salad, and bread at a nearby Italian restaurant. He patted her hand and comforted her as she relived the trail of clothing that had led to Jen's bedroom that night. Then she told him of her dream and the building she was buying for the antique shop. He summoned the waiter and ordered a bottle of red wine to celebrate. He could hardly contain his excitement for her.

"Well, London, even though there won't be an engagement party, it looks like I'll still be able to plan a different type of celebration for you this year. You must let me help you with a grand opening event for the new store," Jon pleaded.

"There's no one else I would rather have catering the event. I was thinking we could have a masquerade ball the night before the grand opening. What do you think?"

"Oh, darling, I think that's a fabulous idea."

"Okay, good. Then for the grand opening, I want to hold a silent auction for several unique pieces. The competition will get wealthy customers eager to buy and interested in the new store, not to mention raise money I need to get inventory. I have Max Callaghan doing the renovations on the old building."

"Oh my, Max the mountain man? Now, London, I don't want to see you rebounding so quickly into his arms. I see the way you're glowing. Make sure you channel your energy into your new venture and not into his pants."

They laughed together, but she made no promises. They sat plotting the events together all afternoon until she finally headed home, eager to research the countless French antique vendors and to start placing orders.

Her email inbox had several new messages from Deacon. She moved them to the trash bin without even bothering to open them. She surfed craigslist and eBay, saving potential items to her browser favorites. Her list grew as her eyes began to glaze over. She'd almost forgotten how early she had gotten up that morning. She yawned and clicked a few more times when something caught her eye. She found the most perfect Louis XVI crystal chandelier. The "buy it now" price was right and she placed it in her cart. She almost clicked to pay, then hesitated. She was a little superstitious at times and didn't want to jinx anything by jumping the gun. Although it was also an auction item, she noticed that it wouldn't be sold for a few more days, so she saved it in her cart and logged off. No sense in buying it before she had the building in her name.

She was exhausted, yet her mind was still frenzied with excitement about the wonderful changes in her life. She got ready for bed and picked up a good book to help her wind down as she settled in. She adjusted her bed lamp and read a few pages. Her eyes were blurry and she was easily distracted by the noise of the frigid winds blowing outside. She glanced over at the dresser and the box with her engagement ring in it. She rose, walked over, and tucked it away in the drawer as she blinked back tears. She paused at the mirror, giving her reflection a confident smile of approval, then crawled back into her warm, cozy bed. She read a bit more and then dozed off halfway through the first chapter.

She awoke to darkness, startled and alone. She was unable to recall her dreams or what had caused her to jump. She was still overly exhausted from the emotional roller coaster she'd been riding the past several days.

She got out her toy and inserted it deep inside herself, letting the vibration bring her the release she so needed. She rested a while longer, waiting for the sun to rise again.

Today was the day she would become the proud owner of the modest building that she would transform into Le Magasin d'Antiquités. She finally arose to shower and get dressed for her appointment to close on the purchase of the building. She put on a black skirt with black tights for added warmth, and her new long, charcoal gray sweater. She cinched up her belt and selected some coordinating silver jewelry to complement the silver accents on the sweater. She slipped on her new black over-the-knee boots and checked the mirror. Looking and feeling fabulous, she called Mr. Thomas to make sure their meeting was all set. He answered on the first ring, confirmed that everything was in order and told her that he would meet her at the bank. She bundled up in her black imitation-fur coat and selected a stylish purse and other accessories from her recent shopping trip. She grabbed a yogurt with granola from the refrigerator and she was ready to roll.

The bank was a short jaunt from the château, and she got flutters in her tummy as she pulled into the parking lot. Most of the staff knew her well, as her grandmother used to do business there. London received several warm greetings as she walked in and Mr. Thomas was in the conference room, waving her over. The meeting was brief as there was no mortgage involved. She signed the papers, the funds were transferred, and Mr. Thomas handed her the deed. She also transferred the remaining dividends into a new bank account strictly for the business. She thanked everyone and sashayed from the bank, feeling euphoric.

She headed over to the sign maker, arriving a bit early for her appointment. She had sketched a rough draft of her ideas. She wanted to create a black sign in the shape of the Eiffel Tower, with Le Magasin printed vertically and d'Antiquités curved across the bottom in gold elegant lettering. She discussed her business plans briefly with him and how she was considering selling jewelry in addition to furnishings. He suggested including small symbols on the sign depicting furniture and jewelry with splashes of red to add some color. He worked up a sample of the graphics on the computer screen, and she was pleased with their final creation as she placed the order. She was ecstatic about her decision to include jewelry sales in the new store. It added new challenges to the adventure, and she couldn't wait to begin another treasure hunt online.

When she got back to her store, she looked at the bare walls and saw the blank canvas of possibilities. She called Max to let him know the building was hers. He congratulated her and shared in her excitement for the project. He was anxious to begin and was in the area, so he offered to stop in to discuss their time line and the extensive ideas they both had rolling around in their heads.

She wandered down to the basement as she waited for him. She explored the basement further as she had noticed some items stored down there. They were covered in dusty tarps at the far corner, and her curiosity was sparked as she proceeded to reveal what had been left behind. She tugged at a canvas and to her surprise, she unveiled the old jewelry showcase that had belonged to the previous tenants. It was elaborate and brought back many fond childhood memories as she recalled peeking through its glass, marveling at rubies, diamonds, emeralds, pearls, and ornamental pieces that captured her attention and inspired her imagination as a little girl. She was stimulated by this discovery as she heard footsteps upstairs.

"London?" She heard Max call out in his deep, sexy voice.

"I'm down here, Max. Hurry, come see what I've found!"

Max hustled down the staircase to find London beaming at him. He looked exceptionally handsome today in blue jeans with a casual sweater, a bulky black leather jacket, scarf, and gloves . . . not his normal work clothes. He was even clean-shaven. *He sure cleans up nicely,* she thought. She was animated, talking fast, enthusiasm radiating from within her as she filled him in on her latest decision to sell jewelry and how it must have been meant to be as the display case was left behind.

"Slow down, slow down." He laughed at her as he looked over the case.

She took a deep breath and giggled. She was overcome with excitement.

"It's good to see you so happy, London. And yes, this looks to be in good shape too. I think it's a great idea since this used to be a jewelry store. You'll broaden your market and increase traffic through the new store," Max said approvingly.

"I just can't wait to get started on everything!" London exclaimed, bursting with exuberance.

Max flashed an affectionate smile. He shared in her eagerness and she was glad to have him helping her achieve her dreams. With his strength and proficiency in construction, and her creative flair for style, she knew anything was possible.

They proceeded back upstairs to discuss building materials and the floor plan again. Max brought up some pictures on his tablet and London showed him her selections for black and white ceramic tiles and parquet flooring to emulate the style throughout Le Château. They browsed images of the palace and he made notes of the details as she pointed them out. He suggested they take a trip over to the local building supply so that she could look at some of the items and ensure the actual textures would be right.

"Good idea," she replied, looking forward to going just about anywhere with him at the moment. They climbed up into his pickup truck together. As they pulled out of the snowy exit, Max discussed the limited parking area with her and asked if she planned to acquire the adjacent vacant lot. He explained that not only would she need the space for her customers, but it also would be helpful when he brought in his construction equipment. She hadn't thought about it, but she agreed that it would be worth buying. She always hated jockeying for a parking space at her favorite stores, and she wanted her new place to offer a pleasant and relaxing shopping experience from beginning to end.

As they drove, she called Mr. Thomas to inquire about the availability of the vacant lot. She was pleased to find that it was available and she informed him that she would take it. As she hung up, she remembered the crystal chandelier on eBay and felt a sense of urgency. She didn't want to miss out on it.

"Can I use your tablet real quick to make a purchase?"

"Sure," Max replied. "What else are you buying today?" he asked with a sarcastic grin.

"Oh, let me show you!" she responded as she pulled up her virtual shopping cart. He was impressed with her choice. Relieved. She was now the owner of a Louis XVI chandelier, her very first purchase, and she explained her plans to have him hang it in the room where she would have the dining service set up.

They spent what seemed like hours at the supply store, exploring all of her options for building materials to incorporate into the interior of her new tiny palace. By the time they left, it was already afternoon and he drove her back to the antique shop. She pressed the auto-start button to warm up her SUV as they sat talking in the parking lot, watching more snow begin to fall. She realized that she hadn't eaten anything all day except yogurt and she was famished. She also realized that she didn't want to go home alone.

"Would you like to join me for lunch at my place? I have a new recipe I'd like to try and maybe you can help me in the kitchen. You're such a great cook. . . ."

Max hesitated, studying her face for a clue of what the menu choices might be today. He nodded as a smile spread slowly across his face. "Sounds good, I'll follow you."

She watched his truck behind her in the rearview. It was a sexy ride that suited him. She'd been able to resist him at the store since her mind was so focused on the business, but she wasn't so sure her defenses would be as strong at home.

They were quite a team in the kitchen together as they whipped up a spinach-and-bacon quiche. They brushed against each other as they worked closely preparing lunch. She watched his fingers touching the food. She remembered how he touched her the day of the rainstorm a few months ago. He looked up at her as he whipped the eggs. His rhythm duplicated his thrust. After he placed the quiche in the oven, he took out some crescent rolls, opened the container, and took out the dough, his fingers molding it into mounds, then cutting it into small round rolls, and finally placing them on the cookie sheet. The quiche was delicious. They tidied up the kitchen together and she filled the coffee machine to brew a cup.

She stood at the counter, rinsing the sink and running the disposal when he came up behind her. He massaged her shoulders and she went limp. He kissed her on the back of her neck, sending chills across her body. His body pressed against hers and she could feel his heat. She turned around to face him, their eyes locked, and her breathing became sporadic. She kissed him on the lips just as the coffee was done brewing. She smiled and slipped away from his grasp. Saved by the cup.

She looked out to see the snowfall increasing, then turned on the weather channel. A winter storm was moving in. Max said aloud what she was hearing.

"Looks like I should stay for a while." She nodded, smiling at him as she strolled back to the kitchen.

He started a fire in the fireplace while London retrieved his coffee and put a bottle of wine in the refrigerator to chill. Big snowflakes blew by her window in gusts as the wind howled. She brought him his coffee and they sat down on the sofa by the fire. He flipped channels on the TV, each one beeping and flashing the weather alert across the bottom of the screen.

Before long, the only light around them came from the TV and the fireplace. Max caught her staring at him and smiled, touching her cup with his. "Only now am I noticing what a resemblance you have to Robert Redford," she said.

"You're kidding, right?" he said.

"No, of course not."

"A toast," he said, changing the subject, "to your antique shop and new adventures."

"And blizzards," she replied as she snuggled in next to him, pulling the blanket down over her lap. She took his cup and hers, setting them on the side table. She turned back, cupping his face in her hands as she kissed him hard on the lips. He grabbed her forcibly and kissed her back. They played with each other's tongues; then she sat on his lap, kissing his face and neck. He tasted so good, and felt even better.

He touched her arms, his rough fingers on her tender skin making chills run up and down her spine. He cupped her face with his strong hands and kissed her again and again. He took his hands and went under her sweater to undo her bra. She slipped her sweater over her head and dropped it to the floor. He put his hands under her breasts, cupping them. Her mind flashed back to the molding of dough as he continued to fondle and then sucked on her nipples, bringing her to such hotness she thought she might just pass out. She moaned as the wind howled and whipped harder at the windows. As another wicked storm brewed outside, worse than the last one they experienced together, a fury raged inside of her with a desire to be ravaged by this gorgeous, rugged man.

She was at his mercy, and he was grateful. He toyed with her and she could feel his hardness beneath her, throbbing to escape. She smiled as she moved sensually on top of him, riding him, moving her hips up and down and doing a lap dance on him. He reached inside of her skirt, touching her with such a fury that she became savagely aroused. She tugged at his hair and kissed his ear, his neck, his face, his mouth. She tugged at his lip with her teeth and that pushed him over the edge. He grabbed her and with swift motions, he removed his clothes and pulled up her skirt. He pulled her down onto the Persian rug in front of the fireplace. His bare body was as beautiful as she'd remembered. She had nearly forgotten his size and was delighted to see that his hardness was ready to mount, but he toyed with her, delaying the pleasure and making her work for it.

They kissed and fondled each other. She was ravenous as she licked the end of his maleness, slowly opening her lips and sliding them over the end. She swirled her tongue over and over his prize as he slowly went into her mouth. It filled her as she sucked on it; he moaned with pleasure.

"God, London, that feels so good," he said, his voice anxious and strained. He rolled her onto her back as she continued to play with him. He moved to the part of her body that needed attention so badly. He inserted three fingers deep inside her. She pleaded for more. He kissed her fervently as her mind checked out of this world. Nothing else mattered but the wonder of him and the feeling he was generating between her legs. She wanted him in the worst way. He kept himself away from her, his hardness taunting her, teasing her, holding her back from satisfaction. She was about to explode if he didn't give it to her soon.

He looked down at her smiling face and pulled her toward him, opened her legs, and touched her wetness with his tongue. She was uncontrollably stimulated. He sucked and licked on her while she squirmed, moving into positions that were sexually pleasing. She was panting and agonizing to feel him. When she couldn't take any more, he mounted her and slowly pushed his hardness deep inside her. She groaned as she felt him sliding deeper, inch by inch. She clenched his arms, gouging his skin with her nails. He went faster and faster until she screamed in ecstasy. "Oh, Max, now!" she shouted as she climaxed and he filled her with his juices. They fell into a pool of wetness, spent and exhausted. Her fantasy was now fulfilled as he pulled her over to him. They lay in each other's arms, completely relaxed. *What a wonderful night*, she thought as she snuggled deep into his arms, tugging the blanket to the floor to cover them. They cuddled in the firelight, listening to the wind howl and the fireplace crackle. He touched her face gently and stroked her hair, admiring her beauty. He truly was an Adonis, and a gentle giant. As the fire died down, he got up without a word, scooped her up, and carried her to the bedroom. He wrapped his body around hers and covered them with more blankets as they drifted off to sleep.

All too soon, the night was over as she awoke sleeping in his arms. The storm had dumped nearly three feet of snow overnight and they were overwhelmed by the sights outside. A few tree branches had blown across the yard and the snowdrifts were more than four feet high, including the one outside her front door. The wind was still gusting as London brewed some coffee. Max built a fire and made some calls. She toasted English muffins and they chatted at the table as they ate. Max said that he called his crew but they wouldn't make it over to plow them out until tomorrow. The transportation department was scrambling to get the main roads cleared and wouldn't get to side roads until much later in the day.

They decided to make the best of a day off and reminisced about snow days as children. They watched TV by the blazing hot fire, took a steamy shower together, and made love all afternoon. The evening disappeared as they cooked, ate, and polished off a bottle of red wine, making for a wonderful day together.

The next morning, London heard the plow trucks. She jumped up to chat with them over the intercom. Max bundled up and headed out to shovel around the gates before London pushed the button to open them. Soon the driveway was noisy with plow trucks and snowblowers to the rescue. Max came back inside once they'd left, stomping off the snow at the doorway, waiting to say good-bye. She came over, still in her silky black robe, and kissed him long and hard before releasing him. Leaving her side wasn't easy, but he had a few things to attend to at his office before heading over to the antique shop that afternoon. She missed him even before his truck was out of sight, but she knew she would see him again very soon as her exciting new adventure continued.

Chapter 13

ANGEL FOOD CAKE WITH
BERRIES AND CREAM

January blew by like the blustery winter wind but had been a blur of intimate bliss mixed with business for London. Research, ordering, and deliveries consumed her days. The renovations kept Max very busy too and allowed them time together daily. She had convinced herself not to overanalyze their relationship. She wanted to form a friendship first. She was just enjoying each day, savoring each moment. He seemed to value her hopes and dreams as he helped to make them come true.

Max and his crew had started by cleaning and preparing the basement so that she would have proper storage for the vast inventory that was being shipped in. They had also roughed in the loft upstairs and quickly installed the royal parquet flooring. The work was coming along nicely and she was able to begin furnishing the shop. She was excited to finish the apartment, which she was decorating partially like Queen Marie Antoinette's bedchambers as she persisted in re-creating the inspirational dream she'd had.

She was in no hurry to rent out the loft yet, as it gave her a cozy place of solace to retreat to, somewhere she could organize her thoughts while the dusty, noisy remodeling continued on the first-floor partitions. She loved the view of Tarrytown from the window where she had set up a small but dignified desk that resembled the *bureau du roi*, Louis XV's rolltop secretary. From her seat at the window, she could see the delivery trucks rolling in alongside the building each day, loaded down with her treasures. She bounded down the stairs like an animated child to meet the deliverymen every afternoon, and the construction crew gladly assisted with moving the furniture to the basement.

She had found just the right table and chairs for the dining room—an eighteenth-century oak buffet parquetry table with eight white straight-back chairs. There were bamboo-armed chairs for the ends of the table. She also found a jam cupboard, an early twentieth-century beechwood bergère, a Louis XV–style cane bench, and a signed bamboo armoire of Napoleon III. Her search continued for a Parisian bookcase and Persian rugs.

She was delighted with a canopy bed she'd located for the loft. It was the perfect shape, and she planned to have it adorned in gold and painted with pink roses and greenery. She'd ordered the ideal curtains to drape over the canopy, while Jon had introduced her to a talented artist, Christopher, who was confident that he could mimic the regal and elaborate walls of Queen Marie Antoinette's bedchamber.

The surroundings were transforming into her vision; images in her mind came to life all around. She would walk into the shop to find Max and his crew working away. He looked hot in his tool belt and construction gear, perspiring slightly, hammering away as his muscles flexed, the master of every situation he oversaw for the project and his staff. He was so intuitive; she felt he could almost read her mind as he re-created in the physical her mental pictures of the palace. His ruggedness was really beginning to grow on her, and she enjoyed getting to know him better as he thrived within his element. She found him irresistible. She would saunter up the stairs, shooting him a seductive look, then send him a text message that she needed to meet with him. He would sneak away to join her in the loft and together they had succeeded in breaking in the new bed.

Valentine's Day would soon be here, but it fell on a week-night. Max had suggested that they celebrate throughout the weekend and enjoy a romantic dinner together on Saturday night. She was relieved to have so many distractions to prevent Deacon from coming to mind too often, especially around Valentine's Day, which always made her think of him. Her new true love was her store, and Max was a great companion in the adventure.

She awoke at the château and decided to take a break from the shop to unwind for their weekend together. Max would be out all day bidding new jobs for the springtime as his crew continued at her store. She got up, put on some music, and took a long, simmering bath to soothe her achy body and her mind, which had been working overtime. The morning was dreary and overcast. She already had candles blazing, flickering on the cream walls and marble pillars surrounding the sunken tub. Romantic music and perfumed bath oil permeated the air as she sipped on a mimosa and floated amid the bubbles.

She closed her eyes in a feeble attempt to stop the thoughts of Deacon as they drifted in. The pain he brought still lingered, as did her love for him. She fought back tears as she downed her mimosa and refilled the flute from the champagne bottle she'd placed beside the tub. She shook him off with thoughts of Max. She began scheming of how to surprise him on Valentine's Day. Since they were already going out on Saturday, she planned to cook dinner at home on Tuesday night and come up with an interesting surprise for his dessert. She emerged from the tub and toweled off as she watched herself in the mirror. She decided to crawl back into bed, feeling peaceful in the tranquility of the room, and she drifted back to sleep.

A lover appeared in her dreams, but his identity was hazy. He took her from behind, kissing her neck as she felt her body go completely limp. He made love to her with his hands, his mouth, and then his body. He brought her emotions to their highest point and left her passions wild. He penetrated her deeply while her mind searched for something to hang on to, but there was nothing. Just puffs of smoke on a cold winter's day. Her fantasy disappeared with the sunlight.

She awoke again in the late morning hour to a wet bed. She reached for her toys in the nightstand and brought herself to climax.

She heard the intercom. There was a delivery at the gate. She jumped from her bed, somewhat startled as she threw on her robe and raced down the stairs.

"Flower delivery for Ms. Shelby," the man stated.

She pushed the button to allow access to the circle drive as she grabbed her purse. She pulled her robe tie tightly as she humbly greeted him at the door, digging for a few dollars to tip him. He took the gratuity and smiled as he handed her the vase bursting with a bouquet of two dozen red roses. A heart-shaped card dangled down the side by a red ribbon. She shut the door behind him and closed the gates as he exited. She placed the flowers on the table and flipped the card around, which simply read, THINKING OF YOU, LOVE, MAX.

He had personally signed the card, which meant he took

the time to personally stop in at the flower shop and make the arrangements. She fondled the tiny card, tracing the contours with her finger, pondering for a moment about the shape of a valentine heart. She smiled as she thought, *Love isn't perfect, because if it was, this would just be a circle. But like a heart shape, love has its high points and its lows.* Max's sensitivity softened her heart. She called his cell phone to thank him, but she got his voicemail. She knew he was busy meeting with potential clients, so she left him a sexy message.

She got dressed, freshened up, and headed out to the store for groceries. Back at home, she put away her purchases, lit a fire, and curled up with a good book. She had to restrain herself from logging on to the laptop in search of more antique treasures. She could lose herself all day on there and she really needed to take a break. Max called to let her know he was on his way back to the area, but he had a long drive ahead of him. He had bid on several potential jobs that would be enough to keep him busy all year if the contracts were awarded to his firm.

She invited him to join her, saying that she had picked up an assortment of brochettes from the butcher to grill for a quick and easy dinner. He was starving and couldn't wait to see her. She put the skewers into a tangy marinade with lots of spices, then slipped into some silky pajamas and lounged on the sofa to watch TV as she waited for him.

When he finally arrived at the château, she realized how much she'd missed him. Even though he was usually working at the store while she was preoccupied with orders and research, they were always together and it felt strange to have been apart.

"Thank you again for the beautiful roses," she said as she wrapped her arms around his neck and kissed him. He hugged her, picking her up right off the floor as she wrapped her body around his. Their lips never parted as he carried her upstairs to the bathroom where they stripped down and indulged in a sizzling shower together.

Afterward, they dried off and slipped back into cozy pajamas to cook dinner. Max bundled up to grill the brochettes on the back deck while London slipped a loaf of French bread into the oven and opened a bottle of wine. She lit the candles on the dining room table and turned down the lights.

They sat at one end of the table together, their legs intertwining as they sipped their wine and chatted about his day. London sliced the bread and buttered it, then held a piece in front of his mouth. He smiled as he took a bite, licking the melting butter from her hand and nibbling at her fingers. He pulled a succulent chunk of beef from his skewer, smirking at her, and touched it to her lips. She licked it, then bit into it, tearing off a piece with a wild look in her eyes. They continued serving each other back and forth, the intensity growing between them. He was ready for round two before the food was even gone. He carried her over to the Persian rug in front of the fire and ravaged her wildly, exploring every curve and groove of her body with his tongue. She moaned in ecstasy, begging him to take her. He turned her over on her knees and took her from behind, one hand on her hip and the other tangled in her hair to hold her in place as he rode her hard, and she climaxed, screaming through multiple orgasms. They collapsed in the firelight for a while before finally finding their way up to the bedroom.

In the morning, they slept in late together. Max was due to be at the shop to check on the crew's progress, but he was in no hurry. He said he would also stop by his place to pick up his tux for their dinner date. "I have a special surprise for you tonight. I'll pick you up about seven o'clock for dinner," then he slipped away before she could drill him with questions about his plans. She went upstairs to select her attire for the evening and was shocked to find a beautiful corset on the bed. It was pink silk with black lace trim and pink ribbons woven through the garment and tied into a bow. Beside the corset, he'd left a note, CAN'T WAIT TO SEE YOU WEARING ONLY THIS AFTER DINNER TONIGHT.

She didn't know where he was taking her for dinner. He would only tell her that it was five-star and formal. She retrieved an elegant black lace evening gown she had never worn from the back of her walk-in closet. She slipped into the corset and tried the gown on over it. She looked like royalty as she spun around, holding her hair up to show off her enticing neck. She hung up both garments, quickly threw on a casual black outfit, and raced off to the spa to be pampered for the day. She wanted a stunning French manicure and her hair done in an elegant updo to complement the gown.

On her way back from the spa, feeling invigorated, she grabbed a quick lunch with Jon and filled him in on the progress at the store and her Valentine's Day plans. Jon was delighted to inform London that he and Christopher had become exclusive since last month when they had met with her. She was thrilled to see him settling down and seeming so contented.

As she drove home, she passed the store and saw Max's truck out front, but refrained from stopping in, as she knew she would get caught up with work. She wanted to focus on their romantic evening together. She raced home and took a short nap, sitting up slightly and resting carefully so as not to disturb her hairstyle. It was tough to sleep in the upright position and her mind was racing with thoughts of the store,

Max, and dinner. She loved the fact that he was so secretive and wanted to surprise her, but the curiosity was killing her. She drifted away briefly and dreamed of the hidden passageways in the palace again. Each time she revisited the dream, she explored new rooms and discovered amazing treasures that filled her with wondrous intrigue.

She awoke feeling pleasantly relaxed and refreshed. She flicked on the TV for the weather report while she brewed a cup of coffee. She gazed out the window into the sunset and was glad that the weather would be calm and mild for the evening. It was still snowy and chilly, but nothing new was expected to fall for at least a few days.

She slipped into her new, luxurious lingerie, and her royal full-length black velvet gown with a sweetheart neckline, and one dangling diamond necklace that filled in the opening. She spun and danced around before the full-length mirror, admiring the work of art the hairstylist had created. The chignon swept up gracefully with just a few wispy strands escaping that were softly curled into cascading spirals. She added a few finishing touches to her makeup and checked the time. It was 6:45. Her excitement grew as the minutes ticked away. She retrieved a chic pair of sparkling stilettos, opera gloves, and a matching handbag to complement her gown, along with a faux-mink stole to drape over her shoulders. She looked simply divine as she floated down the staircase.

She looked out the window and opened the gates as she saw headlights approaching. To her surprise, a stretch limousine entered the drive and circled around to the front door. She watched as the chauffeur came out to open the door for Max. He stepped out, adjusting his tie and looking debonair. He strolled up to the door as she opened it. They gasped together and smiled as they looked each other up and down.

"Thank you for the lovely corset," she said as she extended her hand.

"You're welcome, darling. And I must say, you are simply breathtaking this evening," Max replied as he took her hand, kissing it gently and eyeing her as if he could see right through her clothing.

"A limo, Max? You really didn't have to."

"I want you to feel like the royal queen that you are. Your chariot awaits, my dear," he said as they made their way down the walkway. The chauffeur stood rigid like a British soldier, then leaned over with his white glove to open the door for London.

"Madam," he said with a nod.

"Thank you, sir," she responded as she eased into the seat.

She put up the privacy window as they drove to the restaurant. She eased her gown up slightly, causing the side slit to fall open, revealing her silky black thigh-highs. He studied her as she caressed his thigh. He popped the cork off a bottle of expensive champagne and poured a glass for each of them. She sipped at the bubbly, then leaned over to kiss him, the sweetness of the aphrodisiac moist on her lips. He returned her kiss and held her close.

"You'll have to save that energy a little longer, London," he said as he flashed her a devious smile. She pouted slightly for a moment as he laughed at her.

"So where are we going tonight?" she asked with impatience and anticipation as she gulped her champagne, trying to stifle her urge to attack Max right there in the backseat. He looked delicious.

"It's a surprise, but we're almost there," he reassured her.

She peered through the darkness, trying to figure out where their path was leading, but the view was primarily obscured by numerous mature trees that lined the roadway. After only a few minutes, the driver soon turned and followed the pathway leading up to the Manor Hotel & Spa, a majestic estate situated on one of the highest elevations in Tarrytown.

London's eyes gleamed as she caught her first glimpse of the grandiose architecture, and Max squeezed her hand in his as he studied her childlike reaction. Although the Manor was close to her château, London had never visited it, and she now wondered why she hadn't. The spectacular fortress was illuminated and she was captivated by its magnificence.

"I thought gallantry would be proper for an exquisite dining experience for my queen this evening," Max said.

"Oh, Max, it's beautiful! Thank you," London exclaimed, radiating amazement and overwhelmed with infatuation.

They had a view of the Hudson River Valley and the Manhattan skyline. They were led into the dining room where they were seated at their candlelit table by a stone fireplace. London admired the beauty and charm of the neoclassical style as they settled in by the cozy fire crackling beside them. Max ordered wine and then reached across the table to hold London's hand.

"So what do you think?" he asked, smiling at her astonishment.

"It is stunning, Max."

He pointed out the rich wood panel accoutrements and explained that they were first owned by Louis XIV. They had been brought intact to the Manor when it was first built more than a century ago. London was impressed. He enlightened her with interesting facts, including that the estate spanned fifteen tranquil acres and the prestigious facility had been awarded countless times for its unique distinction, respite of refinement, and luxurious, old-world elegance.

"You sure know a lot about this place, don't you?" London smiled.

"Well, I've done some work here in the past and got interested in its history."

The waiter returned with their wine and reviewed the marvelous choices with them from an array of unique Auberge-style natural French cuisine. He explained that the establishment prided itself on an innovative seasonal menu and cuisine based on locally sourced ingredients. London selected the loin of Colorado lamb with matsutake and edamame purée, and Max chose the New Zealand free-range venison loin with butternut squash, Brussels sprouts, and applewood bacon hash.

London felt intoxicated by the fantastic good food and the ambience was just a bonus, as their extraordinary evening was winding down. Max was a little rough around the edges, but he certainly had excellent taste and etiquette. He was full of secrets and surprises and she became more attracted to him with each passing day. She was relieved to know that he wasn't simply after her body, or her money. His company was doing well and she knew he was stable and self-sufficient. He also seemed to respect her for all of who she is.

"Now, I had considered reserving a suite here for tonight, but I have yet another surprise in store for you before the night's over."

He thanked the waiter and accompanied London back to the awaiting limo. Max put on some music, for a short ride to Le Magasin d'Antiquités. The lighted sign was installed and gleaming down at her. "Oh, Max! Thank you. When did you have time to put the sign up? The sign maker did such a wonderful job." Max climbed out, taking her hand and helping her from the car. She stepped out to admire the handiwork from a different view.

"I'm not done yet, you know."

"There's more?" London probed.

"Yes, follow me please, madam," Max replied in his pretend accent again as he guided her inside the shop.

Max adjusted the lighting and as her eyes focused, she looked down to see a trail of soft pink rose petals scattered before her, leading her up the staircase to the loft. Chills ran up her spine. He followed closely behind, helping her to hold her gown as she ascended the staircase. They paused at the large wooden door of the loft.

"Close your eyes," Max said.

She did as she was told and he reached around to open the door before her. She gasped. "Oh, Max!" The headboard was gleaming gold and adorned with roses just as she'd wanted. And the walls . . . they were absolutely striking. They were bejeweled with golden accents and overlaid in tapestry-like designs. The room had become an almost mirror image of the queen's bedchambers.

"But-but how?" London stuttered in disbelief. "How did you and Christopher get this all done in just the past two days?"

"Well, remember the Louis the Fourteenth wood panels tonight in the dining room at Gallantry that were transported and affixed to the walls of the Manor?"

"Yes," London replied, her brain still processing the majestic beauty of her surroundings.

"Well, that inspired me and I worked with Christopher last month on the idea. He did all of the painting at his studio and we brought them here and simply attached them to the walls."

"Oh my God, Max. It is absolutely amazing. Thank you so much."

London wrapped her arms around his neck and kissed him.

She released him and gazed into his eyes, stunned by his ardor. She strolled across the room, floating on a cloud. Max walked over to where he had a tall pedestal beside the bed. On it was a champagne bucket and he popped another cork, letting the fizz run over into the bucket below. London rose to retrieve her flute and toasted Max.

She was now eager to show her appreciation and honor his wish to see her wearing nothing but the lovely pink corset he'd given to her. They made love until the early morning light crept into the cozy loft. London rose, drawing the elegant canopy draperies around them as they snuggled together in the darkness to sleep the day away.

London awoke to the fragrance of coffee. Max smiled from across the room, sitting in an eighteenth-century cream velvet Louis XV armchair, dressed in his tuxedo again, the collar of his shirt hanging open with several buttons undone and a newspaper across his lap. He had picked it up along with some breakfast from Jon's bakery. "Good morning." She smiled shyly as she got up, stretching.

They talked about the plans for her shop. Max broke down how he would take out the side wall, use the archway of the fireplace for the entrance to the addition, and rebuild another fireplace where she was going to put the front room. She had planned on the front room being on the right of the entry to the shop with a kitchenette along part of the back. There would also be two small French-styled bedrooms. One would be formal and one informal, and both would be located behind the front room, which would now have an entry that duplicated the rainbow design to match the opening in the other room. Max said he could build the new addition this week and bring over matching bricks from the demolition job.

Max invited her to see a movie with him that evening. He had a few things to tend to that afternoon, and offered to take her to the château in his truck, which he had parked at the store the night before. She didn't have a change of clothes and felt obvious—in the daylight wearing an evening gown—but got a kick out of the naughtiness of it.

Back at home, she took a long hot shower and enjoyed a light lunch before having a nap on the couch.

She woke up in time to get ready for the movie. She slipped into a soft black skirt with a sweater. She zipped up her high boots and bundled up in a wool jacket, scarf, and gloves.

Max picked her up right on time and they headed out. The lobby was bare as they walked in to purchase their tickets, then they headed over to the concession counter for some popcorn with extra butter and two colas. They entered the dark cinema, finding their way down the aisle and stopping halfway to slide into the aisle seats. She was surprised to find the theater so empty. London felt it was due to the snow warnings.

She found the trailers boring and waited for some excitement as she felt a tickle on the back of her neck. Max stroked her hair, nuzzled her neck, and whispered in her ear.

"You smell so good."

His lips brushed her neck and the heat of his breath made her purr. She dipped her hand into the popcorn and grabbed a mouthful, smiling as she pretended to ignore his advances. Her eyes were fixated on the screen but her tummy turned to jelly. He dipped his hand into the popcorn and whispered, "Should have had some chocolate drizzled over the top."

She smiled and said, "Go buy your own popcorn. I've got to keep an eye on my weight."

He laughed. "I'll keep an eye on your weight for you." He chuckled and grabbed some more hot buttered popcorn.

"Sure you will, and I'll give you something else to drizzle chocolate over."

He kissed her on the cheek and leaned toward her. When he went to reach for more popcorn, she had moved the container closer to her breasts. He touched her arms with his fingers and moved them up and down her arm to her hand. He then circled his finger around hers, sliding it up and down to symbolize what he wanted. He kissed her ear, and then licked it, nibbling on the end of it, exhaling across her skin. He gave her mini kisses all over her neck, moving her hair from one side to the other.

He moved her skirt higher up on her leg, moving his hand to her inner thigh as he tapped her lightly to open them for him. Her knees trembled in anticipation. He reached between her legs, touching her hot sex, then brought his fingers to his mouth to taste her juices. He savored her for a moment as she watched him, her tummy tingling, then he went for more popcorn and gobbled it up. He reached back down, fingering her and gently moving her lips apart, touching her with his buttery fingers, then bringing them up for her to taste. She licked them clean and moaned as he touched her again. She was hot and wet and wanted him desperately as her mind recounted last night's events. He had her under his spell and she was at his will.

She slid down in the seat, opened her legs wide, relieved that no one else was in the theater so that they were free to explore each other. He rubbed her, moving his hands so he could enter her with his fingers. She moved her bottom so he could penetrate her even farther. She wanted him so badly. He kept on playing with her, her juices flowing as her wetness covered his hands, his lips on her neck, his breathing accelerating with heated passion. He dipped his hands deep into the popcorn tub where the hot butter pooled at the bottom, then he slid down on the floor in between her legs. He rubbed her sex with his warm buttered hands, then put them in his mouth to suck the butter off. She grew wilder with desire as she watched. He penetrated her with three fingers, slowly at first, then pumping harder as he leaned in to suck on her button. His tongue ravaged her as his fingers were thrusting in and out, over and over until she threw back her head, her body releasing into climax as she shuddered under this control.

To her surprise, he brushed his hands off with a napkin and walked out of the theater, giving her only a smile. She looked at the screen just as the movie *The Girl with the Dragon Tattoo* was showing a sexual scene. London adjusted her skirt and looked up at the movie screen as she awaited Max's return. She became engrossed with the film even though she'd missed the first ten minutes or so. Max must have been very quiet with the door when he reentered the room because he startled her when he snuck up behind her and whispered in her ear in a sultry voice.

"Hey, baby." He laughed as he came around to sit beside her with another bucket of popcorn in his hands. "This batch has chocolate drizzled over it," he said with a grin as he consumed a handful. She reluctantly reached over, taking a handful for herself.

"Mmm, that is yummy," she said, reaching for more.

They indulged back and forth, eating popcorn and gulping their sodas, but London was hungry for more of something else, and the action in this movie wasn't helping her at all. She set her popcorn in the adjacent seat and put her soft drink in the cup holder. She reached over, rubbing his thigh around the bucket of popcorn until he handed it to her and she stacked it on top of hers. She caressed his bulge as it grew higher, begging to escape from his pants as his breath quickened again. She flipped the armrest back and leaned over to unzip his pants, releasing his throbbing giant as she eased down to wrap her lips around it, stroking it with her buttery, chocolatey fingers. She took his hardness deep into her throat, her lips tight around his throbbing head as she sucked him with her mouth. He was gasping for air, tugging at her hair, and she was unrelenting with her rhythm. He moaned and quickly released his prize into her mouth as she savored the warm, salty treat. They both sighed as he adjusted himself. They settled in, trying to catch up on the plot and watched the remainder of the film.

He drove her home and she invited him in to stay again. She didn't want their night to end. He stayed over and caressed her to sleep with a glorious massage. She slept peacefully all night, wrapped in the warmth and safety of his strong arms.

Monday morning, she awoke happy to find him beside her. She looked down at him while she rested on her elbow. He was handsome in so many ways: his strong jaw, his messy blond hair, and his rugged features. She watched him sleeping until his alarm went off. They shared a quick breakfast over coffee before he headed out to work at the store all day, and London had plans to prepare for a special Valentine's dinner and surprise dessert.

The morning had suddenly disappeared as she'd lost herself on the laptop making purchases for the store. Her cell phone rang and it was Max calling. He explained that some of the guys on his crew had an extra ticket for the hockey game that night and wanted him to tag along. He knew it was last minute and wanted to check with her to see if she had anything planned.

"I don't have any plans, until tomorrow night," she said

seductively. "Go have fun, Max. You haven't been out with your buddies in a long time."

"I might be really late getting in, so I'll probably just stay at my place tonight, okay?"

"Sure, thanks for letting me know, you're not obligated to. Thanks. Please, have a great time!" she urged him.

"Okay. I look forward to dinner at your place tomorrow night. See you then, darling."

London decided to call Paris to see if she would join her on a shopping trip. They had so much catching up to do, as she hadn't seen her since the Christmas party. She was available and they went together to the adult novelty shop, perusing the aisles for an hour and a half, giggling and marveling at the toys, lingerie, and gag gifts. They had a great time, and London found the perfect black-and-white French maid costume that would make her Valentine's dinner complete. She even purchased a French tickler to tease Max with for their special evening.

Throughout the shopping adventure, London filled in Paris on the devastating breakup with Deacon, the threesome with Jen, and then the news of the antique shop. Paris was thrilled that London and Max had reunited and felt it was exactly what she needed after what Deacon had done. They were famished after their escapade and stopped in at a Japanese steakhouse for an eventfully delicious dinner. They loved the social atmosphere and watching the chefs cooking, juggling knives, and putting on a show.

London dropped off Paris, went home, and headed to bed. She wanted to be well rested for another eventful evening tomorrow. She sent Max a text: Thinking of you. Good night. He quickly replied: You're always on my mind, London. Good night.

The day flew by as she checked over some online orders and

coordinated with Max at the store about the deliveries. She was happy when it came time to get ready to party. She went to her closet to find something she could use to disguise her maid costume. She found an old shirt to go over her outfit that would work. This would be a fantasy to end all fantasies. She was anxious to get cooking. Her body was already simmering. All she could think of was Max and his arms, his lips, and his wonderful hardness entering her. She was becoming obsessed with him.

She tidied up her home and placed wood by the fireplaces. She took out new vanilla candles and placed them around the house. She put clean sheets on the bed and pillows. Picked out a special CD of romantic music, and then stepped back to make sure she hadn't missed anything.

She was fixing herb-roasted Cornish hens with wild rice to serve with white wine. She did some more vacuuming and cleaning and set the long glass table with sheer gold-and-black place mats under gold chargers and black plates. Gold-rimmed goblets sat by each plate, and her gold-plated silverware provided the finishing touch. The new centerpiece was designed out of gold and black leaves with a cream-colored candle in the middle. She stepped back to see how lovely it was with the lights off and only the candles and the fireplace blazing. She sat down with a book to read while she waited for the evening to begin.

He would be arriving by 6:00, so she put the Cornish hens in the oven at 5:00 and put on a romantic CD. Night was falling as she took a hot perfumed bath, put on her maid's costume, fishnet stockings, and covered it all with her huge sweatshirt, casual pants, and slippers. She placed her spiked heels by the bed for a quick change later. Soon she saw his headlights shine down the driveway. She sat in her chair with her book and a blank expression on her face.

"Hey, baby, I'm home. I really missed you last night."

His words made her smile. She placed her book on the table and welcomed him with warm kisses as he placed his jacket on the tree stand, holding her with one arm around her waist.

"Must be you missed me a little bit too," he said as he grinned. She went to the refrigerator and got out a bottle of wine and poured them each a glass while he took off his work clothes and grabbed a quick shower, slipping into a burgundy velvet robe.

"To tonight," she said with a suggestive wink. "Happy Valentine's Day."

They talked for a few minutes before she excused herself from the room. She reemerged to reveal her maid's outfit. He raised his eyebrows in pleasant surprise as she waved her French tickler at him. She went to the coffee table and bent over to show him that she wasn't wearing panties. He walked over to her, bent down, and kissed her hotness. She moaned and turned around, kissing him again. Her tongue searched for his tongue and his arms went around her waist as he pulled her into him. She snuggled in his arms, but then she backed away, putting her finger to her mouth and saying *Shh* as she led him to the dining room. The candles were glowing and the fireplace was blazing as she pulled out his chair and kissed him again and again. Sitting on his lap with her special spot next to the one thing she so enjoyed. She smiled, knowing how much he would love this evening.

She got up and brought in the main course. She placed the food in her mouth, and with her finger she rubbed the rim of the goblet. She made love to him in her mind all throughout dinner. Afterward, she took his arm and led him upstairs to the bedroom, where she undressed him and laid him on the bed. She massaged him with hot perfumed oil as she rubbed his arms, legs, and back. Her body moved around his, her hips swaying in a belly-dancing way. She then rolled him over to sit on him with her hotness on top of her prize for the night. She kissed him again and again as her lips found his hardness. She kissed it and licked it with her hot, wet mouth. She got up, leaving him breathless as she lit more candles and turned off the lights. She left the bedroom for a moment and returned, shaking a can of whipped cream. She kissed him again and then sprayed cream all over his throbbing maleness, placing a cherry on top.

"Too bad only I get to eat dessert tonight," she said as she lowered her mouth over him and plucked the cherry, laughing as she ate it. He smiled and closed his eyes, squirming in anticipation of her next move. She removed the whipped cream with her tongue from the top of his phallus and down his shaft to the bottom like she was licking an ice cream cone. She sucked him tenderly, licking again and again as the remaining cream started to melt. She followed the cream to the bottom of his shaft and, with her mouth and tongue, she sucked the melted cream. She then went back to the top of his hardness and down to the bottom over and over until he was all clean. He squirmed and sighed. She was driving him crazy. She stuck her finger deep inside of herself to wet it, then reached around to his ass and inserted the finger as he groaned. She moved her finger all around inside him as she continued to suck him savagely. She felt him throb and stopped.

She got up to put on some music as he whined, begging her not to stop. He wanted her to finish him, but he enjoyed her dancing as she watched him stroking himself. She was rhythmically moving all around the bed, slowly taking off her clothing and dropping it to the floor, leaving a path as she tickled him teasingly with her new toy.

She mounted him, sliding his hardness deep into her body as she grinded into him. She felt him throb and a deep moan came from within. She withdrew her body.

"*No, London,*" he pleaded, but she was going to make this one night he'd never forget. She again placed her hot lips on his and kissed him. He had had enough of her teasing as he flipped her over with a firm grip and pulled her to the end of the bed, thrusting his hardness deep inside her. She gasped softly as he went even deeper into her. He moved, rubbing her breasts, sucking on them and kissing her, then flipped her over, taking her from behind, stabbing his hardness deep inside her sex while he touched her clit. He massaged her, moving on top of her body. She admired the shadowy images on the bedroom wall, reflecting two mingling bodies that in themselves were sexually artistic. He went faster and harder into her body, while she shook from the passion and her growing emotions.

"London, come for me, baby," he whispered in that sultry voice that made her explode with emotion. Together they screamed as the release happened over and over again, their bodies trembling as the juices ran out of her.

The blazing flames of the fireplace competed with the two of them in a rhythm of love. She looked at this man, the light in his face, the release in his eyes. She knew the night was a success and she felt immense happiness in his arms. She took a deep breath and looked again at her lover. He glistened in the candlelight, his eyes opened wide, full of wonder as he gazed back at her, his breathing beginning to stabilize.

She rose from the bed, tugging his hand and pulling him to follow her to the bathroom. He complied, slipping out of their bed of disarray. The candles cast a glow of warmth on the cream and marble hot tub and tiled floor. The flickers were like his tongue working magic on her sex, her arousal zone. She stepped into the large marble Jacuzzi, holding on to his hand for balance. He slid into the tub, pulling her to him as they bonded together. They kissed each other over and over again. She could feel him rise as he rubbed against her. He rubbed her back. He turned her around and fondled her breasts down to her passion zone. He rubbed her front. She turned around and stood in front of him. Putting her hands on his shoulders, she slid on top of him, rubbing him with her body, her hot spot responding with more juices than she ever thought she had.

She slid around him, opening his legs to the flow of water. She watched his member moving up and down with the water bubbles. She was behind him now, tantalizing his butt by moving her hands in his sensitive areas. She reached up on the edge of the tub and pulled down a toy. She turned it on and slid it down to his ass, rubbing it around. She felt him grow more excited. His hardness standing tall, wanting, pleading, she inserted the toy inside him.

He yelled, "London, what are you doing? Oh God, baby!" He rode the wave, moving and trying to get to her as she slid under the water and out of his reach. She held on to the string connected to his toy. He tried to grab her anywhere he could, but she just laughed as she dodged his grasp and slipped away. She pulled out the toy and placed it back on the edge of the tub. She felt him grab her from behind, turning her around to kiss her.

"Oh my God, London, I've never wanted anybody as much as I want you," he said breathlessly. He placed her legs around him as he penetrated her. He held her close and he took her, filling her with his pleasure. She rested her head on his brawny shoulder, pondering how she would allow him to be in control of the next round. They rode the flow of water and just sat back, looking at the candles glowing, watching them flicker as they rested, floating in a pool of passion. He touched her, caressed her, and played with her nipples, her breasts, her neck, and her tummy. He reached down to her sex and fondled her and he rubbed her tender spot. He put his fingers deep into her, moving them around touching her. She moved around his body, kissing him more, but then she pulled away and excused herself. He looked puzzled as she stepped out of the tub to put on her robe.

"Meet me downstairs in about five minutes. I'll call you." She entered the dining room and took the dishes off the table. She laid out a red plastic tablecloth and brought in the dessert. She had whipped up an angel food cake, broken it into pieces, covered it with whipped cream and vanilla pudding, and sprinkled strawberries, raspberries, and blueberries over it. She took off her robe, sprawled herself across the table and spread the delicious mix all over her nude body, especially in all the hot spots, topping it off with extra whipped cream. She looked luscious. She opened up her legs, letting the pudding drizzle down in between them. Satisfied, she called out to Max.

"Ready, hon." He appeared in the doorway, his mouth hanging open.

"Oh, London, you look delightful and delicious. I don't know where to begin."

He came over and kissed her again and again, licking the cream parts off of her first. He plucked a piece of cake from her breasts.

"Yummy," he said as he licked the cream and juices from her. Then he placed a piece of cake in her mouth, touching her with his fingers as she licked them at the same time, kissing her and licking her until her upper body was all shiny and clean. He bent over her sex, licking the top part and then inside her, where the juice and cream had gathered. He smiled, his face full of pudding, cream, and fruit as he nibbled at a piece of cake. He slid on top of her and placed her legs on his shoulders. His hardness was ready yet again for another round.

He penetrated her again, and she moaned as she touched his private parts, her eyes pleading for him to make her come again. He was moving faster now, and she was again wild with passion. Her moans and groans were getting stronger as his thrusting speeded up. His arms held her close, his lips on hers, the shadows of the candles and the fireplace making the room a golden passion pit. He placed his hands under her butt and pulled her closer as he slid deeper inside. Her legs started to shake, her eyes closed, her mouth smiling as she came with him . . . no yelling . . . no screaming, just a wonderful, warm, silent orgasm. He kissed her deeply, their breathing slowing as he looked down into her eyes. They giggled as they tidied up the table, and themselves, then snuffed out the many candles burning everywhere before grabbing a fast shower to wash off all the dessert and then crawling back into bed to retreat. As London curled up into his arms, she noticed a large box on her nightstand.

"Max, what is that? That's not another gift, is it?" she said in disbelief, her voice strained with exhaustion but excited nonetheless.

"It is," he said.

She leaned up on her pillow to click on the lamp. She fondled the ribbon tied into a perfect bow before untying it, eyeing him with a smile of curiosity as he watched her with heavy eyelids. She opened the box to reveal an exquisitely extravagant faux-diamond necklace draped over the velvety frame inside the box. Hundreds of Swarovski crystals hung down, arranged in an elaborate, glistening design of festoons, pendants, and tassels—a replica of Marie Antoinette's scandalous necklace.

"Oh, Max, it's beautiful! Thank you," she said as she kissed him.

"And so are you, London," he said as he stroked her face. "I hope you'll wear it for the grand opening of your new store."

"I certainly will. And do you know the story behind this necklace?" she inquired.

"I do." He smirked. The two chatted about how it was the necklace that the jeweler made up for the queen to get her in trouble and how Marie Antoinette had never really wanted it when it was later offered to her. Max noted that the queen had actually settled down with her children by that time and had no interest in such extravagance any longer. They giggled about the scandal that surrounded it, but London quietly wondered to herself if Max was implying something much more profound with his reference to settling down with children.

London climbed out of bed and walked over to the mirror to model the necklace. "It's so gorgeous. I can't imagine how any woman wouldn't want to wear it. It will be perfect with my ball gown. Simply fabulous! Thank you again," she said as she placed the box gently on the nightstand. She snuggled back into his arms, her body fatigued, but her mind afire again with thoughts of the store and jewelry! She needed to shop for jewelry in the morning. She drifted off to sleep, returning to the palace of her dreams for another wondrous journey in search of hidden jewels.

Chapter 14

SPICY BACON AND CHEESE OMELET

London awoke to the heavenly smell of bacon frying. She smiled and didn't want to get out of bed. She listened to the birds happily chirping outside her window and thought about how quickly spring had arrived. Max had been getting busier at work, bidding new jobs while his crew was hammering away to finish up her store this month. She cherished her moments with him, especially since they had become less and less frequent. She sometimes wondered if he also had someone else in his life, someone he cared for deeply, but Max was not one to divulge his previous relationships. Anytime she had inquired, he'd clammed up or changed the subject. She still thought of Deacon, so often, and uncertainty swirled through her mind. It was hard to stifle her feelings, but she kept herself busy with Max and stayed preoccupied with the store. Max broke the silence, wiping away her contemplations as he burst into the room, carrying a breakfast tray.

"Good morning, sunshine." He grinned as he served her breakfast in bed. "Hope you're hungry."

"I'm always hungry for you," she replied with a smirk.

"Thank you. Everything looks and smells so wonderful!" She sat up eagerly, propping up her pillows.

Max was a fabulous cook, and he had whipped up a bacon-and-southwestern-cheese omelet with English muffins, orange juice, and fruit. He joined her on the bed with the tray and their meals. They sat together eating and laughing as he fed her grapes and bites of the delectable omelet. As they were finishing up, she noticed Max gazing at her.

"What?" she asked as she felt herself blushing, a rare occasion.

"I'm just admiring how gorgeous you are, even first thing in the morning."

She blushed harder as she sipped her orange juice. "Are you sure that's all it is?" she inquired. "You sure look like you have some deep thoughts going on in that head of yours."

"Well, there is something I'd like to ask you."

"Okay, go ahead." She encouraged.

"Easter is this weekend and I've been thinking . . . would you like to join me at my parents' home for Easter Sunday brunch?"

She was tentative because unlike her, Max had come from a very large, very tight-knit family. She pondered before responding. *I am trying to make fresh new starts in life, and this will certainly be a new experience.*

"Max, you know that big family gatherings are not my thing, but if it's important to you, yes, I'll go with you."

"Thank you, London," he said as his face lit up like a little boy's. He leaned over and kissed her tenderly, then scooped up the tray and headed downstairs. He hollered back to her, "Now get up and let's get moving. We need to go check the progress at the store." She groaned and giggled as she dragged herself from the warmth of the covers. She showered quickly and dressed casually, and they drove separately to the shop, as Max had other responsibilities to tend to in the afternoon.

She was pleased to see the renovations progressing. The wall was out and the new addition was roughed in. The walls would soon be finished and the floors would be laid. The walls of the front room would mimic French walls, creamy white with wainscoting trimmed in gold gilt. The bow window in the front room would be all leaded glass. London had a picture that she was obsessed with, and she shared it with Max to explain the images she had in mind for the dining area and front room. He was impressed with her interior design vision and agreed that it would be doable, with Christopher's artistic help of course. She found the photo so inspiring that she had decided to change the entry flooring to cream tile with small burgundy squares. Also pictured were two burgundy love seats, along with a table and chairs, which she wanted to locate and incorporate into her own plush setting. Max suggested neoclassical design columns and a gas fireplace to complement the room, and she agreed. The ceilings would be done in wainscoting squares of cream-painted wood to accentuate and offset the room. She smiled to herself, filled with delight as she looked around the vacant room, envisioning her dream as he helped her to make it a reality.

Everything was coming together nicely, and she had to order more furniture today. Max consulted with his foreman on the progress and goals, then let London know he would be working very late that evening as he had several more projects to bid. He planned to stay at his place, as he had some things there that needed taking care of too. He kissed her good-bye, and she wanted to cling to those soft, warm, inviting lips. But she knew their work would never get done if she got aroused now. She headed home to work, where it would be quiet.

She spent the afternoon making several phone calls, researching and ordering more furniture, and chasing down some divine eighteenth-century jewels she'd found online. She was now having everything shipped to the château as she had succeeded in filling the store's basement wall to wall with treasures. She was stashing the vast overflow of inventory in the pole barn behind the château, which was spacious and offered plenty of storage space for her additional antique reserves.

She also called the specialty printing store to order invitations for the masquerade ball grand opening. She requested that the fleur-de-lis emblem, signifying French heraldry, be printed on the front in raised gold print. The printer complimented her selection. She also explained that the date had not yet been determined, but that she would fill in that line with calligraphy later. She wanted to have them printed now so she could do the addresses, and then all she would have to do is fill in the date.

She then proceeded to call Jon to discuss plans for the ball. He suggested meeting for dinner and asked if Christopher could join them. She was glad to have the company for the evening, and additional input from Christopher to help with brainstorming ideas for the special event. Jon asked London to meet them at the 1117 Club in Manhattan. It was once a glamorous speakeasy, and Jon had worked there a few years back, early on in his career. She was ecstatic as she loved the ambience of the famous restaurant.

London freshened up and dressed in a black cocktail dress, stilettos, and her faux-mink stole. She was excited for a night out, and the fact that the snow had all finally melted away. She decided to break out the Beemer again, and soon she was racing down the interstate toward the city. The speed, combined with the cool night air, was exhilarating. She arrived at the Club feeling divine, with a hint of spring fever setting in.

London was surprised to find the place jam-packed on a Monday night. She found Jon and Christopher already cozy in a booth across from the bar, and they both jumped up to hug and greet her. Jon selected a chardonnay and ordered for the three of them, including Caesar salad, seared scallops, and classic crème brûlée. Dinner was marvelous, and the conversation was even better. The Club was so fun, with toy mobiles dangling from the ceiling, and the atmosphere was playful and inspiring. They indulged in yet another bottle of wine and chatted freely over plans for the masquerade ball, decorations, hors d'oeuvres, wine selections, servers, and more.

Jon reminisced about London's grandmother and how London had inherited her excellent taste. Jon explained to Christopher that Grams had passed on just a few years back from breast cancer. London talked about significant donations she had made over the years to breast cancer research and how she remained hopeful that one day a cure might be found. Christopher sat listening as the two chatted. He was moved by their discussion and he finally spoke up.

"How about making the Saturday sneak-preview event a silent auction, with a portion of the proceeds going to benefit the foundation?"

"That's a wonderful idea, Christopher," London replied.

He explained that he had been involved in many similar charity functions in the past and could assist with the arrangements. London was thrilled and felt even more excited knowing that she would be supporting a good cause in the process of opening her store. She was relieved to have their help, as they were both so talented and capable. Jon mentioned that he and Christopher had talked about how she needed an assistant, someone to help her run the store. They suggested that Christopher take the job. It would help him supplement his income from his artwork, and he loved the way the loft had turned out.

After much discussion, London welcomed Christopher as her first employee. He would live in the loft and could use part of it for his studio, with the awesome view. She offered to even let him stage and sell his paintings in the store, which had lately begun to resemble artworks found in the royal palace as he'd been so inspired by the work he'd done on the walls and canopy bed. Christopher shared London's passions for France, French architecture and design, and he was quite knowledgeable. She was delighted to have him aboard and could certainly use the extra help at the grand opening. She'd been having such a great time she hadn't noticed how late it had become. She ordered a coffee to go, bid them adieu, and headed home to the château, exhausted and ready for a good night's sleep.

The next couple of days flew by as London worked feverishly planning, ordering, and researching. She was frequently called out to receive more deliveries and she directed the unloading at the barn, excited to inspect the quality of the various antique furnishings and amazing jewelry she had discovered. Max had been working at the store and was busy planning for his next projects.

Before she knew it, it was Thursday afternoon and London hadn't seen Max in what felt like forever. She was happy to finally see a text message from him: Meet me at the store, 5:00 p.m. this evening. Can't wait to see you! She dressed casually and headed out, stopping to pick up the invitations, which were already printed, then proceeded on to the store. On the way, she saw Max's truck at the park. She pulled into the parking lot and got out. There was commotion everywhere. London snuck over to the concession stand at the edge of the field to watch, pulling her hoodie over her head in the hopes that Max wouldn't recognize her. She helped herself to a soft drink and a hot dog smothered in relish, then tried to blend into the crowd that had gathered as she observed Max surrounded by a number of little boys. They were little league toddlers, and he was patiently fitting them with their uniforms and coaching them. She moved closer and overheard him talking.

"Hey, this fits you perfectly," he said as he opened up another box of shirts and pants. Max placed a baseball hat on the little guy, then patted him on the head. The boy ran out onto the baseball field, excited with his new outfit. He waved frantically at his mother to watch him. London's heart melted as she watched Max. She saw an expression she had never seen on his face before, a look of peaceful satisfaction. She puckered as she took another bite into the bitter relish, cringing as she realized her dreams were shattering. She knew Max could never be the one for her as she could never give him a child. She got back into her car, her eyes tearing. She sat watching the activities on the field, blissful children in the beautiful park, flowers blossoming, seedlings sprouting up, and nature coming to life all around her.

London pondered a recent discussion she'd had with her doctor regarding children. She'd explained the horror stories her grandmother had shared. London's mother had severe issues with high blood pressure, seizures, and toxemia, or pre-eclampsia as it was now known. The condition had advanced to eclampsia and London's mother had nearly died several times during the pregnancy and childbirth. Her mother spent weeks in a coma after giving birth. Everyone had been concerned for the two of them, especially for London because she had missed out on critical bonding time with her mother in the first weeks of her life. Thankfully, her mother had recovered well, but many relatives had experienced the condition in London's family, and some of the women had even died giving birth decades ago. It was undoubtedly hereditary, and the family history made it probable that London would experience the same complications.

London was never sure if she even wanted children in the first place since much of her own childhood had been so horrific and traumatic. She didn't feel confident about her own ability to raise a child and wasn't sure she wanted to risk her life to have one. After learning of the hereditary condition, she had all but written having a family right out of her mind. She recalled how very professional the doctor was, informing her of many options such as surgery, in vitro fertilization, adoption, and more, but London glazed over, hearing only bits and pieces of the information. She felt that the condition was simply confirmation from a divine source that she was not meant to have children, a fact that she had pretty much already come to terms with quite some time ago. She had thanked the doctor and let her know that she would follow up for further consultation if she ever changed her mind.

Despite her strong internal coping mechanisms, London still felt tears forming in her eyes as she watched Max on the distant field. *Damn useless hormones*, she thought. She knew she would have to set him free soon, but she didn't know exactly how. She looked at the clock. It was 4:30 p.m. She started the Beemer and drove to the store.

The building was almost ready, and she reveled in the beauty and the spaciousness of the rooms. So much had been accomplished since she had been there on Monday. Max arrived shortly after her and was watching her admire the wonder of his work.

"Like it?" he asked as he moved closer to her, massaging her neck and shoulders, sending chills up her spine

"Yes, Max, it's wonderful." She smiled as she turned around and kissed him.

"Mmm," he whispered. "I'd love more of you right here." He cupped her face and kissed her on the mouth. She responded with a warm, tender kiss in return. He reached down under her buttocks and pushed them toward him with such strength that it took her breath away.

"Let's try to stay focused," she said in a scolding tone as she smiled and gently pulled away. She was busy visualizing her furniture in the building and he was simply distracting. She continued to walk the floors, pointing to where she was going to put everything. Max followed closely behind and whispered in her ear.

"I want you tonight."

She just smirked as they wrapped up their review of what remained to be done. After they'd finished, he followed her to the château. On the way, she drove past the Sweat Shop, a private exercise club, and she smiled, remembering when she'd had had quite an affair with her kickboxing trainer from the club. That affair had lasted about a year and the sex was wonderful, but he got serious and she backed away. He just wasn't what she wanted. He was too into himself, always primping and preening, and it bothered her after a while. Once the passion had subsided, there was nothing left. He was all brawn with no brains or romance.

She smiled and shook her head at how promiscuous she had been and the lifestyle she used to live. Thankfully, she had matured and finally realized that many men were not her answer to finding happiness. Only the right man would make the difference. She thought, *You choose your own happiness and the path you choose is the one you live*, another quote from Catherine's *Life Lessons*. She had now chosen a path that was leading her to a more stable lifestyle.

London pulled into the driveway as those memories drifted away. Those days were gone. She was feeling contented with Max, but still thought of Deacon, the love of her life, every day and how much she missed him. She still clung to the hope that he would somehow find his way back into her life. She also worried about how serious Max seemed to be getting, especially with the invite to his family gathering. *How can I ever tell him that we would never have a family of our own? He adores kids and it would break his heart.*

She went inside and distracted her thoughts by starting to cook dinner while Max showered. She smiled as she sat down at the table, feeling a tingle in the pit of her tummy. Max dressed and went back down to the garage. When he reemerged in the kitchen, he was holding a bouquet of flowers in his hands. He gave her a light kiss as she thanked him, then she turned to finish preparing dinner. He grabbed her, turning her back around to kiss her again, more passionately this time.

"No little peck kisses for me, sexy lady," he said.

She smiled. "But what about the dinner?" She tried to turn away again, but he held her tightly as he kissed her again and again. She succumbed to his advances. He carried her upstairs, where he placed her on the bed.

"The stove is still on," she pleaded, dazed from his intoxicating kisses. He put his finger on her lips to shush her, then left the room. Upon returning, he continued his sexual advances on her, as her body reached out for his in return. He slowly undressed her, then pulled his clothes off and carried her to the shower, where they both enjoyed the warm water on their bodies. He knelt down and opened her legs as his tongue found its place. He licked her intensely as she pulled his head toward her breasts. She felt uncomfortable not having his hardness in her hands, but he soon returned to her lips with wet, warm kisses. They engulfed her to the point of her not caring about anything else but the desire between her legs. He pulled her to him, grabbed her ass, and lifted her up.

As her legs went around him his maleness entered her and she screamed with delight. He held her there as he pumped into her hard, slow strokes, his hands holding her up in the air and his hardness penetrating her to the depths of her body. She was in another world, one she so enjoyed as he continued to take her this way. He finally sped up as she felt herself submitting to him. Her body shook from the passion and the climax she was feeling. This was the part she loved so much . . . these feelings . . . she did not want to come again right now, her nipples—her button—her body all ready for another explosion that was oh so close.

She finally let go as she yelled, "Yes . . . oh my God!" Her body shook as he shot into her. She could feel it as her muscles tightened and relaxed, milking his maleness for all it had. He held her tight, their juices mixing and trickling down her legs. The warm water touched her sensitive skin, his kisses calming her down, while his hands were massaging her butt and her back. Her body responded by relaxing in his strong arms. He gently set her down and held her close as they stood in the warm mist. He opened the shower door and placed a terry cloth robe around her and grabbed one for himself. He pulled her to him and kissed her again. They left the bathroom together and walked down the stairs.

"How about ordering pizza for dinner?" he said as he looked at the cold, half-cooked food on the stove. He picked up the phone as she smiled and nodded yes with a wink.

She snuggled in his arms, eating pizza and drinking red wine while watching the blazing fire. He finally carried her up to bed, and together they collapsed with exhaustion into the coziness.

London woke up on Good Friday to Max's whistling coming from the kitchen. She put on her robe and found him standing by the stove making scrambled eggs with ham and cheese, toast, and bold Brazilian brew. He had cleaned up the mess from last night and everything looked sparkling clean. He served her, kissed her warmly on the lips, and joined her at the table, all set with place mats and the flowers he had bought last night.

"This is wonderful," she said as she took her first bite. He smiled. It had been a long few days without him. She watched him eat with great gusto as a nagging feeling crept over her. Her mind revisited the little league game from the day before and her heart ached. She knew that his love for children would eventually come between them. She admired his features, so strong, yet he was so kind and gentle. He was not a very complicated person at all. He was confident, he knew what he wanted, and he knew how to get it. She smiled to herself as she realized she was also becoming very confident in herself, with much thanks to him.

She browsed through some photos she had on her cell phone of the merchandise she'd ordered. "Look, Max," she said as she shared the pictures with him of the articles that were stored in the pole barn.

"Most of them are here," she said. "I'm just waiting for a few more pieces, and then I'll have them all." He looked at the many beautiful purchases and nodded approvingly.

"You know, we can start to move most of these articles and furniture in by the end of the month." As he spoke, London's eyes sparkled as if he had turned on a light inside her. She could hardly wait! "Would you like me to install the chandelier today?" he asked.

"Oh yes, and may I watch too? Then when I get home, I'll prepare the invitations to be sent out for the ball, now that I know when the store will be finished!" she replied eagerly.

"I'll protect the chandelier with a plastic tarp in case of some dust from the drywall and sanding of the walls and floors, but they're coming along well." London finished her breakfast, watching Max in the pole barn, loading the chandelier. He told her that he would wait for her to arrive at the store before he hung it, so she hurried with the rest of the cleanup, dressed, and met him at the shop.

The little French antique store was finally taking shape. She could not help but feel nostalgic as she watched the parquet flooring being laid in the dining room. She so appreciated Max's employees working on Good Friday. They didn't seem to mind, and she knew that Max took good care of them pay-wise for their efforts. Everything brought back memories of Versailles, especially the chandelier, which Max was now hanging. It looked quite elegant in the dining room. The transition from that to the tile that was going into the front room was dramatic. Stepping down one level, there was a formal front room that put one in a different world. The wall of leaded glass windows was to the right and the fireplace setting was on the back wall, with shelves for knickknacks and one large portrait of Louis XV over the mantel, which completed the room. Backing out of the front room and stepping up past the entrance way was the doorway to the dining room. She was very pleased. The fireplace was gorgeous and the burners were already installed. The artificial wood was ready for lighting with the push of a hidden button to ignite the gas fireplace.

The wainscoting was done to perfection and the pillars framing the doorway were the perfect touch.

She thought about the masquerade ball. The gathering would be held in the store on Friday night before the grand opening on Saturday, which was the sneak-preview auction. Then on Sunday, sales would take place. She couldn't wait to write the invitations, and that job would be done this weekend. She enjoyed the artistic pastime of writing calligraphy, appreciating what Grams had taught her. She was very talented. She also planned to stamp each envelope with a wax seal of the king of France. She would have them in the mail by Monday, in plenty of time for the first weekend in May. Max headed out to another job, and she was excited to get back home to start addressing the invitations.

Saturday evening, Max called and asked London to meet him at Pop's Pool Hall. He was heading there with his crew for burgers and beers. She dropped her pen and tucked the invitations away on her desk. She threw on sexy jeans and sweater, jumped in the Beemer, and raced to the bar. She parked and popped her trunk. She took out her leather bag with a pool stick that she always carried with her. It had been a long time since she had seen Pop, her friend, and tonight was a good time to visit with him. When she opened the door, Pop was standing in the corner. "Well, these old eyes can't believe what they are seeing," he said as he walked around toward her and gave her a big hug. "Hey, hon, how are you doing?"

"I'm great, and how about you, Pops?" She smiled, remembering he had been one of her grandmother's lovers. In his prime he was a handsome dude. Now age and drinking had taken its toll. "How's business?" she asked.

"Could be better; business is not like it was when you were

here. What are you doing with yourself these days? Staying out of trouble, I hope?"

"I'm trying. I'm opening up a new business down the street from you in a few weeks. It's an antique store."

"Sounds like a full-time job." He laughed, showing his lack of teeth. She hugged him and walked over to the pool tables. She was looking for Max and wanted to run a few pool balls at the same time. It had been a long time since she had visited the old pool hall. Pops and her had a close friendship. He had showed her how to play pool several years ago. He kind of took the place of her dad. Looking over the pool hall, she didn't see Max. She walked around the tables, rubbing her hands over the felt, feeling the rim. Then she laid the leather bag down, unzipping it. She pulled out her pool stick and put it together. It was her favorite stick. It had been a graduation present from Pops and it was accurate. She chalked up the end of the stick as Pops racked up the balls.

He watched his prize pupil approaching the head ball. Her breasts almost touched the table as she bent down, with the pool stick projecting from her hand. She slid it slowly through her fingers back and forth a few times. A few guys walked over to watch her, and she recognized some of them from Max's crew at the store. She felt their eyes on her as she stroked the pool stick in and out many times. She finally hit the ball, with a crack that shocked them all. She walked around the table, her body moving slowly as she eyed her next shot. She had an audience and she was thriving on playing up to them.

She looked toward the doorway and saw Max and Bud enter the poolroom. Max walked toward London and asked her if she would like to play him. She agreed, knowing he was a top pool shark. She had him rack them up again. He hit the head ball and the other balls went scurrying all over the table. He chose solids, which gave her stripes. He walked around, eyeing the best shot he could find, one that would put his cue ball right where he wanted it for the next shot. He hit the ball and it went in where he wanted it to, but the cue ball didn't stop where he had hoped it would. It was London's turn. She eyed her play and hit it right on target. Max looked at her like he had been slapped. She ran the table for a few minutes. When it was his turn, the cue ball was far from where he wanted it and he missed, which set her up perfectly. She made the shot and ran the table, putting the eight ball in the side pocket.

He looked at her devilishly. "Let's play another one," she suggested as the two other men left the room, leaving her and Max alone. He agreed and went behind her, whispering in her ear.

"If I win, I get you for the night." She couldn't let this go. She enjoyed Max so much and wanted him in the worst way. He walked around the table behind her, touching her butt as she bent down to hit the ball. His touch sent chills up her spine. She missed on purpose. He had a wonderful run on the table. It was her turn as she lined up her shot, bent forward, and moved her butt, tantalizing him on purpose. She spread her legs far apart as she placed the pool stick between her two fingers and slid it in, looking him straight in the eyes. She looked at the shot and let it go. Her ball went in the pocket and the cue ball replaced itself where she wanted it. She moved over for her next shot. She closely eyed the shot as it was the one she was famous for and she could make it easily. After studying it for a moment, she decided that he was more important than winning. She let the stick go, missing the shot completely. It was his turn. As he rubbed past her, his hardness began to show. She wanted him so badly and smiled at the effect she was having on him as he finished the game and won. He came over and grabbed her around the waist and kissed her passionately. "You have teased me enough for one day, my precious one. Now you're going to pay." Together they walked out of the hall to separate cars. He followed her home, both of them speeding down the road.

They walked hand in hand inside, where he kissed her as he took off her clothes piece by piece. He carried her up the curved staircase to her room, kissing her and nibbling on her neck all the way up. He laid her on the bed, pulled her toward the end of the bed, where he undressed and entered her. She murmured, "This was well worth losing a pool game for." When he was done, he pulled her to him and held her tight into the early night. She enjoyed him again and again. Afterward they went down for dinner dressed only in robes and slippers. He whipped up grilled steaks on the barbecue and she challenged him to another game of pool afterward. They got up and went back down to her pool table. She racked up the balls, and as she lay on the table to make a shot, he came up behind her, took his foot, and separated her feet while he rubbed his hardness between her legs. She ignored him, and when it was his turn, she walked behind him to rub his ass then reached in between his legs and grabbed his hardness. It was her turn again when he walked behind her, separating her legs, inserting his hardness inside her, pumping her as she lay on the table enjoying the wonderful tingle when he hit her G-spot that made her shake and grip the edges of the table. He took her this way short of making her come. She moved off the table over to the bamboo love seat, where he whispered in her ear, "Come for me, London." She gave him his wish with her screams of ecstasy. Back and forth to the pool table, she beat him seven games to one, between all the lovemaking. He smiled, knowing he had been hustled by the best. They went to the bedroom, their hands clasped, and he held her through the night.

They awoke Easter morning, dressed in their finest spring attire, and drove into town to Max's parents' home for a holiday gathering. The smell of brown-sugared ham baking in the oven filled the air along with the sounds of shrieking children running through the house. Max had five brothers and sisters, some of whom London knew from their school days, especially his sister Marie. They had been close back then. Most of his siblings were now married with children. Max had a total of twelve nieces and nephews. All the children, with the exception of the two tiny infants, came bounding into the family room to greet their uncle Max. He was besieged by a troop of toddlers as they tackled the gentle giant to the floor. They rolled around, laughing and wrestling.

London was overwhelmed by it all. She struggled through numerous introductions to his family members, attempting to make conversation as the nosy sisters and sisters-in-law cornered her with prying questions, hinting about Max getting married and having his own little family soon. London avoided the subject as Max swept in to save her. He took her by the hand and together they snuck out to the backyard.

"Will you help me with setting up the Easter egg hunt? I have to hide all one hundred and fifty of these eggs for the kids."

"Sure." London giggled, and they proceeded to conceal the plastic eggs filled with treasures all around the beautifully landscaped yard.

"Sorry about my sisters," Max said. "They want so much for me to settle down. I should have prepared you for the onslaught."

"Yes, a little warning would have been nice," she said with a smile.

Marie emerged to help them. She too was apologetic for the interrogation London had been subjected to.

"Marie is the only one who understands," Max said. "Since she hasn't settled down yet either," he explained.

"Max, I wanted to tell you that Mom invited Madison and Mikey to join us for dinner tonight," Marie said, her eyes fixated on his reaction.

"Oh, wow! Are they back from Texas?" His voice quavered.

"Yes, Mom and I saw her at the grocery store on Good Friday. She spent several months with her family over the holidays, but she finally decided to return home last week." Marie continued as London listened, curious as to whom they might be talking about.

"How is she coping, and how's little Mikey?" Max asked, and London noticed the genuine concern in his voice.

"She seems to be doing well, they both do, and she looks fabulous," Marie said, shooting London a glance.

"Max!" called a voice from the house. "We need you in here for a minute."

"Ladies, duty calls." Max chuckled as he bowed out gracefully, leaving London at Marie's mercy.

"So, London," Marie asked, "how have you been?"

The two of them chatted, catching up on the lost years between them. Marie eventually segued back to explaining who Madison and Mikey were.

"You remember Michael, Max's best friend from high school, don't you?" Marie asked.

"Yes, I sure do," London replied as she tucked another egg behind some blossoming lilies of the valley, the fragrance drifting into her senses.

"Well, he joined the Navy after high school and was stationed in Corpus Christi, Texas, for a while, where he met his wife, Madison. He eventually moved back up here when they had their first child, Mikey Junior. Max was very close to them and looked after Madison when Michael was deployed overseas. Sadly, Michael was the victim of an IED attack a couple years ago."

"Oh, that's terrible," London said, suddenly feeling the devastation of Max's loss. "I wonder why he never told me."

"He doesn't like to talk about it much. The funeral was devastating for everyone," Marie explained. After a long pause, Marie boldly asked, "London, do you love my brother?"

Shocked by her forwardness, London hesitated to respond. "I'm not sure. I love being with him and I treasure our time together, but I'm not sure if we are truly in love. Why?"

"Never mind, I'm sorry to be so blunt."

London's mind raced as Marie continued on, trying to change the subject to idle chitchat. Finally, they had reached the bottoms of the seemingly endless baskets of Easter eggs and they headed back inside. Marie escorted London to the bar, where she mixed them each a drink. London was relieved as she downed a nip of the tasty vodka and orange juice. She thanked Marie and slipped away to find Max.

She found him helping with lunch preparations. She sauntered over and pitched in to help in an environment where she always felt comfortable, in the kitchen. Max's mother was scurrying here and there, dressed in her Sunday best, her sweet voice calm and soothing amid the noisy chaos of the household. Max smiled as London stepped in to chop vegetables while he sliced the ham.

The doorbell rang and London's heart stopped. Everything became a blur around her and all the noises seemed to run together as she watched Madison enter the foyer with Mikey. Madison was a knockout, tall and blond, tan, toned, and shapely, looking celestial in a peach sweater with a cream skirt, her slender legs accentuated by neutral high heels. London saw the look on Max's face as he headed down the hall to greet them.

"Max!" Mikey squealed, and ran to throw his arms around him. Max leaned in to catch the little guy as Madison glowed, waiting for her turn to move in for a hug. Max propped the four-year-old on his hip as he walked over to Madison. London watched, taking her eyes away from the vegetables as much as she could without risking cutting herself. Her heart ached at the sight of them, apparently so happy to see each other. She blinked away a tear as she looked back down to focus on the task before her.

The crowd eventually moved into the enormous dining room, where a table accommodated twenty people, and a few smaller tables had been arranged for the children. The feast was amazing, but London had lost her appetite and feigned eating out of politeness. Max and Madison chatted so much London began to feel invisible. *Madison's sweet southern accent could charm the pants off any man*, London thought. Part of her wanted to hate this beautiful woman who came in and took over her date for the day, but seeing how happy they were together something inside her felt a sense of peace too.

Madison mentioned some repairs she needed done at her house. Max assured her that he would be over soon to take a look at it. Feeling like a third wheel, London excused herself to the bathroom to freshen up and take a breather from all of the commotion. As she was returning to the group, Marie reappeared.

"Ready for another yet?" she said as she waved her empty glass.

"I sure am," London said.

"London, I know you and Max have been seeing each other for a few months," Marie said, pausing as she poured their drinks. "Max told me all about you and your antique store and the wonderful times you two have been having together. But I wanted to prepare you."

"Prepare me for what?" London asked.

"Well it's obvious, isn't it? Max fell in love with Madison," Marie said, her voice in a hushed whisper now. "He was so attentive, caring for her and Mikey after Michael was gone. Madison was in mourning and felt it was too soon for a new relationship. Last year, she decided to go stay with her family for a while to sort out what she was feeling, and Max didn't know if she was ever coming back or not. But now that she's back . . . well, I think he has his answer."

London was dumbfounded as she tried to process Marie's ramblings. "So you think she's back to claim him?"

"I do. Oh, London, I'm so sorry. I know Max wanted to marry her, and he was torn about it too, but Mikey already thinks of him as a father figure since he was so young when it all happened. Max was lost without Madison when she left, but I think you and your project at the store saved him from his loneliness. My mother didn't know he was bringing you to brunch today, or she might not have asked her over."

London took another large gulp of her drink, the vodka beginning to numb her senses and dull the impact. "As a matter of fact, he saved me too, Marie. I was feeling pretty lost myself when we teamed up together."

"I just wanted you to be aware. It's possible that they might reunite. They both come from big families and both have talked about wanting many more children. They have so much in common. Madison just wasn't sure about anything back then. And I'm sure Max didn't want to tell you, as he wasn't sure how things stood or if she would ever be back."

"Well, I've had my own demons that I've been contending with and I haven't told him everything either. I guess we will have to have a long talk later tonight. Thank you, Marie. Thank you so much for your support today."

"London, please call me if you need to talk about anything after tonight."

"I will. And I hope you will join me at the grand opening of the shop next month too. It's going to be amazing and you won't believe all the wonderful things your brother has done with the building."

London made her way back to the group and pleasantly socialized with her usual charisma. After their meal, she blended into the crowd and watched as the little children scavenged for Easter eggs in the backyard. Her heart melted as she watched Max and Mikey together, and she carefully studied Madison. They were perfect for each other, and as much as London cared for Max, there was no denying it.

She observed him walking them to their car as they left the party. He stopped at his truck to grab something, piquing London's curiosity as she moved closer to the window. She watched as he emerged from the cab with a uniform, hat, baseball mitt, and ball. Little Mikey jumped up and down, overwhelmed with joy, and gave Max a big kiss.

When the event finally wound down, she and Max said their good-byes to his family and headed back to the château. She couldn't wait to get back to the comfort of her home, and she had so much to get off her chest when they arrived. They were both quiet on the drive home, which felt exceptionally long. Max parked the truck out front in the circle drive and London realized he wasn't planning to stay over.

"Max, could you come inside so we can talk for a little while before you head home?"

"Sure," he replied with a weak smile through the look of grief and shock on his face.

They went inside, where he lit the fire and London brewed coffee. They snuggled in on the sofa to chat. After a long hesitation, Max mustered the strength to finally speak.

"Oh, London, I'm so sorry I never told you about Michael, Madison, and Mikey," he said.

"Max, it's okay. Marie filled me in at the party."

"She did? So you know . . ."

"Yes, Max. I understand."

He was soft-spoken as he quoted, "If you love something, set it free. If it comes back to you, it is yours. If it doesn't, it never was." He paused for a moment as the words sank in to the air between the crackling sounds of the fireplace. "I let them go, London." His voice caught and she could see the glimmer of tears forming in the flickering firelight. "I thought they were never coming back."

"Max, please don't be sad. You should be celebrating right now. By the way, I saw you at the baseball game on Thursday."

"You did?"

"Yes, I've been searching the depths of my soul since then, trying to find a way to tell you this. Max, the truth is, I will probably never have children. I knew after seeing you with the boys that day that I could never give you everything you need in life. You're a family man and you're meant to be a father someday. You deserve to have that." London took a deep breath before continuing.

"I will admit that Madison was a huge surprise, and it was

awkward meeting the way that we did, but I'm so happy for you. I want you to go to her and Mikey tonight. You belong with them, and it's a blessing from heaven that they returned to be with you."

Max blinked away the emotions that were beginning to consume him. She leaned in, wrapping her arms around his neck, hugging him tightly as she rested on his burly shoulders of strength one last time. He embraced her, holding her close as they both quietly sobbed tears of pain and joy together. She finally pulled back, resting her hands on his shoulders and looking deep into his eyes.

"Max, we've been here for each other and we've helped each other through some very tough times. I can't thank you enough for your support and understanding after what happened to me with Deacon and Jen. You have helped me turn my life around and given me hope for the future. I only wish I had known what you were really going through all this time so that I could have been more supportive, but I think I understand why you kept it to yourself. I won't hold you back from your true love, Max. Madison is your fate. I know you love me, and I love you, but we are both still madly in love with other people. We will always be friends, and we had the most amazing affair two lovers could ever ask for." She smiled as she brushed away another tear and forced her best smile. "But I do hope that you might still help me to finish the store and see me through to the grand opening."

"London, you are amazing. I don't know what to say except that my crew and I will certainly be there to help you every step of the way."

"Thank you so much. I don't know how I would do it without you and your brawny team." She gave him a tender and final kiss. "Now go!" she ordered, giggling as she rose from the sofa, pulled him up, and guided him to the door anxiously. As he walked out, he stopped and turned around. He grabbed her, embracing her, his breath hot on her neck. She whispered in his ear, "You were never mine, Max. Now, go be free."

He turned to hide the tears that were streaming down his face and walked to his truck. She watched out the window, closing the gate as the lights on his big truck disappeared into the darkness. Her heart ached as she strolled across the room to fetch a box of tissues. She stopped on her way to the sofa to pour a glass of Deacon's fine scotch, then snuggled down with the remote. She flicked on the TV, searching for distraction from the deep thoughts that overwhelmed her mind. She scrolled through the guide and stopped at the movie classics channel. She mused at the irony of the title of a 1957 film, *An Affair to Remember*. It had been one of Grams's favorites, and she recalled watching it many times with her. She selected the movie and the opening credits appeared on the screen.

Cary Grant reminded her a bit of Deacon with all his glorious charm. She lost herself in the story, only needing a few tissues along the way as she was whisked off to France and back to New York with Deborah Kerr leading the way. Knowing how the film ended, London drifted off into a deep and peaceful sleep to visit her palace of refuge. She was enchanted to find Deacon waiting there for her in her dreams.

Chapter 15

MASQUERADE BALL AND SUCCULENT FEAST

The weeks passed by fast, and the following night was the ball. London's antique shop was ready for the event. Max had kept his promise and was very helpful in making sure everything was in order for the deadline. The responses she'd received from the invites to the ball were overwhelming. She was excited about the day her business would be in full swing and the party where her guests would be wearing masks and eighteenth-century costumes.

The local costume store was delighted, and as a consequence had already become a fan of London and her new venture.

She planned to hand out prizes at midnight for the two best costumes. She had found the gown of her dreams and would be dressed as Marie Antoinette. The dress was a gorgeous cream satin number with faux pearls and diamonds throughout the bodice, and lace at the end of the sleeves. The food was also inspired. Her fruit cake was to be designed after the Eiffel Tower, coated with sugar glazing and adorned with removable mini lights. It had sounded amazing, and she couldn't wait to see it. The front room would be decorated like the Hall of Mirrors ballroom—miniature, of course, but elegant just the same. She could hardly sleep that night, like a child on Christmas Eve.

On the day of the ball, she arose and headed to the store to finalize the details. The decorators had placed French chairs along the mirrored walls, making the room look huge. Next to the French sconces on the walls were gorgeous masks of gold and cream. Her ceiling-to-floor windows accented the French theme. She placed crystal and gold beads, which hung from the sconces to the chandelier, in the dining room. When London entered the front room, which had been transformed into a ballroom, her heart skipped a beat. The makeover was awesome, and she couldn't wait for the evening to begin. She had hired a string quartet that would sit in the kitchen area, out of the dancing area yet microphoned to be heard. Everything was perfect. So she left for home to get herself dressed and ready for the event.

Her dress had been delivered with a bustier, farthingale, slips, shoes, and wig, all boxed and ready to adorn her body. She retrieved the necklace Max had given her and smiled, fondling the glistening crystals as she set the box beside her costume. She jumped into a warm, scented bath as the room glowed in the flickering candlelight. Her body felt so excited, yet so relaxed. She couldn't believe how calm she felt at that moment. But the evening's anticipation was slowly building, and she began to tingle all over. She closed her eyes as she pictured herself in the majestic gown and envisioned the grandeur of the evening.

She got out of the bath, dried herself, and went into the bedroom to get dressed when she was interrupted by a buzz on the intercom. *I wonder who that could be*, she thought. The voice on the other end of the speaker was a lovely lady from the costume shop who had offered to help her with her dress.

London opened the gates and ran down to open the door. The woman introduced herself as Gabriel and explained that her services were part of the costume rental agreement. London accepted gratefully, as putting on all the garments required two people. Gabriel held the undergarments for London as one layer after the next was draped over her body. She was girdled and tightened up within the layers until she felt just like a marshmallow. The cream satin dress was placed over her head and her bosom popped out at the neckline. Her skirt flowed down to the floor with pearls and faux diamonds in flowered forms. Her sleeves were tight at the top, flowing into ruffles of lace and pearls. Her neckline was plain, but her faux-diamond necklace from Max amply filled the space. She tried to sit but failed as she puffed out like a cotton ball, sending her and Gabriel into a fit of giggles. After her make-up was applied and the faux-diamond earrings were affixed, Gabriel adorned London's head with the fancy wig. She spun around and . . . voilà! She was Queen Marie Antoinette! She slipped her feet into the cream satin slippers and was ready for the evening.

She traveled to the party in a horse-drawn white carriage. She felt as if she was on her way to the Palace of Versailles right down the street. When she entered her store, people were already dancing. She was amazed at how beautiful they all looked in their noble attire, their faces disguised by their masks. The store was glistening, thanks to Jon. She was announced and all the guests bowed. One of the guests reached out his hand, inviting her to dance. He waltzed her out onto the cobblestone sidewalk. She believed it was someone she knew, but he didn't have his telltale cologne on. He wore gloves, and had done a good job of disguising himself. She thought she knew who he was, but she was not sure; however, it had to be someone she'd invited.

"I think I know who you are, but am so enjoying the game. Don't tell me," she said with a smile. He whisked her back inside. As they danced around the floor he held her close, but he spoke not a word, which added to the mystery and intrigue of his identity. After the song ended, he slipped away.

She walked over to the table of tasty hors d'oeuvres and decadent desserts. The cakes looked especially inviting, and she giggled to herself as she said, "Let them eat cake!" There were petits fours, cream puffs, éclairs, strawberry shortcake, and six bowls of whipped cream amidst the other tantalizing foods that surrounded the magnificent fruit cake replica of the Eiffel Tower. The tiny lights on the centerpiece twinkled, reflecting onto a large, sterling silver coffee service set and crystal goblets full of champagne and white wine. She took a flute of champagne and sipped it along with some whipped cream and strawberries, remembering a movie she saw where the leading man told the woman that "strawberries bring out the taste of champagne." She nibbled as her dancing friend came back over. He dipped his strawberry in her whipped cream and rubbed it against her neck, then gave her a lick. He nuzzled her from behind, kissing her shoulders, her neck and her cheeks, his breath hot on her ears. She wanted to take his mask off and let him kiss her lips, but she would have to wait until midnight when everyone would remove their masks together.

He again took her in his arms and they danced around the floor. His lips were on her neck as his hands caressed her back. His charm and attentiveness had her so hot and wet that she almost came right there. Their bodies glided across the dance floor as he led her outside, where he kissed her bottom lip. She knew from the feelings she felt down deep he had to be Deacon and played along. She wanted more and couldn't wait for midnight to arrive. He reached under the layers of her dress, touching her between her legs. Her every thought, nerve, and emotion was on fire with desire, her resistance was gone, and all she wanted was to be fucked, now, and for a precious moment forgot where she was.

"Please," she whispered to her masked friend, who led her back inside. One part of her body had been brought to life, while the rest of her was dying in agony to feel his touch. The ball would soon be over and she could then take advantage of her new mystery lover. He danced with her again, his embrace reassuring her that this would be a night to remember. She felt her body slip away on a cloud of passion. He held her close, kissing her bare shoulders. His gloved hands were soft and gentle, and he held her with the greatest of care. He kissed her, tonguing her when nobody was looking. Her heart pounded so hard she thought everyone could hear it. He kissed her cheeks as he brushed against her face. *Oh my God,* she thought, *if it doesn't get to midnight soon I will simply die.*

"*Bonsoir, mesdames et messieurs.*" She changed to English. "Welcome, guests. What a wonderful gathering and how beautiful you all look. I can only imagine how dances back in France must have looked. I would like to say a special thanks to Jon and his staff from Creative Catering for the gorgeous decorations and delectable food." She led the crowd in accolades and smiled. "Now the moment we have all been waiting for, the drawing." London's dear friends Grace and Brent Cosgrove easily won the contest. Grace floated across the floor in an emerald velvet gown donned with tiny emeralds graced by a lovely diamond-and-emerald necklace and earrings, her hair piled up high with an emerald broach in the middle of the front with a long emerald feather. Brent had on a light green velvet jacket with a cream ruffled shirt that flowed out of his jacket at the neck and sleeves, tight knee-high light green pants, matching high socks, and buckled shoes. Grace's gown and his suit were tailor-made, and she was a vision of loveliness in her dress. London awarded them with their trophies that showed a French couple dancing. They proceeded to lead the group back onto the dance floor in a waltz. When the song ended, it was five minutes to midnight. The countdown started: four, three, two, one! Everyone removed their masks and smiled as the festive masquerade came to a close. London's eyes darted around, searching for her mystery man, but she couldn't see him anywhere. The ball wound down as guests came over to thank London. She bid them farewell, with smiles and laughter, her eyes still searching for her partner. After the last visitor exited the store, Jon offered to drive London home. He assured her that the wonderful waitstaff would clean the store and Christopher would secure everything and lock up.

At the château, Jon came inside to chat. London poured them each a glass of wine, and they talked for a while. She explained the story to him about her split with Max. They'd both been so busy that she hadn't even had a chance to fill him in on the details. Jon was comforting and shared in her sorrows. He changed the subject as he inquired about the mysterious man who had swept her off her feet at the ball. Her face lit up as she told Jon she didn't know who he was, and sadly, he'd disappeared just before midnight. However, her gut feeling told her it had been Deacon. They were both exhausted from all the excitement and intrigue. Jon helped her out of her heavy dress and was soon on his way. London poured another scotch and headed up to bed.

Saturday morning, she awoke feeling groggy for a moment as her eyes adjusted to the daylight. Then she realized, *Today is the Grand Opening of Le Magasin d'Antiquités!* She got ready fast, grabbing a yogurt for breakfast and a sandwich for lunch.

Max and the movers showed up, and she opened the gates, then watched as they took the furniture out of the pole barn and loaded it into the truck. She was excited that her dream had finally come true. She packed her dress and decided to change at the store after everything had been moved into its proper place.

When she arrived at the shop, Christopher was waiting at the door for her. Together, they directed placement of the precious antiques and soon the store was full of beautiful items. She polished the tables while Christopher cleaned the glass door on the book case. She placed statue heads on pedestals, and a centerpiece on the dining room table. Max grinned at her as he hung a few pictures. Soon everything was ready and the clock read 1:00 p.m. The opening would be only from 2:00 to 4:00 p.m. that afternoon and nothing would be sold yet. People could tag and bid on their choice of items and the winning bidders could claim their merchandise on Sunday, with the proceeds of the silent auction of the Louis XV picture going to the shelter. She walked through the building, looking at each piece in different rooms, admiring it all and wishing she could keep several of the items for herself. Tomorrow, she would have to part with them, only to replace them with other items that were equally as lovely.

She looked at the heavy chandelier with its crystals glimmering in the sunlight, prisms reflecting rainbows over the walls. She turned to admire the elegant French front room. She loved and appreciated the beauty that Max had captured in remodeling the building. He'd brought her such happiness and she hoped that he had found his happiness too with Madison and Mikey. Her mind drifted to thoughts of Deacon. She smiled as she thought of the mystery man again, wondering if it could have been Deacon and how she'd hoped to find him when the masks were removed, but alas it didn't happen.

London looked at her watch impatiently. She had a little more time to kill, so she retrieved her sandwich and sat at the dining room table to eat. She took in the surroundings as she munched quickly, then headed to the powder room to change clothes. The lavatory was finished in striking black and gold contrasts. The black wallpaper had pink flowers and ribbons of gold and pink that complemented the black pedestal sink and golden fixtures. The lighting consisted of two crystal sconces and a small chandelier hanging in the middle of the room. London quickly changed into her Marie Antoinette costume, minus the tedious undergarments, as she thought it would be fun to dress up one last time before returning her costume. She left the room to promenade around her new store.

It was nearly time to open the doors for business. London took in a deep breath as she looked out the window in surprise. The line of customers had already formed outside on the sidewalk. *No need to keep them waiting any longer*, she thought. She opened the doors and welcomed her guests to the sneak-preview auction. She and Christopher guided patrons and clarified the auction process. They could bid and sign a tag for certain items, and if their bid won the item, it would be held for them to pick up the following day. Christopher was instrumental in providing the historical and intriguing facts behind each unique piece, and London was impressed. He had really done his homework. Familiar faces from the previous night's ball appeared, voicing comments on the party and how wonderful it had been. Items were being tagged fast and the bids were increasing with competitive fury. She was certain that all of the items would be gone by the next day, and she was relieved that she had wisely doubled her inventory so that she would be able to replace most of the treasures.

London noticed that Jen was in line to bid. She hadn't seen her since that fateful night at Jen's apartment. London's blood boiled, but she maintained her composure.

"Everything looks great, hon," Jen said as she approached London, expressing her enthusiasm over the new store. "And I love your sign! It's so creative. The whole store is just so original and amazing!"

London smiled, feeling catty as she remembered the night of their threesome.

"Thank you," London replied curtly. "I even have an authentic eighteenth-century guillotine down in the basement that I'd like to show you later."

London smirked and diverted her attention to a patron with a question. Jen kept waiting around and following London. The distraction was beginning to annoy her as she attempted to review her inventory plans.

"London, we really need to talk," said Jen, toying with her purse straps.

"I really don't know what to say to you, Jen," London replied as she walked around marking items in her book.

"I am so sorry. Please accept my apologies. The tryst was my entire fault. I seduced him and encouraged him to come over to my condo. You know, Deacon is beside himself with grief since you two broke up," Jen pleaded.

"I really don't care. He showed me just how little he cares by having a fling with you. Seeing him in bed with you . . . Oh my God, Jen! You knew how much I loved him and you didn't even care. How could you?" London tried to walk away, turning her back as tears began to form.

"London, wait," Jen continued. "I talked to Deacon today. He's distraught and talked of moving back to England soon. He's lost and devastated without you, and I just don't want to see you lose him forever. I could never take him from you, and not for a lack of trying. I'm sorry for what I did, but please hear me out. You've wrecked him, London. He will never be able to love another woman again, ever. He only wants you. You mean the world to him." Jen paused before finishing catching her breath. "Please, London, just promise me that you'll go see him and hear him out before he's gone forever."

London spun back around. "Thank you, Jen. I may go and give him one last chance, but I'm not so sure I can ever forgive you. Now please, I have a store to run here, and now is neither the time nor the place for this nonsense."

Jen nodded apologetically and excused herself. London watched Jen exit, feeling overwhelmed with betrayal, but realizing that Jen was right. London was mired in a tunnel of confusion and guilt. She would talk with Deacon if she could muster the strength to face him. She walked around lighting candles for atmosphere, the fragrance filling the air with soothing comfort. Oddly enough, the name of the candle was "Ol' France," which made her smile. The dining room was already full of people looking through books and drinking coffee. She had installed a cappuccino machine in the corner by the bookshelves near her window seat in front of the bow windows. She strolled over and poured herself some. She sipped it, savoring the heat and moving her hands up and down the warmth of the cup. She thought about Deacon and the first time they'd met as she rubbed her finger around the rim of the cup, around and around until her mind was satisfied. She put it back up to her lips, letting the foamy liquid slide down her throat. Her heart and body ached for Deacon, and she was torn as she attempted to disguise her turmoil. Part of her still loved Deacon madly. He was her true soul mate. She smiled as she blinked away her tears.

It was almost 4:00 when Christopher touched her arm, bringing her back to reality.

"Today was an amazing success. We made fifteen hundred dollars on the portrait of Louis XV for the shelter," he said.

"Oh, that is wonderful. Thank you so much for all your hard work, Christopher," she replied.

He was so intuitive and he offered to close up shop if she wanted to escape early. She accepted his offer. She changed out of her dress and headed to the château, stopping only to return her gown at the costume shop, where she thanked them for their assistance with the ball.

Back in the comfort of her home, she indulged in a hot bath, dined alone by candlelight, then curled up by the fire to sip on yet another tumbler of Deacon's scotch, the only substitute she seemed to have for his touch lately. Before retiring, she retrieved her engagement ring from the drawer. She crawled into the comfort of her bed, admiring the beauty of the glistening aquamarine gemstone in the lamplight as she drifted off to meet Deacon in her palace of dreams.

Sunday morning arrived early and she awoke to the intercom buzzing. "Yes?" she asked.

"You need to open the gate so we can transport the replacement items you need for your store."

She realized she was still clutching the engagement ring and quickly tucked it into her purse as she hit the remote control for the front gate. The sound of the trucks invaded her quiet morning. After a cup of yogurt, coffee, and cereal, she showered and dressed with excited haste, readying herself for yet another busy day. She straightened up and left for the shop, eager to make her first sales. The ride to the store was exciting as she thought about all the changes that would be made. She also felt somewhat saddened about selling some of her loveliest things. That was the one drawback to this business . . . falling in love with the furniture. Each piece was so special that she would buy them all if she could, but she knew her home would soon become crammed to the rafters. She giggled at the ridiculous thought of becoming such a hoarder.

She walked in to find that Christopher already had the fireplace blazing and the cappuccino machine brewing. She placed an open sign on the door for her customers, turned on the music, and lit the scented candles. They were ready for business. She and Christopher chatted. He had overheard Jen's comments the day before and encouraged London to consider going to see Deacon, just to be sure about her feelings.

Two and a half hours later, her store was empty. All the wonderful French antiques had been sold and the workers were bringing in new items to replace the original ones. She marveled at how the room's ambience changed with the new furniture and the colors blended with each and every piece. She changed the flowers, moved a few knickknacks around, and added a new statue. A bust of Marie Antoinette on a Corinthian column pedestal was now in front of the doorway leading to the front room, and next to it London placed a bouquet of yellow roses, which picked up the colors from the Monet *Water Lilies* painting that hung over the fireplace, replacing the portrait of Louis XV. What a change! Her previous theme had been mauve and pink, her preference, but now green and yellow were the predominant colors and she enjoyed the transformation.

Her day was beginning to get very exciting, with many sales. The drivers were constantly running back and forth from her house to replenish the inventory, and then back out to make deliveries of the French treasures to their new homes.

The store's ambience changed continuously. It seemed that just as she had gotten used to a certain look, poof, the items were sold. It was great for business, but tough on her. She liked her comfort zone, and the ever-changing adjustments were a bit difficult. She kept reminding herself that this was business, not personal, and that she would have to adapt. She walked around the dining room table, touching the crystal center-piece. It shone so brightly, accompanied by the chandelier above. It seemed that they were competing for wall space to cast their rainbows of colors.

Suddenly a familiar and powerful fragrance engulfed her senses, stopping her dead in her tracks. She turned around to see Deacon standing before her. She wanted to embrace him immediately, but she didn't. He smiled at her, clinging tightly to a small box in one hand and a vase of flowers in the other. She stared at the bouquet of lilies mixed with English daisies, afraid to look into his eyes lest she fall into his arms. She moved along the table, adjusting the place settings and trying to stay focused. He set the gifts down on the table in front of her and pulled her to him. His lips took over and she went limp. Customers stood watching, envying what they were witnessing. He was her love and that was all that mattered to her at this moment. When he finally released her, she gasped for air. He turned without a word and made his way out of the store, debonair as he ever was. She was breathless and speechless as she watched him go, her heart crying out as her body stood frozen. She felt like a pull toy with her emotions, and for a moment she was ready to just leave the store and follow him, but she knew she had to stay for her patrons. She watched him cross the street, climb into his car, and drive away. She felt warm and fuzzy as she composed herself. She spun around, still blushing, and waited on another customer as people passed by smirking at her.

When she finally had a moment for a break, she decided to open the gift Deacon had left. Christopher was at her side, the curiosity killing him as she opened the card attached to the small box. The handwritten card read:

Congratulations on your new store! I will always love you, London. Please forgive me. I can't wait any longer. Meet me for dinner tonight at my place if there's still a chance for us. If not, I will be bound for England tomorrow morning. Yours Forever, Deacon.

She and Christopher both sniffled away their emotions. "Open the box!" Christopher said.

She proceeded to peel back the ribbon and open the box to reveal a pair of gorgeous antique earrings. They were eighteenth-century Victorian natural pearls, each surrounded by nine glistening rose-cut diamonds in a pendant-style classical round cluster. They were exuberating with royal baroque grandeur, and his thoughtfulness melted her heart.

The rest of the day went by slowly. She was overcome by a sense of urgency to get to Deacon. Finally, Christopher rushed her out to be with him and assured her that he would take care of everything. She put on some lipstick and primped her hair before she ran out the door, jumped into the Beemer, and raced off toward his condominium. She couldn't drive fast enough and wanted to be in his arms now. When she spotted his place, her heart skipped a beat. She got out, walked on rubbery legs up to the door. She pushed the intercom button and heard his response, his deep voice sending shivers up her spine. "Hi, it's me, London." He buzzed her in. As she entered, she found him juggling with cheese, crackers, wine, and glasses in his hands. She took the wine and glasses from him as he bent down to kiss her lips. They turned to place everything on the table, then melted into an embrace. She put her arms around his neck as they kissed. He struggled to remove her coat so she could feel his body, a feeling she had missed for so long. Finally, with his help, she dropped the coat to the floor, their lips staying pressed together. They made their way to his bedroom, their clothes dropping to the floor behind them in a trail until they were nude. Meanwhile, his mouth explored her body. He ignited her as his tongue glided over her neck, her ears, her breasts.

She fondled his hardness as his hands pulled her into position at the end of the bed. His ultimate goal was to get inside her as quickly as possible and make her his again. She obeyed without hesitation. She was ready and opened her legs to welcome him. With one swift plunge he entered her, riding her wildly as they climaxed together moments later. In that wonderful moment of harmony, their souls reunited. He collapsed on top of her, kissing her tenderly with those lips that she had been longing for. He began to apologize for his haste and for his past indiscretion, but she placed her finger over his lips.

"All is forgiven, my darling," she said with a gentle smile.

He relaxed as she snuggled into his arms. After a long silence, she finally spoke. "I thought you invited me here for dinner," she said with a smile as the heavenly fragrance of food came wafting into the room.

"Dinner is on its way," he said with a smile. He put on his robe as the buzzer rang and he opened the front door. Five men in waiter uniforms shuffled in, bearing trays loaded down with enticing cuisine. They set up the table and poured the wine. She was thrilled knowing that he had put so much thought and effort into planning this wonderful evening. She slipped on a robe and walked over to the table. Beside the gourmet feast she noticed a mask lying on the table. It was the mask of her mystery man from the costume ball! She could only smile at him as he caught her glance.

A succulent pheasant was lusciously displayed under a glass dome, garnished with wild rice, and accompanied by brioche, white wine, and chocolate mousse for dessert. She was very pleased. She sat down to dine in her robe, knowing that the first round of sex was just a pressure release and that the main course would follow once dinner had settled. She cut the pheasant in small pieces, placing each one on her tongue. The moisture stayed on her lips as she took her tongue and slowly licked at the juices. She picked up some wild rice and placed it on her tongue. She casually chewed the meat and rice with deliberate allure, tantalizing him with every bite. She picked up the goblet and placed it on her lips, letting the liquid run down her throat as Deacon watched her, knowing that she could stop traffic with the way she was eating. He followed her every mouthful, and as she took her last bite, he moved over to her, cupping her face and licking the juices from her lips. His tongue invaded her mouth, and her body responded to his just as he'd hoped for. He clung to her lips as he got up, then let go as he cleared the table and brought over the dessert.

"I want to feed you," he said as he pulled her chair from the table, turning her toward him. He took a spoonful of chocolate mousse and placed it in her mouth, following it with a kiss. He spoon-fed her each and every bite, her body wanting more than dessert. Then she proceeded to feed him as the intensity grew between them.

She helped him clear the table, and he touched her every time they were near, his hands traveling over every part of her aching body. She was still amazed by the way they connected. He grabbed her, kissing her as he untied her robe. He pulled her to him, caressing her breasts as he bent down, taking a nipple in his mouth and encircling it with his tongue. He sucked it until her knees shook. He carried her into the bedroom, his lips never leaving hers. He gently placed her on the bed, kissing her, fondling her and tasting her juices. He buried his face in her breasts, licking and sucking them feverishly, then returning to her mouth and back again. She was lost in a state of euphoria as her world fell away once again. There was no house, no sound . . . nothing but the flickering of the candles and the hot, intimate forms that molded together as one on the bed. She placed her arms around his shoulders, pulling him closer. She felt him come alive as she kissed him and moved her attention to his throbbing hardness. She took it into her hands, rubbing it up and down as he positioned himself to lick her legs and everything in between.

She took his hardness in her mouth, touching it with her tongue, going around the ridge and behind it, her lips lightly sucking on it, licking it like an ice cream cone, round and round, up and down. The precum forming on the tip was in her mouth and she sucked at it hungrily. He licked inside her legs and all the way up to her passion pit. He loved her zone, and he especially loved what he could do with it. He toyed with her button, stimulating it as she squirmed and moaned in ecstasy. Much to her delight, he sucked on it as he fingered her at the same time. Her attack on his maleness grew more intense. She nibbled at the tip, her lips slowly parting as she drew him all the way into her mouth, the tip touching the back of her throat. Deacon moaned, pulling her tightly to him, not wanting any space between them. She sucked on it until he stopped her. He turned her around and placed his lips on her mouth, kissing her with such passion that she felt it all the way to her toes. She could feel him throb and knew he was ready.

He pulled her to the end of the bed and placed her legs on his shoulders as he entered her. She moaned as he moved her into the position that gave him the greatest penetration. It was like his sex had a mind of its own and had found its way home. He rode her like a stallion, his eyes burning deeply into hers as if he were recording this moment for eternity. He continued to watch her every reaction, her every movement. She watched his eyes, his mouth, and the fiery thrusts of his body into hers. Her body responded, accepting its invasion, holding on to him as tightly as she could. She watched the sweat beads forming on his forehead, knowing that the moment was close. They screamed as he exploded, shooting into her, her body responding with her own climax, her legs shaking, her body jerking and contracting, squeezing every last drop out of him.

He fell on top of her as she wrapped her arms around him, their juices mixing together as they trickled out of her. She didn't want to move. She wanted to stay in this moment of peace and tranquility forever. However, reality always sneaks in, as Deacon got up on one shoulder and hesitantly asked, "What happened to Max?" he brushed her hair from her glistening face.

Her first impulse was to ask, "How did you know?" But she took a breath and began to tell him that she cared for Max and tried to give the relationship a go. But ultimately they wanted different things. London proceeded to share the story, and how they had both realized they had to move on as their true loves awaited. "Max's true love returned to his life, she wanted children and I didn't, plus Max knew I had never forgotten you, which was true."

"You know, I'm not necessarily against the idea of having children with you," Deacon said in response. "I know you had expressed your concerns to me before about the hereditary condition you may have, but I will be there for you. And we could always consider adoption," he suggested.

"Maybe someday. . . ."

"But first things first," Deacon said. He rose from the bed and put on his robe. He sat her up in bed, wrapped the blanket around her, and placed a gentle kiss on her lips. She was amazed at the magical power he still had over her. He knelt before her and gazed into her eyes, the moonlight and candles casting a glow over his handsome features.

"London, I love you with all my heart. The last few months were awful. I felt like a piece of me was missing, and the almost funny thing was that when we had the threesome, it kind of made me feel you didn't care who I was with, so I felt being with Jen was all right, but believe me I will never be with anybody but you for the rest of my life. London, will you please marry me and spend the rest of your life with me? I will always be here for you, no matter what happens, and I want no one else in the world but you. It has always been you, sweetheart. I might have been confused once but never again."

"Oh, Deacon, yes! Yes, I will. Sex, passion, and desire mean nothing without love; the genuine, deep feeling of two souls intertwined forever, unconditionally."

She leaped from the bed. "I'll be right back," she said, leaving him still kneeling with a puzzled look on his face. She ran to retrieve her purse and returned breathless as she handed him the ring box. He smiled as he opened it and slipped the ring on her finger, kissing her again. He climbed back into bed beside her and held her, their hands clasped together.

"How about a honeymoon in France?" he whispered.

"That sounds perfect. I can't wait to go back," she replied with delight.

"But what about your store?" he inquired.

"I have Christopher working with me, Jon's friend. I'm sure he wouldn't mind covering things for me for a little while."

She snuggled into Deacon's embrace. She had finally found her mate and her favorite flavor, and now . . . they would taste life together.

Acknowledgments

My life has been blessed by many angels. Some very close and others far away but very helpful. I wish to use this page to send my warmest thanks to them, you all know who you are.

We all have dreams and my dreams have come true, thanks to Robert L. Fenton and Deborah Lee Watson of the Fenton Entertainment Group, Inc., and Simon & Schuster: Malaika Adero, who opened the door; Jhanteigh Kupihea, who has continued to work with me to fulfill this dream; and D.J. DeSmyter, who continues to work with me; plus the staff at Simon & Schuster. A million thanks.

To all who read my words, never give up on your dreams, they do come true.

Special acknowledgements and recognition for those artists who seem to find words to fit all moods: Charles Kelley, Dave Haywood, and Hillary Scott's "Need You Now," sung by Lady Antebellum; Rihanna's "Rude Boy"; Sammy Fain and Irving Kahal's "I'll be Seeing You," sung by Billie Holiday; John Waite's "Missing You," sung with Alison Krauss; and Frank Loesser's "Baby It's Cold Outside." I would also like to give a notable thanks to *The Girl with the Dragon Tattoo*, which I mentioned in one of the chapters.

About the Author

Antoinette is a nom de plume for a lifetime resident of the Midwest. She is an avid reader—imagination has always played an important part in her life—and she enjoys classical music and history.